I0699645

Kingdom

of

Forgotten

Curses

Courting Books Publishing

Kingdom

of

Forgotten

Curses

Beauty
&
the Undead
Beast

Autumn Kaufer

ISBN: 979-8-9867469-8-2
Cover image & design by: A.R. Kaufer
Courting Books Publishing
First edition, October 6th, 2023

Contents:

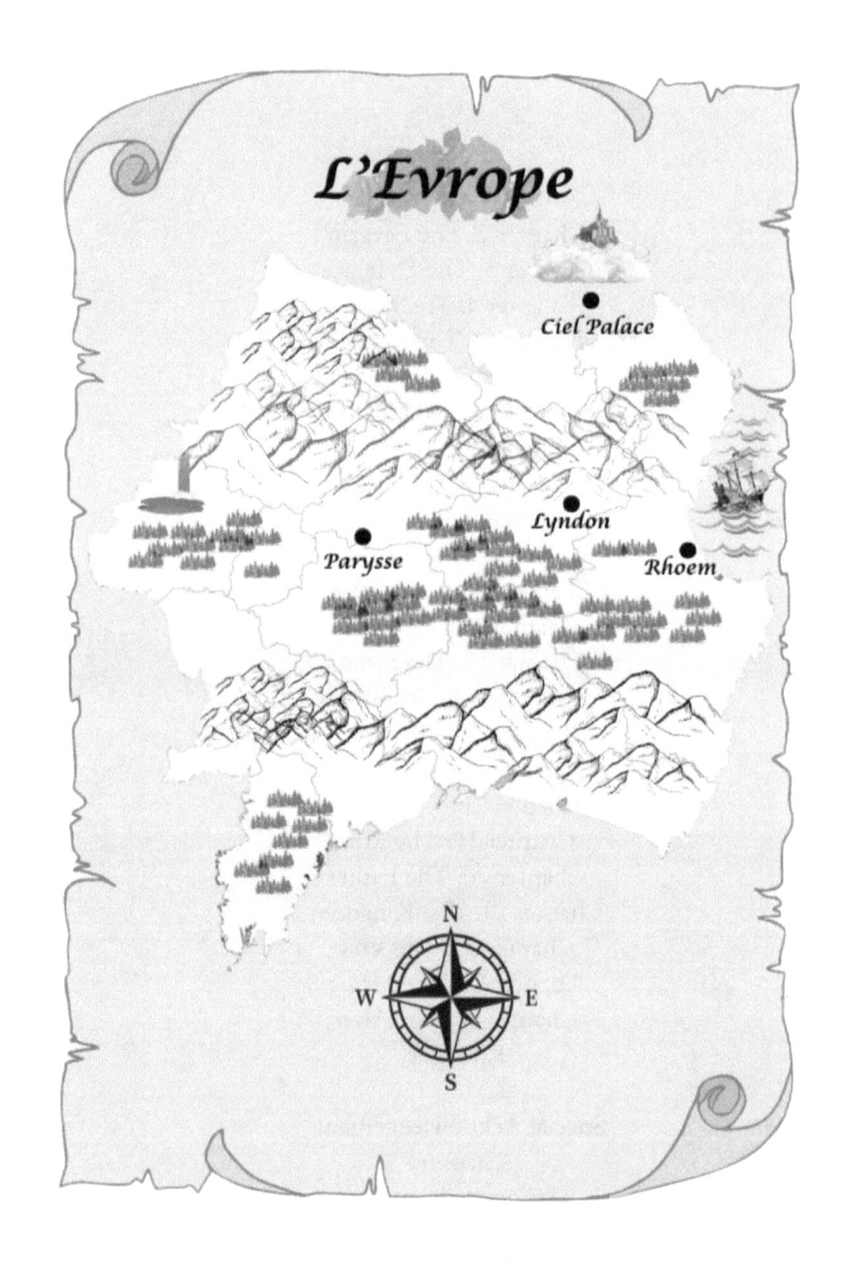

L'Evrope
Ciel Palace
Lyndon
Parysse
Rhoem
N
W
E
S

For Gran, who instilled in

me a love of stories

and fairytales.

This is for you,

for showing me worlds

beyond my wildest dreams.

Once
upon
a
time....

**"Do you believe in destiny? That even the powers
of time can be altered for a single purpose?"**
-Bram Stoker, *Dracula*

Prologue

he bell tolled as the masquerade party reached its crescendo. The prince watched in fascination as the women danced together. He lavished in the expensive wine, and when he stood up, he swayed for a moment. With a devious grin upon his face, he approached them. They bowed before quickly retreating in fear.

A woman in a luxurious red gown with dark hair plaited down her back stared at his grey mask, noting how simple it was in comparison to his fine clothing. His suit was a rich black velvet with crimson embroidery and a matching silk cravat.

Disappointment filled the prince when he lifted his glass to his lips, only to find it empty. As he searched for more wine, Celine, his trusted servant, interrupted him. She was older than him and had cared for him for as long as he could remember. Her hair was golden and her eyes bright blue. Her uniform was the same as all his servants, plain black to blend in. When she was close enough, he pulled her to him in a tight embrace.

"There you are. We need more drinks," he said as everyone cheered and raised their glasses.

She took a moment before facing him. "Mi'lord, there is an urgent matter which requires your attention."

"More important than this celebration?" he asked with a hearty laugh. "Yes."

At her tone, he turned serious and followed her. As they left the ballroom, he stumbled over the legs of a man passed out from the wine and slumped against the wall. The prince saw who it was and rolled his eyes, annoyed but not surprised.

They entered the foyer of the extravagant chateau. The floor was marble, white with grey and dark blue streaking through it. The trim around the entryway was dark wood, nearly black in the low light. Celine turned on the overhead chandelier, and the prince was surprised by what awaited him.

A woman stood, wearing the uniform of his sworn enemy, grey armor with red accents, and a torn white banner soaked in blood was draped over her shoulder. Her light brown hair was damp and matted to her skin. Her green eyes studied him for a moment, and her mouth was taut with pain.

The prince turned to Celine. "What is going on?" he demanded.

Before she could answer, the stranger spoke up. "I apologize for coming like this, but I had nowhere else to turn. I am wounded, and I implore you to give me aid."

The prince scoffed. "Do you know where you are?"

"I do," she stated plainly.

"Hmm, since you came here, perhaps you have a death wish? I could kill you where you stand."

"I came for help," she tried again, wincing in pain.

"Why would I ever help you?"

"Because I believe there is kindness in you, even if you refuse to let anyone see it. I believe everyone is capable of change. Even a blood-thirsty soldier like you."

His body shook with laughter. "You truly are pathetic. Why don't I throw you in my dungeon for the night and see how you fare?"

She held his gaze. "Help me, please."

As he debated how to proceed, he noticed her blood leaking onto the floor. He sighed and shook his head in disgust. "You are ruining a rug far more valuable than you."

She glanced down before smiling at him. "Do we not like blood?"

His eyes burned into hers as he stepped towards her. "I love blood. What I do not love, however, is the sight of my fine rug being bled on by the likes of you. Now leave before I do something about it."

"You refuse to help me?" she asked in quiet disbelief.

"You are lucky that is all I do. Get out."

"Please, I implore you," she tried once more.

"Get lost!" he snarled.

"Well, aren't you quite the beast?" As she stepped back, she was encompassed in a white light, nearly blinding him. Her wounds healed. She stood before him in a silver gossamer gown, and her eyes sparkled in the light of the chandelier. Two white faery wings were upon her back. "Now you see me as I truly am, what say you?"

Left speechless by the sight of her, he could only shake his head while his mouth hung agape. He collected himself before slowly approaching her. "Fae haven't dared enter these lands in a century," he murmured in disbelief. "Who are you? What do you want?"

"Who I am is unimportant. It's *what* I am you should be concerned about," she said as she lifted her silver wand. "I am here to show you the light. Your bloodthirsty ways have gone on long enough. I cannot stand back and watch from the shadows any longer while you murder countless innocents. I came to give you a chance, to see if you could be redeemed."

"No, you have the—"

"Stop!" she commanded. "You will not interrupt me, muritor. Hmm, muritor, a mortal being, yes," she said as she studied him for a moment. "That will do. Perhaps you wish to beg for my favor, instead? Kneel before me, and I shall grant you mercy."

"I have knelt for kings, as was my obligation and duty. I will never kneel to a woman, least of all you." Defiance blazed in his stare.

"Still, I give you this chance. Will you put a stop to your warmongering, to your murdering of innocents? Do you seek redemption for the men, women, and children you have butchered?"

He swallowed hard at her words, regretting he had come with only Celine. "No, I'm telling you, I'm not—"

"So be it." She pointed her wand at him, speaking softly in the fae language he did not understand. Her magic flowed into him.

Frozen in place, his mask melted against him. First, it spread over his face and down his neck, infusing the grey color into his skin. His arms went rigid as it continued into him until it covered him in its entirety. Dread filled his stomach when he looked down at his hands. Small silver scars appeared, covering nearly every inch of him, and he cried out.

"What are these?" he demanded.

"Each scar is a mark of your cruelty, of an innocent life snuffed out by you."

He went to protest, but his mouth spread open, and his canines stretched out into long, sharp fangs. Celine watched in shock and horror as the events unfolded before her, no longer recognizing him as the master she cared for.

The faery raised her wand to her. "No!" Celine cried out, unable to move as the magic flowed through her the way it had the prince.

"You, and all who serve him, are forced to stay here. You cannot leave these lands. To do so would result in dire consequences. Instead, you will serve him as you have, trapped with the man who has caused so much harm. That is your punishment."

Party guests had gathered nearby, curious to see what was happening. Upon the sight before them, they quickly fled in terror. Only the servants remained, trapped in a chateau that would be filled with endless despair. The clock struck midnight, and the faery smiled at the prince.

"Perfect," she said as she approached him. "Happy birthday, Your Highness."

"What did you do to me?" he growled.

"You have been cursed."

He looked at Celine, but instead of seeing his faithful servant, he could only hear her heart pounding as her blood flowed through her veins. The roar of her pulse nearly drove him mad. He gripped her wrist and dragged her to him.

"How can I serve, master?" she asked, keeping her head down.

"Look at me!" he commanded.

When she raised her head, he saw the vein throbbing in her neck and could not stop himself. He dove in, his fangs penetrating her skin. His tongue lapped at the blood, and his need grew as he fed. Upon hearing her heart pounding against him, he pulled back. Shame ripped through his very core, and he shoved her aside before rushing towards the faery.

"You made me into a monster!"

"Perhaps you should know better, that appearances can be deceiving," she said with a smile. "You are now a vampyr. Cursed as a nemuritor, an immortal, who feeds upon the blood you love so much."

"I demand you undo this at once!" he cried out in despair.

"You can demand all you like, but the curse cannot be undone by me."

Dracke turned away, his mind battling his heart, knowing he had no choice. "Then how?" he asked, seeking even the smallest amount of hope for his dire situation.

"It requires two things. One, a pure, selfless act. Two, someone must fall in love with you, unconditionally and of their own free will, and they must tell you so. Both must occur before midnight on your one hundredth birthday."

"And if they don't?" he asked, swallowing hard.

"The curse will become permanent. You will remain a vampyr while your staff turns to statues, surrounding you and reminding you of both your cruelty and your failure to save them."

"Is that all the curse will do?"

"No. You, your staff, and your chateau will be forgotten by the people. You will become a thing of legend, passed by, and ignored. Your kingdom will be frozen in eternal winter, as ice cold as your very heart."

"Wait, how can someone love me if I am forgotten?"

"I guess you will have to figure that out. Unless you break the curse, I will not see you again until your one hundredth birthday."

He opened his mouth to speak but decided he would not subject anyone else to this curse. Fear ripped through him, and he charged at her but stopped when she vanished. Stripping out of his jacket and shirt, he rushed to the mirror. His reflection sent a wave of disgust crawling through him. He rampaged through the chateau, ripping doors off their hinges and destroying any mirror he saw as he cried out in rage, unable to bear the sight of the beast staring back in return.

"Who gave thee permission to gather my roses? Is it not enough that I kindly allowed thee to remain in my palace? Instead of feeling grateful, rash man, I find thee stealing my flowers! Thy insolence shall not remain unpunished."

-Madame de Villeneuve,
Beauty and the Beast

Chapter 1

The Rose

our Majesty," Marius said as he examined the tattered document on the desk. "Who is—" He lifted it closer, adjusting his small, silver frames as he attempted to make out the writing. "Prince Dracke? I don't believe I've heard the name before."

"He is but a legend, so I thought. Why do you ask?"

"According to this, he nor anyone from his family has paid taxes."

"In how long?"

"Ever."

King Willam approached Marius, richly dressed in a fine navy-blue suit and matching cravat. Willam was young for a monarch but more than made up for it with experience. As ruler of the muritor lands, he had managed to keep the peace during his reign. His pride was apparent in his manner of dress, in the way he carried himself. He kept his light brown hair, mustache, and small beard neatly trimmed.

"Majesty?"

"Apologies," Willam said, glancing at the desk. "Why so many books on fae legends and myths? What is that to do with the law?" he asked, lifting up a dusty volume.

"It's tied together," Marius answered, taking the book, and returning it to the stack. He held up the document in question.

Willam carefully took the paper and read it. "Ah, my. I thought he and his family were mere stories. I have not heard mention of them in a long time."

"Who was he?" Marius asked.

"The legend goes, he and his family were once the original rulers of these lands. They were cruel beyond words, marching on neighboring villages to demand blood sacrifices." He shook his head. "I really don't wish to discuss it. What matters, however, is this oversight needs to be addressed. You must go there, not only to inquire about payment, but you must tell me everything."

The excitement in his voice surprised Marius. "Your Majesty?"

"Who is in charge there? What is the state of the chateau? I demand a full report as soon as you've returned."

"Of course."

Willam looked at Marius for a moment, noticing how grief had aged him in only a few short years. His grey suit needed to be replaced, and his loafers hadn't been shined in at least a month. His hair was salt and pepper, while his face was well-groomed, contrasting his worn appearance.

"I also recommend you dress a little... nicer, in case there is still any royalty or nobility left there," Willam suggested.

"Yes, Majesty. I wonder what it looks like?"

"A land beyond a great vast forest, surrounded by majestic mountains with flowers of frailty and beauty."

When Willam smiled, his green eyes danced at the thought of learning what had transpired in Parysse. Growing up, he had heard legends of blood-drinking demons and murderous tyrants. As far as he knew, those were nothing but stories told to scare a young prince.

"I will set off at once," Marius responded, pulling Willam from his thoughts.

"Good man," he said, as he glanced at the stack of books again. "You know, there hasn't been a fae sighted in our kingdom in nearly two hundred years. Why the fascination?"

"There hasn't been a reported sighting," Marius clarified then gave him a reassuring smile. He gathered his things, tucking the book of fae legends into his bag, and left the palace, curious about the mission laid out before him.

Riding to his estate, his thoughts drifted to his family. How would they react to learn he would be leaving again so soon? After the loss of his wife, he rarely traveled far. The king was understanding and only too happy to cater to Marius. Gratitude filled him at the thought, but he knew in this instance, he had to follow through.

Tufts of snow swirled around him as the wind chilled him to the bone. In town, he gently kicked his heel into the side of his steed to encourage him to speed up.

He arrived at his manor, and his youngest daughter greeted him. She approached to help him from his saddle.

"Bellamina."

"Welcome home."

"Thank you, my sweet Bells."

She smiled at his nickname for her. She was dressed in a fine silk gown, gold with a dark brown embroidery matching the curls nestled around her face. Her lips were the perfect shade of pink, and her hazel eyes lightened or darkened, depending on her mood. The entire village was enthralled with her beauty.

"Of course, Father." She reached for his bag.

"Leave it. I'm not staying, I'm afraid."

"What? Where are you going?" she asked as they walked towards the manor.

"I'm going to Parysse on assignment for His Majesty."

Bells swallowed hard at the news. "I understand."

"For now, I need to pack warm clothing and change before I head back out." He clasped her hand as they entered the foyer. "Thank you for welcoming me home, Bells." He kissed her forehead before meeting her gaze. The sorrow that weighed heavily on her reflected in her eyes. "Are you doing all right?"

"Yes," she responded softly.

The foyer was open with dark wood floors, grey walls, and arched doorways. An entry table in the middle of the room normally held a vase with fresh-cut roses, Bells's favorite. After she had returned, they were the first thing to make her smile. Since they were out of season, a bouquet of snowdrops graced the table instead. Her father had instructed fresh flowers to be put out every other day for his daughter.

He lifted her chin gently. "How are you?" he asked again, unable to hide his concern.

She pulled away, not meeting his gaze. "I am fine," was all she said as she went into the kitchen to fetch him stew and bread while he packed.

He dressed, then joined his daughters in the dining room. While he ate, he noticed his other two daughters clutching each other and pouting.

Marie was the oldest, dressed modestly in a pink cotton gown with her dark hair tied up in a bun.

His middle daughter, Elise, was dressed in a blue silk gown, matching her eyes. Her hair was plaited down her back.

"Do you have to leave again?" Marie asked.

"You've just returned!" Elise exclaimed, taking her sister's hand.

"I know you two are worried about the upcoming ball. I will return in plenty of time. I give you my word, we will attend it together. I have to go to Parysse now."

"Bring me back furs," Marie demanded.

"And fine silks," Elise added.

"Whatever you desire," Marius answered.

The girls perked up and gave their youngest sister a knowing smile. She ignored them as she stood to walk with her father to his horse.

"Are you sure you want to go alone? It will be dark soon."

"Bells, I know you are a talented rider, but I am fine to go on my own. You worry too much." He clasped her hand, wishing to see her smile once before leaving again. "What would you like me to bring back? Don't think it escaped my attention you asked for nothing."

"Return here, safe and sound. That is all I desire."

"Very well. I promise I will." He mounted his horse, looking at her once more before heading away from the manor. The road ahead would be long in the chilly evening, but excitement crept in at the thought of going on an adventure.

Upon his arrival, Marius pulled out his pocket watch, pleased to see he had made the trip in less than an hour. The doors to the gate swung in, and he tried to spot whoever opened it, but his horse quickly led him up the path. A thick forest lined both sides, and the trees still bore leaves that were weighted down with snow.

The entire chateau was white marble, blending in with the snowflakes swirling around him. Even in the blaring tufts, bright pink and red roses grew on their bushes, climbing along the trellises. At the entrance, a man with long grey hair and thin in the face appeared, wrapped in a dark cloak.

"How may we serve?" he asked.

"I need to see whoever is in charge here," Marius explained as he dismounted.

"I will take excellent care of your horse. Please, go inside and warm yourself."

"Thank you," Marius said as he walked towards the entrance. Like the gate, the doors opened to him with no one in sight. He paused for a moment before stepping into the foyer, where he was greeted by Celine. "Good evening," he offered.

"To you as well, sir. You are here to see the master?" she asked.

"I am."

"Please, follow me." She led him to a parlor with a roaring fire. "Sit and recover. He will be with you shortly."

"Thank you."

Marius removed his coat and hung it on the rack beside the fireplace. The room consisted of dark wood walls and trim, with an antique secretary desk by one of the windows. He sat in the plush chair directly in front of the warm blaze. Between exhaustion from his travels and the comfort of his current position, he slumped over and fell asleep.

"What do you want?" the voice bellowed across the room and startled Marius awake.

He jumped to his feet, turning and trying not to stare as fear crept through him. The man who stood before him, though to Marius was more beast than man, was dressed in stately robes with a small, jeweled crown upon his head.

"My apologies. I am Marius Renfield, barrister to His Majesty, King Willam. He sent me here to discuss taxes." He glanced up when the prince laughed.

"Of all things!"

"I apologize, but—"

"Nonsense. Let us discuss the matter at hand."

Celine walked in. "Would monsieur care for some wine or mead?"

"Coffee, if it is available," Marius requested as he followed the man to his desk. He had organized the documents by the time Celine returned and handed him the warm mug.

"Is that all, sir?" she asked.

"Yes, thank you."

"Are you sure? I can have a meal brought in."

"Thank you, but no." Marius intended to get what he needed, then stop at the local inn for the rest of the night before returning home the next morning.

He took a sip, drinking in the deep, rich flavor as he tried to push down his fear. The voice in his head told him to leave immediately, but he knew he could not. He would never refuse an order from his king.

Marius cleared his throat and handed him the first document. "May I ask your name?"

"I am Prince Dracke."

He nearly spit out his coffee. "Um, but he… I thought he was merely a legend. You can't possibly be—"

Dracke chuckled softly. "It matters not, but I assure you, I am who I say I am."

Marius stared for a moment, wanting to doubt his identity, except he wore a crown of sparkling jewels upon his head. "Of course. Thank you."

Dracke read the documents while Marius finished his drink. "Everything appears to be in order," he said as he handed the papers back to Marius. "The compensation shall arrive tomorrow. Now, was there anything else?"

To avoid the prince's gaze, Marius stared down into his empty cup. "Um, no, Your Highness. Thank you."

"Monsieur Renfield, is something the matter?"

He swallowed hard before looking into the monster's silver eyes. "No. Thank you for seeing me on such short notice," he managed, gathering his attaché. "And the hospitality."

"Of course."

Marius blinked in disbelief when Dracke vanished. He shook his head and quickly made for the door, telling himself it was a combination of exhaustion and nerves.

The frigid air blasted Marius in the face as he walked outside. He shivered and gripped the collar of his coat, grateful to be leaving the chateau. The man in the black cloak approached, leading his steed.

"Thank you."

"Yes, sir. A fine horse you have."

Marius smiled and gave the man a small nod as he attached his bag to the saddle. He was about to mount, but the roses caught his eye.

This would surely make Bells smile. She would love one. I should ask. A shudder wove through him at the thought of seeing the prince again. *It's just a rose. I won't disturb him over such a trivial thing.*

He walked up to the bush, looking at the roses until he found the perfect one. Carefully, he twisted the stem, removing the rose and—

"Now you are stealing from me?"

Terror shot through Marius as he turned to face the prince. "N… No, Your Highness. I… my youngest daughter, Bells, loves roses, and…" His heart pounded so loudly in his head, he could hardly hear himself as he tried to stammer out an answer. "I apologize, but I was simply—"

"This I will not tolerate, Monsieur Renfield."

Before Marius could offer another plea, Dracke grabbed him by the collar, and they vanished.

Chapter 2

The Bargain

ells stood before the window, worry drawn across her face as she watched the snow fall and waited for her father to return. She resumed her mending as her sisters discussed the approaching ball. They had been chatting about it non-stop since the invitation had arrived.

"Do you think Jonathan will be there?" Elise teased as she ate her second scone.

Marie blushed as she nearly dropped her book. "What?"

"You know he likes you."

"He mentioned once my eyes reminded him of the sky, that's all."

Elise giggled. "So, when are you two getting married?"

Marie stood up and shoved the book back onto the shelf. "Stop being a brat! For being the middle child, you act more like the spoiled baby in the family."

Elise let out an exaggerated gasp as she stood. "I'm simply asking a question," she said with a pout.

"You should be more concerned whether Sir Arthur will be there," Marie shot back.

"How dare you?" Elise snapped.

Bells sighed. "Both of you, stop. Father should've been home by now."

"He's fine. He said he would be back before the ball. Why do you worry so much, *Bells*?"

She cringed at Elise's use of her nickname, as her father was the only one who called her Bells. "Because…" she took a breath, "I just do. I am going to find him myself."

"You don't know where he went," Marie pointed out. "Only that he is in Parysse."

"Then I'll go to the palace. They will tell me."

The two older sisters exchanged a glance before erupting into laughter. "Little Bells, going to see the king? Oh, I would pay a hundred gold to witness it myself!"

"Elise, stop. I mean it. I am going to find out. You can both stay here, gossiping and talking about boys."

"Ugh, why are you always so serious?" Elise asked. "What, did your sense of humor die, too?"

Marie gasped softly, about to speak up when Bells turned to Elise. "You need to grow up!" she snapped as she ran from the drawing room.

Bells went upstairs to change into warmer clothing and pack a bag. In the stable, she saddled her horse, and rode towards the Ciel Kingdom, determined she would find out about her father.

She distracted herself from the cold by watching the people coming and going from the shops in the village. A few had closed recently, and a line of beggars waited for food at the mission.

The market in the center offered smoked meats and baked goods, then there was the clothing shop, a tea house, and of course, her favorite, the small library. As the village disappeared behind her, she followed the path in the woods, her face numb from the biting wind. She rode on, knowing something was wrong, and she had to find her father.

Bells's breath caught in her throat when she arrived at the fae gate which would transport her to the Ciel Kingdom. It was a large, circular area with blue magical rings. She closed her eyes and said a silent prayer before leading her horse into it.

A moment later, they arrived at the floating city. She stared in disbelief at the clouds billowing beneath her horse's hooves. She gathered herself and followed the smooth, dirt path that led her to the palace, which took up most of the isle. A small sigh of relief blew from her lips as she approached the gate to the Ciel Palace.

"Halt! State your business," ordered the guard nearest her. His armor was silver with leather cords, and a blue banner with a white tree growing from a cloud embroidered on it was draped over his chest.

"I am looking for my father, Marius Renfield, barrister to the king."

"Yes, I know the name. He has not been here for nearly a week."

"Nor has he returned to his home," Bells explained.

"Hmm, this does warrant concern. You may go in." He started to gesture but couldn't help staring at her for a moment, shifting on his feet before raising his hand to alert the guard.

The gate opened, and she coaxed her horse inside. At the palace entrance, she dismounted and was grateful when a stable hand took the reins. She went to the large front doors and was surprised to simply walk inside. Unsure of where to go, she loitered in the grand entryway for a moment to gather her bearings.

"Is it really you?"

She turned to see the young prince. "Your Highness, how are you?" she asked with a bow.

The boy approached, fourteen years in age but older in spirit. His chestnut brown hair was neatly trimmed and contrasted with his pale face and bright green eyes. He ran to her and hugged her. "Very well." His black slacks and dark blue shirt were pressed and smooth.

"You are almost as tall as me! How you have grown."

He smiled. "What brings you here?"

"My father has not returned."

"Then we shall see mine and figure this out." He took her hand and led the way. "I am sorry I have not been by to visit. Father doesn't let me leave here often, but I enjoyed when we would gather to hear your stories."

"Thank you."

He paused for a moment, a sullen look upon his face. "I am also sorry about Colin."

At his words, she forced a small smile. "I appreciate that, Prince Alain."

She was grateful they continued towards his father's office, as her heart was not ready to talk about the sorrow threatening to swallow her whole. Without knocking, Alain took her inside.

"I said I do not wish to be disturbed!" Willam barked out, not looking up from the documents in his hand.

"Father?"

The king turned and smiled at the sight of his son. "Apologies. And who is this?"

"You forget Renfield's youngest daughter?" Alain asked.

"Of course not. I have much on my plate at the moment. How can we help?"

"My father has not returned," Bells explained with a bow.

"I noticed, as he was supposed to report to me once he did. Hmm, this is troubling." He scratched his chin as he pondered the situation.

"If you tell me where you sent him, I will search for him myself."

Willam looked her up and down for a moment. "Your father has mentioned you are a rather skilled rider. Very well." He leaned over his desk, gathering a map. He showed her where her father was sent. "Shall I send some guards with you?"

She cleared her throat as she shifted on her feet. "I appreciate the offer, but I will be faster alone. Thank you."

"Very well. Hopefully, he is simply being entertained and did not wish to offend by trying to leave. You know how entitled some of the nobility can be." He smiled and winked at Alain, who chuckled in return.

"Yes, Your Majesty. Thank you."

Alain escorted her outside and to her horse, glancing at her from time to time. "I could come with you if you want," he offered, fidgeting with his sleeve.

She gave him a reassuring smile. "Thank you, but I know you are needed here." She mounted and hurried back the way she came, ready to find her father.

Back on solid ground, she studied the map again. She knew how to ride to Parysse, but she was unsure of where exactly the chateau was, and even on the map, it seemed to almost glimmer in and out of focus. She wiped her eyes and shook her head to clear it, then tucked the map into her pocket. Gathering her determination, she rode forward.

She arrived at the chateau, yawned, and scolded herself because she had not stopped in town to rest. Her worry over her father gnawed in the pit of her stomach, and she could think of nothing else. The gates opened when she drew near. She continued along the path through the woods and reached the entrance. The man who had helped her father now proceeded towards her.

"Evening, madam. A bit chilly, isn't it?" he asked with a small laugh. "How can I help you?"

"I am looking for my father, Marius Renfield."

The man stopped for a moment, turning serious. "Right, of course. Please, go on in. I will tend to your horse."

"Thank you." She admired the roses climbing up the pillars of the magnificent chateau, then stepped inside. A woman approached and offered to take her cloak.

"Welcome, madam. I am Celine. How can I be of service?"

"I am looking for Marius Renfield."

"Please, get warm in there," she said as she gestured to the doorway. "My master will attend to you shortly."

"Thank you," Bells offered with a smile, trying to shake the uneasy feeling as she stepped inside the lavish parlor. She knelt in front of the fireplace and rubbed her hands together as she let the warmth comfort her.

"Another visitor. My, my. To what do I owe the pleasure?"

She stood up, about to speak, but her voice caught in her throat at the sight of him. He wore black dress pants and a matching tunic jacket with a deep red cravat sparkling with rubies.

His grey skin was what caught her attention, and she couldn't help but stare before her eyes met his silver ones. The platinum crown he wore upon his head contrasted with his long, raven-wing hair. She took a breath and collected herself before stepping forward and offering a bow.

"I am Bellamina, and I am looking for my father, Marius Renfield."

"Ah, yes. The thief."

She immediately straightened at his words. "I... I beg your pardon?"

"You wish to see him?" Dracke asked, watching her features with curiosity.

"Please!" she begged, her eyes wide and worry drawn across her face.

Her breath escaped when he appeared in front of her and pulled her to his chest, leaving no space between them. They vaolmersed into the tower dungeon, and he pushed her back as he stared down at Marius.

"This is his punishment for his transgression. I do not abide by thievery of any kind." Bells started to kneel, but he grabbed her arm and shoved her towards the door. "I never said you could touch him."

"Please," she begged, her voice hitching as she watched her father, curled up and trembling with fever. "Let me see to him."

Dracke sighed. "Very well."

She hurriedly knelt beside her father with her stomach in a knot. His hair was matted with sweat and his skin was flushed. She looked at Dracke with desperation in her eyes. "He is deathly ill. He needs a doctor. Please, let me take him."

Dracke laughed at the notion. "Why would I do that?"

"Because I am begging you."

"You are not the first woman to beg for my help. I will not yield to you."

"You said he is a thief? What did he steal?" she asked in disbelief.

"A rose."

She gasped softly. "No. He… he would never take anything without asking first."

"Well, he did. Now, he is serving out his punishment."

"What can I do? He will die if you do not help him." Pushing aside her fear, she stood and locked eyes with him. "Please."

"I care not either way," he said with a shrug of his shoulders.

Her eyes closed when she realized the choice she would have to make, what it would take to satisfy the beast. Her breath shuddered as she gathered her courage.

"Take me instead," she said quietly.

Dracke froze at her words, searching her eyes for any hint of trickery or deception when she opened them. "What are you playing at?" he asked, suspicious of her intentions.

She took a step towards him. "Let him go, and take me instead. Please."

"Why would you do that?"

"Because he is my father. I love him dearly, and I will do whatever I must to save him. Fetch a doctor, and I will take his place here."

"No," Dracke responded with indifference.

Her heart pounded furiously. "But—"

"I don't need a doctor." He stepped around Bells and knelt beside her father. "Do you mean it, if I heal him, you will take his place and stay here with me?"

"I swear."

He bit his wrist and brought it to Marius's mouth, making him drink. Bells watched in equal parts horror and fascination, shocked when her father sat up and no longer trembled. Disgusted by the coppery taste, Marius wiped his mouth before he noticed her in the room.

"What happened?"

Bells ran to him, helping him to his feet and hugging him tight. "Father!"

"What are you doing here?" he asked.

"I was worried because you hadn't returned." She cried out when Dracke gripped her wrist tightly and pulled her away from Marius. "Wait—"

"She belongs to me now. She gave her life for yours. So return to your pathetic muritor life and leave us be."

Marius glanced from Dracke to his daughter in confusion. "Bells, what is he talking about?"

"You were dying, and I had no choice. I am taking your place, staying here with him so you can have your life back."

"No!" he cried out, shooting an angry look at Dracke. "Surely you are not so heartless you would tear a child from her father?"

"I am," Dracke admitted with a smirk. "Now, get your goodbyes over with. I am ready to be done with this drama."

Marius stepped forward, his index finger aimed right at Dracke. "If you hurt her—"

"I have no intention of hurting that which is mine," Dracke stated matter-of-factly, his hand clasped firmly on Bells's shoulder.

"Father, please go, while you can," she implored.

"I will return for you. This will not stand." Marius fled from the dungeon, giving her one last look on his way out.

Bells glanced about the tiny cell, fear pulsing through her as she faced Dracke. "I am ready."

"For what?"

"Whatever punishment you see fit," she answered, her voice not much more than a squeak.

Dracke sighed in irritation. "Please, do not insult me." He pulled her to him and vaolmersed her into a beautiful chamber. "This is where you will stay. As you did nothing wrong, I see no reason to keep you in the dungeon."

A sigh of relief escaped her. "Thank you."

"Do not think I am kind nor will I show mercy again."

"Yes, mi'lord."

"Ugh, do not call me that."

"I see by your crown you are some rank of nobility. What title shall I use?"

"Call me Dracke."

"If you insist."

"I do, Bells."

She stifled a sob. "My father is the only one who calls me Bells."

"What should I call you then?"

"Mina," she responded softly.

"Good. Get dressed and meet me downstairs for dinner."

"I will."

He laughed. "Of course. You say that as if you have a choice." He vaolmersed from the room.

The bed had a white canopy with four posts and was covered with a pink duvet. The gold and white armoire caught her eye, and her eyes trailed over to the matching vanity beside it. She walked to the closet and opened the door, smiling at the variety of beautiful fabrics and colors. Her sisters would be envious of the luxurious clothing inside.

"Are you ready to get dressed?"

Mina jumped at the voice, turning around to see the woman who had helped her earlier. "Oh, um, yes."

"Celine," she reminded her.

"Right, Celine. Thank you. I am Mina," she replied.

"Mina, welcome."

They went into the closet together, deciding on a burgundy gown with plush velvet sleeves, open shoulders, and a draping cut. Mina looked at the gowns, realizing they were all in a similar style. She turned to Celine.

"I do not mean to sound ungrateful…"

"What's wrong?"

She sighed. "This isn't proper for me to wear."

"The prince insisted."

Mina's breath sucked in. She knew he was of some importance but had no idea he was a prince. Realizing it would do no good to argue, she simply nodded. She dressed and looked at herself, embarrassed to have so much skin exposed.

Celine smiled. "He will be most pleased."

Mina's breath caught in her throat. "How so?"

"We have not had a guest, besides your father, in a very long time. I heard my master comment he is curious about you."

"Really?"

"Yes. He said you are his new plaything." Celine paused for a moment. "My apologies. I do have trouble keeping my thoughts to myself. Pay no attention to me," she said with a quiet chuckle.

Mina's hand gently gripped her chin as she thought over Celine's words. "I… what?"

"Oh, I must see to dinner. Excuse me."

Mina watched her leave, wrapping her arms around herself. *I'm sure she didn't mean… No, of course not. He is curious about me, she said. Surely, he wouldn't…*

She took a breath and reassured herself everything would be fine. She turned for the door, but her feet refused to move. Her body trembled with consuming fear as she worried about his intentions with her. The bed was as far as she walked before she collapsed onto it, crying into her pillow, and wishing more than anything she was back home.

"Why are you still up here?" Dracke demanded. Her eyes flew open, and she was surprised to see him staring at her. She quickly stood up.

"I… why are you in my room?" Seeing his gaze lower to her chest, she immediately crossed her arms in a feeble attempt to cover herself.

"You are late for dinner."

"That does not give you the right to invade my privacy," she snapped, stepping back. Her hip bumped into the nightstand, and she let out a small yelp in surprise.

"You need to understand this. Everything in this chateau, and I do mean *everything*, belongs to me."

She swallowed hard. "You do not own me," she replied in defiance.

"It is sad you believe that. Now, come with me for dinner," he said as he stepped up to her. Her breathing came in quick gasps as there was no space between them. His cold demeanor did nothing to ease her fear. "Mina, your heart is pounding as furiously as a war drum. Are you so afraid of me?" Her eyes met his, and he immediately stepped back.

"I do not know what you want with me."

He sighed. "I simply want us to spend the evening together."

Her face flushed. "You… what?"

"I am curious to know you. Now, you will join me downstairs." He held out his hand.

Her gaze shifted to his grey fingers, and when she caught him again staring at her, she shook her head. "I will not. I want to eat in here. I am not your plaything to do with as you wish."

"Ah, Celine told you what I said. Interesting. I shall speak to her later. For now, I assure you, it is perfectly safe to join me in the dining room." His hand stretched towards her. "You will join me," he commanded.

She tried to back up farther, only to discover she was completely flush against the nightstand. "No. I will eat in here," she insisted. "Unless you wish to give me proper attire."

"There is nothing wrong with how you are dressed. I enjoy the view, myself."

"Please," she tried, softening her voice. "Give me proper clothes, and I will eat with you."

"You are in no place to make requests. I will say this once. If you do not join me, you will not eat at all."

"Fine," she snapped.

"I will be waiting." He vaolmersed from the room.

Her stomach rumbled while she paced in front of the fireplace with a throbbing headache. She gathered up a nightgown from the armoire and went into the washroom to shower. Once clean and refreshed, she sat in the nook and stared out at the stars in the sky above, wishing on every single one she had never come to Parysse.

Chapter 3

The Defiance

hivering in her sleep, Mina jolted upright when the light turned on. Celine approached her. "Evening, madam. My master said you are to join him for dinner tonight. I am to remind you, it is not a request. It is a command."

Mina discovered that not only did she have no blankets on her, but her nightgown had been replaced. She rushed to the mirror, looking herself over in dismay. She was wrapped in nothing more than black gossamer fabric that crossed down her chest, tied around her back, and fell to the floor. Slits on either side went all the way to her hips. With anger in her eyes, she turned to Celine.

"Who did this?"

"I did, on my master's orders."

"How did I not feel this?"

Celine averted her gaze. "He commanded you to sleep."

"I beg your pardon?" Mina asked with wide eyes.

"He has… abilities, as you've seen. Madam—"

Mina rushed to the closet, and her stomach dropped to see it empty. "What? Where are my gowns?"

"He said until you learn to behave like a lady, you will not dress like one."

A sob escaped her lips when she looked at Celine. "Please, bring me a cloak, a robe, anything!"

"I cannot. He said he was kind enough to let you sleep, knowing yesterday was hard on you. You are now to join him in the dining room."

"I need clothes."

"You are wearing them," Celine said, pity reflecting in her eyes. "I am sorry."

Mina's hands clenched as she flushed in humiliation. "Please, help me."

"Best not to keep him waiting," Celine said as she walked out the door.

Mina hung her head, determined she would do whatever she had to so Dracke would not see her dressed in such a way.

Dracke sat at the table, drinking from his silver goblet. Mina walked in, and he jumped to his feet, unable to contain his laughter at the sight.

"What are you wearing?" he demanded.

She refused to look at him. "Well, since you removed all of my clothing, I had to make do."

"So, you wrapped a sheet around yourself and tied it off? Ingenious."

"You will not—" She gasped when he vaolmersed before her and ripped the sheet away, revealing only the gossamer fabric underneath.

Dracke's eyes lingered for a moment upon her heaving chest, visible through the thin layers. Crying out in frustration, she reached for the sheet, but he vaolmersed away and immediately returned without it.

"Mina—"

"Give it back!" she demanded. Tears glistened in her eyes.

"See, this is why I have to do this. You need to learn I do not answer to you. When you can behave like a lady, I will treat you like one. I asked you to join me for dinner last night. I was polite and civil, yet you refused to come with me. You will pay for your defiance."

"I will not eat with you like this."

"No one said you will," he responded nonchalantly.

Her head snapped up at his words. "What?"

He pulled her to him and forced her to sit. Leaning down, he gazed into her eyes. "You will sit here."

"I will—" Her eyes went wide when she could not move. Panic flooded through her. "What did you do?"

"You are under my command. Once you have learned your manners, then you will be allowed to move about and eat. In the meantime, I want to know more about you."

Her heart thumped wildly in her chest as she struggled against his control. "Please, undo this," she begged, her voice cracking.

"I will do what I want. Now, tell me about yourself."

"I am no one of importance," she answered, squirming in her seat.

"Aren't we all?"

"You're a prince!" she exclaimed.

Her discomfort began to weigh on him as he watched her writhing. He knelt before her. "Who no one seems to remember. See? Unimportant. Now, look at me." Reluctantly, she met his gaze. "You are free." He watched as her body immediately eased.

"Thank you," she said softly. Her fingers trailed along the lace of the table cover. "Why are you forgotten?"

Dracke stalked back to his seat and took a drink. "We are talking about you," he said as he wiped his mouth. "Tell me everything. Where are you from? How old are you?"

"Why should I?" she snapped as her stomach grumbled.

Dracke appeared in front of her and caught her when she slipped from her seat in fright. Their eyes met, their faces barely inches apart. Her breath shuddered as he seated her upright.

"Are you going to continue to be rude? Perhaps giving you a beautiful bedchamber gave you the wrong impression. Shall I toss you in the dungeon until you learn some manners?"

Thinking about her words carefully, she swallowed hard, her head spinning as her stomach gnawed in pain. "My apologies. I'm afraid my hunger is infringing on my ability to think clearly."

He barked with laughter, and she started at the sound. "So I should give you food to make you polite?"

She closed her eyes and hung her head, unable to take the hunger any longer. "Please," she begged.

"Oh, that was painful. Say it again. Beg for food, and I will have it brought in."

Her hands clenched as she bit back tears threatening to escape. "Please," she relented. "Please, give me something to eat."

Dracke snapped his fingers, and a meal appeared on the table. Mina started to question him about how it happened but thought it best not to push her luck. Instead, she looked at the stew, wine, and bread. Her stomach gurgled when the scents invaded her nostrils. She reached for the bread, but he gripped her wrist.

"What are you doing?" he asked.

"You… you said if I said please again, you would have food brought in."

"Yes, I did. I never said it was for you."

Her lip quivered as anger surged through her. "What?" She glanced at the food, her mouth literally watering from the smell. "Why not?" she demanded.

"Because you still need to learn your manners."

"I did as you asked. I begged. I said please."

He laughed. "Yes, and anyone can say please. You were rude and did not answer my questions."

"If I answer them, will you let me eat?"

He thought it over. "Fine." He vaolmersed into his seat and took another sip while he waited for her to answer.

"I'm sorry," she said after a moment. "What did you ask?"

"Hmm, you must be starving. How old are you, and where are you from?"

"I am nineteen, and I am from Lyndon," she quickly answered while eyeing the food.

He feigned a yawn. "How extraordinarily boring you are."

Her hands clenched again. "I know. May I please eat now?"

"No, because you are dull," he said with a laugh. She reached for the bread again, but the food vanished.

"Where did it go?" she demanded. "How did you do that?"

"What part of 'no' do you not understand? You will obey me, draga mea."

"What does that mean?" He only laughed in response, angering her further. "If you aren't going to feed me, and if you think I will continue to be your new toy, you are mistaken!" She stood to leave and immediately fell to a heap to the floor.

Dracke rushed to her and lifted her up. Instinctively, she wrapped her arms around his neck and clung to him, the way she used to when her father carried her to bed. He froze for a moment, unsure how to proceed.

"Mina?" He realized she had fallen unconscious. He vaolmersed with her into her chamber and laid her on the bed, watching her in concern. Her eyelids fluttered a moment before opening fully.

"Hmm, what happened?" she asked.

"You passed out."

"I need food, please."

Dracke's thoughts raced, jumbled together as he thought of her scent and her warmth while he held her. "You are pathetic," he responded as he stood.

"What do you want?" she asked weakly. "You accepted my life, but what are your intentions with me?" Sitting up and collecting herself, she moved to the edge of the bed and looked at him.

"For now, I am simply enjoying tormenting you."

"Why? What have I ever done to you?"

"Because you are mine to do with as I please."

"No," she murmured in horror. "Don't hurt me."

He grew warm as anger pulsed in him. "Have I hurt you yet?" he demanded. She shook her head. "Then stop acting like I will. You will stay in here tonight until you learn your place!"

When he vaolmersed from the room, she laid back down. The hunger pangs consumed her, and she sat up, determined she would find something more appropriate to wear then go into the kitchen for food. She gathered her strength and crept from the room, checking to be sure the hallway was clear.

Just because he moved the gowns, did not mean he got rid of them. She knew they had to be somewhere nearby. She wandered about the chateau, opening doors and checking closets. Relief washed over her when she found a few hanging up, slightly moth-eaten but overall in wearable shape and not nearly as revealing. Knowing she could mend them, she gathered them in her arms and returned to her room, where she slipped on the best-looking one.

Though her hunger was now a biting ache in her stomach, she was determined to find her gowns before going to the kitchen. She headed for the third floor. Someone grabbed her from behind and shoved her to the wall. She turned to Dracke in surprise.

"Where do you think you are going?" he asked, looking her over in the pale blue gown. "Where did you get that?"

"I demand to be fed and clothed," she cried out, no longer caring that tears streamed down her cheeks. "You can at least give me that."

Ignoring her demands, he took her to her chamber, and tossed her to the floor. "I will give you whatever I feel like. Continue in this manner, and I'll throw you in the dungeon, where you won't be wearing anything at all. Do I make myself clear?"

"Drop dead."

The door slammed shut behind him. She ran to it and pulled with everything she had, but it refused to budge. Holding her stomach while she sat on the bed, the pain overwhelmed her. She drifted off to sleep.

The clock chimed, waking her, and she saw the sun would be rising soon. When the door opened, it startled her. Celine crept in, carrying a small plate. "It is only some bread and dried meat, but I know you need this," she said as she handed it to her. "Please, do not tell my master."

"I swear," Mina said, gratitude awash on her face as she greedily ate the food. "Thank you."

"Sleep now. I will speak to him, and hopefully, tonight will be better for you."

"I… Thank you, Celine."

She smiled and left the room. In bed, Mina was content to have something in her stomach as she fell back to sleep.

Mina awoke to sound of the door opening. She looked over, expecting to see Celine. Instead, a man she didn't recognize walked in.

"What do you want?" she demanded as she stood.

"Celine is being punished for disobeying our master, so I was sent to fetch you. He demands you join him in the dining room."

She found she was once again wrapped in gossamer fabric. "I'll dress and come down shortly."

"Yes, madam."

Her impatience grew as he watched her. "I am not dressing in front of you," she said when she realized he was waiting for her.

"My instructions are to escort you down."

"Then wait in the hall."

"I cannot."

She went into the closet, only to see the few gowns she had found were no longer there. Her heart sank at the sight, and she groaned in frustration. A pile of rolled-up fabric on the top shelf caught her eye. It was the same fabric wrapped around her, and she laughed as she gathered it up.

Chapter 4

The Favor

racke stood when she entered the dining room. He drank from his goblet before looking at her. "Took you long—" His head tilted at the sight of her. "What have you done now?" he asked, unable to hide his amusement.

"You left the fabric, so I took the opportunity."

He stepped up to her, walking around and admiring her in a gown of layered gossamer, covering her nearly from her neck to her ankles. "Defiant to a fault." He stepped up behind her and laced his arm around her waist. "Perhaps I should put you with Celine," he whispered into her ear before he appeared in his chair and took another drink.

Mina fought the shudder threatening to swallow her whole. "What did you do to her?"

He laughed. "No less than she deserved. As faithful as they are to me, I do not understand why she helped you."

Mina snorted. "Because unlike you, she has some humanity left within her."

His jaw clenched as he quickly stood up. "I would be careful saying such things."

Looking at the table, she couldn't help but note it was empty, save his usual goblet. "Why am I down here?"

"I thought we could try again. I will have food brought in," he stopped for a moment when she glared at him, "for you to eat if you honestly answer my questions."

She sighed. "All right."

"Tell me what your last job was."

He watched her go rigid at his question, and she turned away. "I would rather starve," she snipped.

"Well, we're off to a great start, aren't we? Hmm, perhaps I can guess. Let's see, well-educated, comes from money. You were a teacher. No, wait, a governess."

When she looked at him, he was caught off guard by the sorrow in her eyes. "How did you know?" she asked.

"A simple guess. Why would you not wish to discuss such a noble profession?"

"Ask your next question already," she demanded.

"That is borderline rude."

Pain ripped through her abdomen while her appetite awoke at the prospect of food. "I don't care. I can't think—" He was suddenly before her with an iron grip on her wrist, and she froze.

"Listen here, draga mea. I do not care if you starve, freeze, or catch your death. You are nothing to me, you mean nothing to me. If you wish to be fed, if you wish to be treated with respect, you will behave. If I have to explain this again, you will be sleeping in the dungeon. Do you understand?"

"I dare you!" she hissed. He pulled her against himself and vaolmersed them into a cell.

"Enjoy," he snarked before he disappeared.

Mina paced the room, touching the walls, and struggling to catch her breath. She approached the tiny window, letting the icy air hit her face as her heart pounded in her ears, and her throat only tightened more. Exhaustion from lack of food crept in, and she passed out, landing with a thud on the floor.

Mina came to, surprised to be in her bed, dressed in a nightgown, and covered with a blanket. She looked up when Dracke approached her.

"What happened?" she asked.

"I was going to ask you. I could hear your heart pounding from all the way downstairs."

"I… I don't like small spaces," she admitted reluctantly.

"I thought you were going to have a heart attack. While I may not care what happens to you, I'd hate to lose my new toy before I've really had the chance to enjoy it." He watched as her face flushed, and she diverted her gaze. "Oh, please. I do not mean like that. Have I given you the impression?"

"The way you make me dress—"

"You must show me you are worthy of proper clothing and food, which so far you have failed to do. All you've done is disobey me. While I'll admit, I do enjoy toying with you this way, I would never take you for myself." He looked away from her. "I find the thought repulsive."

She was surprised that his last words stung a little. "Thank you. I'm sorry."

"Hmm, a genuine apology. Perhaps we are finally getting somewhere." Ignoring the angry stare she gave him, he came to rest on the edge of the bed.

"Please, at least tell me it was Celine who took care of me."

He laughed. "Yes, I revoked her punishment."

"All she did was give me a little food."

"Against my wishes." He studied her for a moment. "Will you get dressed and join me in the dining room? You have real gowns now."

"Why would you do that?"

"As a peace offering. Do you accept?"

"Yes. I'll be down shortly."

"Thank you." He disappeared.

Mina went to the closet and picked out a dark purple gown. She was slipping on black shoes when Celine walked in. Mina gasped softly at the mark on her cheek.

"What did he do to you?"

"I did this to myself, to prove my loyalty."

"You… you burned your own face?"

"It will be fully healed by tonight."

Mina started to ask but quickly thought better of it. "I'm sorry."

"Don't be. I'm glad I helped you."

Celine braided Mina's hair and escorted her to the dining room where she sat across from Dracke. Her meal appeared on the table. She bit her lip, unsure of how to proceed. When Dracke noticed she had not touched the food, he was instantly beside her.

"What's wrong?"

"I don't wish to appear rude…"

"But?"

She looked down. "I do not eat poultry, nor do I drink wine. I am sorry."

"What would you like?"

She told him some of the foods she liked. In response, he had stew, tea, and bread brought in.

"Thank you," she said with sincerity. She ate her meal as he continued to drink. "Are you not dining with me?"

"I am."

She decided not to pursue it. "What do you do around here all day?"

"I sleep."

A nervous giggle escaped her lips. "Apologies. I simply meant, what do you do when you are awake?"

"I walk the chateau, speak with my servants, sometimes read."

"I love to read."

"It has become a good way to… pass the time."

Mina continued to eat, realizing this was the most civil exchange they'd had. "Wait, what day is it?"

"It is nighttime."

She took a breath. "I meant the date."

"Of course. It is the twelfth."

"Already?" She took a sip of her tea, trembling slightly as she set the cup back on the saucer. "I have a favor to ask."

Dracke appeared beside her, sitting on the edge of the table with his arms crossed. "Well, this should at least be interesting."

"I need to go to Lyndon tomorrow. It's important."

"Why do you need to go?"

She clasped her hands and swallowed hard. "Please." A cry flew from her lips when he pulled her from the chair and pinned her to the wall, his hand around her throat. "What—"

"I should've known," he snarled as he released her.

Mina's hand wrapped tenderly around her neck. "I don't understand," she murmured.

"You were only being civil because you wanted something from me."

"No—"

"Don't bother." His eyes met hers, burning red as he stared. "You will stand here until I say otherwise."

He returned to his seat and finished his drink. Her heart thumped, and the sound nearly drove him mad. He watched her writhe against the wall, trying to break free. A smile broke out across his face, followed by a deep laugh. She stopped and glared at him.

"What is so funny?" she demanded.

"You," he answered as he appeared before her.

"I wasn't being nice just to ask a favor. I swear it."

His eyes met hers again. "You will not speak." She stared daggers at him, with her words trapped in her throat. His hand brushed along her neck, then down her arm. Her body tensed and the anger in her eyes quickly switched to unbridled fear. "Hmm, this is so tempting, the things I could do to you."

A tear rolled down her cheek, and she moaned. Her eyes went wide when he vanished from the room, leaving her all alone. The scent of her meal wafted to her, and she was filled with a longing to sit and eat. She closed her eyes, thinking back to one of her favorite books and trying to picture the story, anything but the torture she was enduring.

"What do we have here?"

Mina watched as the man approached her, the same man who had been in her room. She shook her head, desperately trying to pull away from the wall.

"Ah, I see. A treat from the master." He laughed as he walked to her. His hand caressed her cheek. "Hmm, we haven't had any fresh meat in here for a long time." He reached down to unzip his pants. Mina could only cry in silence, unable to make a sound. "What?" the man asked suddenly, his eyes wide. He fell to the floor with a knife in his back. Mina looked up to see Dracke watching her.

"I apologize for using you as bait, but after the way he spoke of you, I couldn't trust him. I would be unable to do anything to stop him during the day." His head tilted. "Aren't you even grateful?" Her mouth opened, but no words came out. "Oh, right. Very well. You are free."

She collapsed to her knees, sobbing and dry heaving. Her body shook as she slowly stood up straight. Her hand hit his face before he had time to react. "How dare you?" she screamed.

"I did it to protect you from him."

"No, you did it as a game."

"I overheard him talking to Mael, our chef. He said he had every intention of taking you for himself. I couldn't let that happen."

"Why not kill him immediately?" she asked with a scoff.

"I had to be sure he wasn't all talk."

"You could've commanded him to speak the truth. It was a game!" she reiterated.

"Fine, I admit. It was both. I was curious to see your reaction as well." He chuckled as his hand caressed his sore cheek. "You did not disappoint."

Mina glanced at the food on the table, but her appetite was as dead as the man on the floor. She took a step, but her legs gave out. Dracke caught her, his face inches from her own. He clutched her tightly before he sat her down.

"Are you going to faint?" he asked softly.

"No."

He straightened up and cleared his throat. "About your request, the answer is no."

"Why not? I think I deserve it after what you did."

"You are not to leave the estate. If you escape, I will drag you and your father here, then I will put you in separate cells. Do I make myself clear?"

"Please let me go tomorrow."

"You keep using that word, as if it will make something happen."

She stood up, keeping his gaze. "Very well. I am going to Lyndon in the morning, and you will not stop me."

He grabbed her arms and vaolmersed her into her chamber, throwing her to the floor. "I'd like to see you try." He vanished.

She ran to the door, but it was locked. She pounded and cried to no avail. Finally, she took a shower and climbed into bed.

Right before sunrise, Celine came in. Mina was in her nook.

"I am about to retire and wanted to see if you are in need of anything?"

"No, Celine. Thank you."

Celine left, but the door remained partly open. Mina walked to it and looked out. She wasn't sure if this was a trap set by Dracke or if Celine was helping her again, but she was willing to take the risk. No one was in the hallway. She went back into her room, shaking her head because she had no real clothing to wear, only the fancy gowns which would not keep her warm. Her shoes were not appropriate for riding, but they were all he had given her.

Downstairs, she found a cloak on a hook by the door. She slipped it on, went outside, and pulled two roses off the vine before going to the stables. Once her horse was saddled and bridled, she climbed on and rode out through the open gate. She clung to her steed as they made their way to Lyndon, shivering the entire way.

Half-frozen by the time she arrived at the cemetery, Mina jumped down from her horse and ran a few circles, trying to warm herself up. She went through the gate, leaving him tied right outside. It didn't take her long to find her mother's grave.

She laid down a rose. "I miss you. I wonder what you would say about this if you were still alive, and Father returned without me. I thought perhaps he would've attempted a rescue, but I believe he is too afraid of the prince. I can't say I blame him."

A few minutes later, she made her way to another headstone. The marble shone in what little sunlight filtered through the clouds. Mina laid her palm on the cold, smooth surface. She set the rose down, spoke a few words while wiping the tears as they fell, then returned to her horse. Her body was numb from the cold and her grief.

A small groundskeeper's shed caught her eye, and she smiled at the smoke coming from the chimney, beckoning her. Without knocking, she walked inside, only to find it empty. She realized he must have been out tending to something and had lit a fire in preparation for his return. She knelt in front of it, warming herself before leaving again. A pair of gloves caught her eyes, and feeling guilty as she did, she slipped them on.

She mounted her horse and made her way back to Parysse.

Celine walked into Mina's chamber and was shocked at the sight. She rushed downstairs. A moment later, Dracke vaolmersed into the room. Mina was curled up on the bed, undressed with only her cloak over her. Her hair was matted to her head with sweat while her body trembled, raging with fever.

He sat beside her, running his hand along her cheek and forehead, unable to believe how warm she was. "Mina, can you hear me?"

She looked at him, her eyelids fluttering. "I'm sorry."

"Because you left?"

"Yes," she answered quietly, her teeth chattering.

"Very well. You know I can heal you, right?"

"Yes."

"But I won't. I told you that you were not allowed to leave. For your disobedience, you are on your own tonight."

"Wait—" But he vanished before she could utter another word. She clutched her stomach and coughed, her body on fire while she froze at the same time. Her throat and head hurt, and everything felt wrong.

Mina stood up, determined to get warm in the shower. The cloak fell away from her as she walked towards her washroom. The shower was dark marble with a copper showerhead above her. She turned on the tap then climbed in, standing under the heated water.

Of course, this was the worst thing she could do for a fever, but she wasn't in her right mind. In her delirium, she enjoyed being under the water, until she didn't. She quickly switched it to cold, but it was too late. Her heart pounded in her ears as the world faded to black.

She managed to shut the tap off, only to lose consciousness at the same time. Dracke caught her before she hit the shower floor. He wrapped her in a towel and carried her to bed, instructing Celine to take care of her. He returned to the washroom and stood still for a moment, waiting for his body to ease. Seeing her had awakened his desire. Though he'd only caught a glimpse before wrapping her up, that was all it took.

"Master!"

He rushed into the room to see Celine sitting beside Mina, her hand on her chest. "What?" he demanded.

"I don't think she's breathing!"

He ran to her, placing his fingers on Mina's neck. "I can barely feel her heartbeat." He bit his wrist and brought it to her mouth, forcing his blood inside her. The bite healed once he pulled away. "There you are, draga mea. It'll be all right now." He turned to Celine. "Bring her up some broth and hot tea."

"Yes, master." She left to see to it.

Mina's eyelids fluttered a moment before she opened her eyes and looked at him. She smiled, taking his hand. "I need you," she said softly.

Dracke immediately stood up. "What?"

She collected herself, realizing where she was and what had happened. "You healed me after you said you wouldn't?"

"I had no choice."

Hearing the pain in his voice, she sat up and stared at him. "What does that mean?"

"You were in pretty bad shape."

"Thank you."

He laughed. "I didn't do it for you. You are still my prisoner, especially now after stealing two more roses."

She gasped softly. "How did you know?"

"I am connected to my land. I know everything that happens here. Now, what did you take them for?"

Mina looked down. "It's private."

"Tell me."

Celine walked in, and Dracke said nothing as she helped Mina with her tray before hastily making her exit. Mina slowly ate the broth, knowing once she finished, he would question her again.

His patience wore thin. "Well?" he demanded when she set the tray on her bedside table.

Mina kept her head down, sipping her tea.

"I will command you."

The cup fell from her hand, shattering on impact with the floor. "I can't," she said, bending down and picking up the pieces. He knelt beside her to help, and she failed to hide her surprise.

"What aren't you telling me?"

She held up her hand to show him the broken cup. "This is me."

He shook his head. "I don't understand."

"I am broken, and nothing will ever make me whole again. I am a river of tears and sorrow."

"You went to the cemetery? The roses were for the dead?"

"Yes," she replied. He gripped her elbow and helped her stand, carefully taking the broken pieces from her.

"Why would you not tell me this?"

"Why do you need to know?" she shot back.

He disappeared, then returned a moment later minus the damaged cup. "Because you belong to me. It is my right to know every single thing you do."

"You don't own me."

Dracke chuckled. "Are we really going over this again? You made the bargain and took your father's place."

"But a life sentence for a rose?"

"No, Mina. A life sentence for theft. You are lucky that is all I did. When I ruled these lands…" He turned away, clenching his hands. "Never mind. Get dressed and meet me in my parlor."

"Whatever for?" she asked with a tremble in her voice.

"Your first lesson." He disappeared.

She dressed quickly, not wishing to anger him further as she hurried down the stairs. He stepped out of his parlor as she approached. Watching him instead of where she was going, she tumbled down the remaining stairs, landing hard on her hands and knees.

Dracke rushed to her but quickly turned away at the blood pouring from the gash on her shin. He scooped her up and practically threw her into the washroom beside his parlor.

"Clean yourself up, foolish girl!"

She rinsed off her leg in the tub, watching in horror as it healed. She realized she still had his blood in her system, and she gagged at the thought. After taking a moment to collect herself, she joined him in the parlor, where he sat in his chair.

"Come here and sit."

She looked around. "There's only one chair."

He pointed to the floor. "Kneel beside me. Now," he growled. She didn't move. "Unless you'd rather sit here." He patted his left knee.

Her pulse raced, but she did as he commanded, kneeling beside him and keeping her head down. "What do you want?"

"To teach you how things will work around here. You belong to me. Your life is mine to do with as I see fit. If I tell you to stay in the manor, you stay inside. If I tell you to do something, you do it without hesitation. You will help me in the library every evening after we have dinner together."

"Help with what?"

"Cataloging my books. I have spent nearly every night in there for… a very long time. I could use your help. In exchange, you will be well rewarded with jewels and fine clothing."

"You'll pay your property?" she asked in disgust, getting to her feet. He was immediately at eye level with her.

"I own you, but you are not mere property, draga mea."

"What exactly am I then?"

"For now, you are my librarian. Follow me."

They left the dining room and went down the hall. He opened the large set of doors and gestured for her to go inside. The sheer size of the library took her breath away.

"This is incredible!"

Craning her neck, she looked up in disbelief at the shelves of books looming over her. Her fingers brushed along their spines as she smiled at the sight. She continued to the wall and glimpsed out of the gothic window at the gardens. A table sat between a set of shelves, dark and sturdy, covered with books and leaves of paper.

"Like it?" he asked as he stepped up beside her, leaving no space between them. His eyes widened when she looked at him and smiled in response. He swallowed hard, trying not to stare at her lips.

"So many wonderful books in here. You have an amazing collection."

He started to return her smile but caught himself, shifting uncomfortably where he stood. "Glad you like it. This is where we will sit and catalog. We will begin tomorrow night."

"In the meantime, would you take me on a tour of the chateau?" she asked, pushing down her nerves.

"Yes." He took her arm and led her from the room. "On the first floor is the library, the dining room, the ballroom, the galley, and the stockroom. The second floor has guest rooms, each one as lavish as your own," he explained as they walked.

"What's up there?" she asked when they arrived back at the staircase.

He glanced towards the third floor. "Nothing you need to see," he answered curtly.

Her throat tightened at his tone, and she forced a polite smile. "Of course."

"It is forbidden. If I find you up there, I will lock you in the dungeon, no questions asked."

"I… I won't go there. I promise."

"Good, now you need to eat before turning in for the day."

Chapter 5

The Library

ina awoke, cold and clammy. She sat up and went to the window nook, admiring the crescent moon. Slipping on her cloak and shoes, she went downstairs and into the kitchen.

Worried she would get in trouble, her nerves were on edge, but a cup of tea was exactly what she needed. The kettle screamed at her. She jumped and quickly removed it from the fire. She poured the steaming water into her cup, savoring the peppermint scent as it wafted up to her.

I don't deserve to find happiness. I will stop fighting him, and I will do whatever he demands. My life has never really been my own, but especially these past few weeks. My grief… my grief and my pain will never leave me.

I still see him, so cold and empty. It's my fault. I couldn't save him, and now, being here, I believe this is my punishment. I deserve to be here, to be tortured and degraded. After all, isn't that what they do to killers?

Once finished with her tea, she washed the dishes. A hand clamped down on her shoulder. "Find everything you needed?"

She turned to see a woman she didn't recognize. "Yes, I made a cup of tea. I… I hope that's all right?"

"Yes, madam. I am Yvette. Let me know if I can assist in any way."

"Thank you." Mina watched her leave, closing her eyes as she tried to calm herself before leaving the kitchen.

As she approached the stairs, her gaze trailed to the foyer, landing on the exit. She knew to leave would mean certain death for her father, and she would not have another life taken because of her. Even saving him, she did not feel it balanced out, nor would she ever be redeemed.

She couldn't go back to sleep, so she went into the library and picked out a book. She sat by the fire, snuggled up, and reading until she nodded off. Which is how Dracke found her when the sun had gone down.

"Something wrong with your bed?"

She startled at his voice, then stood, the book falling to the floor with a thud. Quickly, she picked it up and faced him. "I'm sorry."

"For what?"

"Falling asleep in here."

"Honestly, I can't think of a better place, can you? So many ideas, stories, passions, all in one place."

Mina studied him for a moment. "Are you making fun of me?"

"For falling asleep? No. For looking like my grandmother in your nightgown? Yes," he said with a laugh.

She snatched her cloak off the chair and wrapped it tightly around herself. "I'll get dressed, then join you for dinner."

"Very good. Be prompt."

She rushed upstairs and changed as fast as she could, grateful he kept his word and had provided her with a closet full of fancy gowns. She gripped the handrail as she hurried down the steps, careful not to fall again. Outside the dining room, she stopped to run her hand through her hair in an attempt to smooth it down before stepping inside.

Dracke stood as she entered. She gave him a small bow, then sat at the end of the table. Her meal appeared before her, and she ate quietly. She stopped when she realized Dracke was speaking to her.

"I'm sorry. What did you say?"

He set his goblet on the table and watched her for a moment. "Are you all right?"

"I'm fine," she replied, burying her surprise at the concern in his voice.

"I asked if you were ready to start cataloging tonight."

"Yes. I love your library."

"What's your favorite book?"

She laughed softly. "Oh, I couldn't choose. So many good ones. You?"

He said the name, and the fork nearly slipped from her hand. It clattered against her plate as she caught it. "Mina?"

She set the fork down and looked at him. "Sorry. It's my nerves."

He appeared beside her, lifting her chin so their eyes met. "Are you so afraid of me?"

"No, not afraid," she lied. "Nervous. I don't wish to upset you."

He chuckled at first, but it quickly snowballed into laughter. "Have I broken you in already?"

Her head went down as she folded her hands in her lap. "I told you I'm broken."

Dracke's laughter ceased. "I'm sorry."

She jerked her head up in disbelief, her gaze meeting his as she tried to determine if he was sincere. "Whatever for?"

"Saying what I did. Why are you broken?"

"I'm ready to work in the library when you are," she said, standing and walking past him.

He gripped her wrist firmly. "Tell me."

She kept her eyes on the floor. "Please, please don't make me." She cried out when he pulled her closer, her face mere inches from his.

"Why are you broken?"

"Because I am. Now please, release me."

His hand opened, and she nearly fell as she pulled away. "Fine. Let's go to the library, shall we?" he asked, leading the way.

Mina said nothing as she walked behind him. In the library, he showed her where he had been working. "You cataloged all of these?" she asked as she flipped through the ledger.

"I've had a lot of time to do so, as you see," he said, taking the book from her. "You write the title and author here, the summary from the back cover, and any relevant information, such as genre, year of publication, and so on."

"Where do I start?"

He pointed to a stack of books on the table. "I haven't done those yet. Go ahead while I find more."

"Yes, mi'lord."

He sighed. "Mina, we've been over this. Call me Dracke."

"It doesn't feel… right to address you so informally."

"It's just the two of us in a library. No need for bowing and titles. I insist."

She sat down and began to write, copying the information the way he had. The next book on the pile was a history book. She wrote the title down, then began to read it after she found a section on Vlad from eighty years before. She gasped softly as she read line after line about his cruelty.

"You are here to catalog, not read," Dracke snapped as he snatched the book away.

"You didn't mind that I read earlier."

"Yes, because it was a play. This," he said, holding up the book, "is not for you to read."

"I'm sorry."

"Keep it up, and you will be."

"What do you mean?"

"I mean do as I say or face the punishment."

She shivered as she thought of her father in the tiny cell. "The dungeon?" she asked softly.

"That's a vacation compared to what I would do."

"You say I live here now, and I am here for the rest of my life. Why wouldn't I want to learn more about the history of my new home? I've studied for years, of course, but I've never come across this."

She jumped when he slammed the book on the table. "It is off limits. Do you understand?"

"No," she responded as she stood up. "I don't understand. It's just history. We are in a room literally full of books about it. Why do you care what I read?"

He picked up another book, smirking as he handed it to her. "Perhaps this would be more suited to you."

The cover bore gold roses with silver vines. "My Dearest of Affection: A Modern Love Story." She rolled her eyes. "I believe you have me confused for my sister, Elise."

"Right. Marius did say you were the youngest. How many sisters do you have?"

At the mention of her family, her heart ached and tears welled in her eyes. She took the books and put them on the shelf. She stopped, her fingers resting along the spines as she gave in to the tears falling down. Her shoulders sagged as she buried her face in her hands.

Dracke was unsure of what to say. He sat at the table and continued to catalog, knowing whatever he said or did would be the wrong thing. Once she collected herself, she continued to put away books.

"You seemed to have learned my system quickly," he complimented.

"It's organized and easy to follow," she said softly as she sat beside him. She continued to write until she couldn't stop yawning.

"Mina, the sun will be up soon. Please, retire for the day."

"I have a few more—"

"Go to bed. They'll still be here tonight."

"Yes, Dracke." She watched him for a moment, and when he went back to writing, she slipped the history book into the fold of her gown and quickly left the library.

In her chamber, she placed the book into her nightstand drawer, then changed for bed. She smiled as she tucked herself under the blanket, knowing she would read it once she woke up. She turned off the lamp and started to nod off.

The door slammed open. "Where is it?" he demanded, flipping on the light.

Mina sat up in bed, staring at him with her mouth agape. "Where is what?"

"Don't play stupid with me," he yelled as he snatched her from the bed and threw her to the floor, looking through her blankets and pillows.

"What are—"

"Where is the damn book?"

She swallowed hard but shook her head. "I don't know."

He lifted her by her throat, his eyes red with fire. "Where is it?" he commanded.

"In… in the nightstand."

He dropped her, and she landed hard, yelping in pain. He vaolmersed to the nightstand and yanked the drawer out. It fell to the floor with a clatter as he gripped the book. He appeared before her, grabbing her chin painfully so she had no choice but to look at him.

"Did you read it?" he asked through clenched teeth.

"No," she answered with a steady voice.

He pushed her back as he stood up. "Why did you take it?"

"I… I was curious," she answered as she fumbled to get to her feet. "I have never heard of Vlad—"

"Do not say his name!" He gripped her wrist and threw her to the bed, bending her over it. "Put your hands on the mattress. Now!"

Trembling in terror, she blindly obeyed. "What are you going to do?"

"What you deserve," he answered, as the book made contact with her behind, nearly sending her to her knees. "Will you defy me again?"

"I only—"

Wham! The book hit her again, and she gripped the mattress to keep herself from falling, crying out in pain.

"Answer the question! Are you going to continue to defy me? To steal from me?"

"I didn't steal it! I borrowed it. I was going to bring it back to the library tonight, I swear!"

"Semantics, draga mea. You stole from me, again."

When she turned to face him, the book slammed into her once more. She could no longer stand and fell in a heap to the floor, sobbing in pain. He raised the book above her.

"Do you swear you didn't read it?"

"I do," she said between hitched breaths. "Please—"

He rolled his eyes. "That word means nothing to me, besides a pointless plea. Which I will not give into."

She sat up, wiping her tears, then surprised him when she returned to the bed, assuming the position with her hands on the mattress. "Do what you must."

"I beg your pardon?"

"I deserve it. I deserve every hit, every spark of pain. After what I've done, I no longer deserve mercy nor the right to live."

"It's just a book."

"That is not what I am referring to." She lowered her head. "Please, hit me again. Make me feel physical pain."

"Why?"

"Because then I no longer feel my heart ache. I didn't realize it until now. I want… no, I need to feel something. Anything besides this. It's too much, and I would rather you beat me within an inch of my life than continue to feel this way."

The book dropped to the floor as his mouth fell open at her words. "Mina—"

"Do it!" she cried. "I can't feel like this anymore."

For a moment, he didn't move. He couldn't conceive of what she needed, what would make her feel better. His thoughts drifted back to his mother, and the time he was sad over the family dog dying from old age. He remembered what she'd said and done for him then.

Mina yelped when he grabbed her arm, pulling her to his chest and holding her tightly. "What are you doing?" she asked.

"Let it out."

"What?"

"It's all right. Whatever you have done, you have paid for it. I assure you. Let it all out."

She looked up at him, seeing pain that matched hers in his eyes, if only for a moment before his expression softened. She collapsed against him as she burst into uncontrollable sobs. He slowly lowered them both to the floor, until he was sitting with her in his lap as she wept into his shirt. His arms kept a tight grip around her as he stroked one hand through her hair.

He realized she had fallen asleep. "Everything will be all right, draga mea," he assured her. "You have no reason to feel such pain. It will be all right." He slowly stood back up, laying her on the bed, and covering her with a blanket. Before he left, he watched her for a moment, seeing some semblance of peace in her expression before he turned off the light.

Mina said nothing during dinner. Dracke took a swig, licking his lips before he approached her.

"How are you this evening?" he asked, watching her with intensity. She repositioned in her seat, and she let out a small whimper of pain. "Mina?"

"I'm all right."

"How bad is it?"

She took a sip of tea before meeting his gaze. "How bad is what?"

"Your pain."

"I'm fine."

He chuckled. "Shall I punish you for your deceit?"

"I'm not—"

"There is no point in lying. It's quite obvious." His eyes met hers, burning red. "You will stay seated here." He brought his wrist to his mouth, biting it and offering it to her. She debated for a moment before she reluctantly drank from him. She tried to pull away, but he gripped her face with his other hand, forcing her to consume more than was needed. She mumbled and squirmed as his blood worked through her.

"Why did you do that?" she demanded when he released her.

"You will see. Now, are you ready to work in the library?"

A warmth spread through her, and her cheeks flushed. She quickly drank the water in the crystal goblet beside her plate. "I need a moment." Her thighs clenched as heat rose from within.

He leaned down, his lips brushing her ear. "Whatever is the matter?"

Her breath shuddered as she ached in her very core. Being so close to him, his scent was a mix of copper and pine, as though he had run through the woods. She nearly laughed at the thought. "I need to go." Her hands gripped her legs as she writhed. His blood worked through her, her heart racing as her desire continued to build. "Please, let me go," she said softly, trembling in her seat.

"Why?"

Her face flushed, her eyes widened, and her lips opened. She moaned as her legs rubbed together. "Please," she tried again.

He smiled as he looked into her eyes. "Very well. You are free of my control."

She ran upstairs to her room, slamming the door, then climbing onto her bed. Her hand gripped the hem of her gown and lifted it. Her body ached in a way she had never felt before, and she surprised herself as her fingers began to caress her aching bud. Her fingers slipped inside, while her thumb stroked softly in a circular pattern.

Her back arched in response as the waves of pleasure began to crash upon her. She couldn't breathe, couldn't think, as euphoria rushed through her, taking her over completely. She had never known such rapture in all her life.

When the storm within her finally came to a stop, she went to the washroom to clean up. She finished by splashing cool water on her face before she joined Dracke in the library.

"Have a nice time?" he asked with a chuckle.

"What?"

"Nothing. Here, let us catalog these books."

"I won't read any, I promise," she said softly as she sat beside him.

They worked side by side for a few hours. She came across another history book and looked to see Dracke standing at a shelf towards the back, facing away, and engrossed in a worn tome.

She opened the book. *Vlad was the cruelest ruler the lands had ever seen. Every crime, regardless of how serious or minor, received the same punishment. Death by impalement.*

Mina's breath caught in her throat, and her heart sped up when she realized Dracke was behind her, looking over her shoulder. She quickly shut the book, setting it on the stack with the others. While unsure if he realized what she had read, she knew her heart would surely give her away.

Instead, he said nothing as he sat beside her and continued to work. She finished, replaced the books, and retrieved more. She smiled while she watched him write.

"You have lovely penmanship," she remarked.

He chuckled in response. "Thanks."

"Is it just you in this chateau?"

"What are you playing at? You've met some of my staff."

"I… I meant as far as family. I—" Before she could finish, he disappeared. Her shoulders sagged, and she retired to her chamber, ready for a good night's sleep.

Chapter 6

The Strawberry

fter a few nights of cataloguing, Mina learned how to word her questions to get answers instead of offending Dracke. Feeling particularly bold, she flipped through a history book, finding another mention of Vlad. A drawing caught her eye.

"That's horrible," she murmured in disgust.

Dracke stepped up behind her to look over her shoulder. "Why do you say that?"

"What could these people have possibly done to be tortured like this? It's absolutely brutal."

"Perhaps they were attacking a peaceful land."

"Even so," she said softly. Her lip curled at the sight.

"What would you suggest then, sit down to tea?"

"Of course not."

He sat beside her and trailed his fingers along her arm and shoulder. "What would you do?"

"I would fight for my people, yes, but this is inhumane and excessive."

"According to this, it worked. They lived in peace for nearly half a century."

"Just because it worked doesn't mean it's right."

He chuckled softly. "I love how you think."

"There are women and children in here. It is downright cruel."

Gently, he pulled the book from her grip and laid it on the table. "You don't need to see such things." She started to argue, but he continued. "Not before we eat then turn in."

He helped her stand, and she pulled back to look at him. "What is in your goblet?" she blurted out.

"What?"

"When we… dine together. It's all you ever have. What's in it? Why don't you ever eat?"

"Do you seriously not know what I am?"

She thought of his blood in her mouth, of how easy it was for him to pierce his own flesh with his sharp canines, but she shook her head. She wanted him to tell her. "No."

He sighed. "I do not feel like discussing it now." He said nothing else as they walked into the dining room.

Dracke sat in silence, not engaging when she asked him questions about the chateau or his family. Once she finished her meal, he vanished without a word. She knew he was upset because she asked about his goblet.

She left the dining room and headed upstairs, intent to spend the remaining hour of the night reading in her nook. When she reached the top of the second-floor staircase, her eyes were drawn towards the third floor. Her curiosity piqued at the idea of exploring for herself. *Forbidden.* The word made it even more tempting.

Before she knew it, she was at the top of the stairs. Her heart thudded in fear of discovery, but she had to see what he was hiding. The first room she came to was a large chamber containing only two pieces of furniture. Against the wall was an antique desk, nearly as high as the ceiling, but it was not the piece that caught her attention.

In place of a bed was a sleek black coffin lined with a crimson velvet interior. Mina's eyes went wide at the thought of sleeping inside such a prison. Horrified, she turned away. Her eyes landed on a journal on the desk. She picked it up and began to thumb through it.

I have tried everything, looked through every book, and I cannot find a way to undo this. There must be some way to break—

"What are you doing in here?" a dark, cold voice asked.

Mina slowly laid the book down as gooseflesh raised over her body. The temperature had dropped twenty degrees in as many seconds. The lump in her throat grew as she faced Dracke.

"I… I didn't mean to come up here. I'm sorry," she uttered in unrestrained fear.

"No, you aren't. Not yet," he threatened.

"What are you going to do?" she asked, her voice not more than a whisper.

He vaolmersed right before her with his hand around her throat. "I told you what would happen if you came up here. Do you have any idea what you could have done?" His grip loosened as he stepped back, his eyes burning red at the sight of her. He closed them and turned away.

Frozen inside and out, all she could do was look on, petrified and waiting for whatever punishment he would inflict.

"Please," she tried.

"Leave, now! I am done with you," he commanded, unable to face her.

"I—"

"If you are still here when I open my eyes, you will regret it."

Running on legs that were nothing more than jelly, she gathered her strength and fled, not from the room but from the chateau itself. A blast of freezing air hit her heated face as she charged out into the snowy night.

She only knew to run as fast as she could, not caring she had not grabbed a cloak or coat. Glancing behind as she ran into the woods, she was relieved to see no one pursued her.

As she turned back around, her foot caught on a root and sent her crashing towards the ground. She cried out as her ankle made a sickening snap. Pain shot through her leg, and she realized this could be the end, for she couldn't stand. Her body trembled in the snow as she ran hot and clammy. Her mind slowed as the sobs wrenched from her mouth and eyes.

This is it. I'm going to lay out here, alone and forgotten. The cold will swallow me up, and I will simply cease to exist. Maybe I will finally know what it is to feel peace.

Strong arms gathered her up, tearing her from these thoughts. She cried out in surprise when she was lifted up and wrapped in a warm cloak. Her eyes met those of her rescuer.

"Dracke," she said softly.

He vaolmersed them into her chamber. After settling her onto the bed, he bit his wrist and forced her to drink. Her body grew warm as her ankle healed.

"What were you thinking?" He shook his head. "That was foolish."

"Dracke—"

"You could have died out there!" he yelled. "Why did you leave?" he demanded as he pulled his arm away.

"You… you told me to."

"I meant the room, Mina. Not for you to leave the chateau."

"Oh. You said you were done with me. I thought you wanted me to go."

"That wasn't my intention," Dracke said with a softened tone.

"I'm sorry. I know you told me not to go up there." She wiped her tears as she looked down. He placed his hand on her arm.

"What did you see?"

"A journal on the desk, and the… the coffin."

"Did you read the journal?" he asked. His voice wavered at the possibility.

"No. You showed up just as I found it."

"Good." He sighed in relief. "Was this punishment enough or do I need to remind you why you should never go up there?"

She looked at him with fear drawn across her face. "Please, don't lock me in the awful dungeon. I'll be good. I swear it."

"I'll give you this one chance. Defy me again, and there will be no discussion. Is that understood?"

"Yes, Dracke. Thank you."

"For now, you need food." He vaolmersed and reappeared a few moments later, holding a bowl of hot stew.

"How do you do that?" Mina asked as she sat up and carefully took it from him.

"Do what?"

"Disappear?"

He chuckled as he watched her eat. "I'll tell you about it someday."

She paused a moment, spoon mid-air before she met his gaze. "Can I… can I still help you in the library?"

"Of course."

"I like it in there," she admitted as she ate.

"I didn't before. Since I have the time, I enjoy it as well."

She wanted to ask what had changed, but the pain in his gaze stopped her. Knowing most people saw him as repulsive, she didn't notice so much when she looked in his eyes. Instead, she offered him the empty bowl. He took it, and she thanked him.

"I'll take care of this, then I'll turn in. We'll resume tonight if you are up for it."

"Thank you." She looked away for a moment and took a breath. "Does it… does it make you sick to your stomach, too?"

"What?"

"To… disappear like that. It makes me a little sick."

He chuckled softly. "No, it doesn't. You don't like to vaolmerse?"

Her head tilted at the last word. "Vaolmerse?"

"It means to walk in the veil, to disappear and appear elsewhere, as I do." He smiled before vanishing.

She stood and walked about the room, unable to believe her ankle was completely healed. She startled when he reappeared.

"Are you hurting?" he asked, looking down at her leg in concern.

"No, you healed me," she assured him.

"All get. Some sleep."

After supper, he walked her to the library, where she began going through romantic literature books. After cataloging one, she opened it carefully, and read a scene.

She looks for him, waiting for the day he will return. Her heart aches as she yearns to be in his arms, to have his lips press against her own. She sees him, and she runs to him. They nearly collide as his fingers entangle in her hair while she grips the back of his neck, holding him in a silent promise to never let go. His mouth kisses lower, trailing along her chin and into the crook of her neck.

"Reading anything good?"

The book fell from her hand, and he caught it in one quick motion. He saw the title and couldn't help but grin at her. His smile only grew when she blushed in response.

"Have you ever been in love?" she asked timidly.

His body stiffened at her words. "Love?" he said with a scoff. "I don't believe in it." He took a step back.

"How can you not believe in it? Love will fulfill you, sustain you, and carry you through the darkest nights."

"What was his name?" Dracke asked.

She laughed softly, the sound prickling his skin. "Oh, I've never been in love."

"Then how do you know it's real?" he asked.

"Because I've seen it. Before we lost my mother three winters ago, she and my father would look into each other's eyes, and you could see the love between them. It was so strong. I have waited my whole life to find a love like that."

"I wouldn't hold my breath." He opened it and scanned a few pages. "To look into your eyes is to see your soul. To look into your heart is to see your love." The laugh flew from his lips before he could help himself. "Really?"

She took it and shot him a dirty look. "I think it's sweet," she said as her fingers brushed along the spine.

Before she could stop him, he had the book in his hands and continued to read. "Her lips consume his as her nails dig into his back. Her hips raise—"

"Dracke!" she cried out, her face flush and her body feverish in response. "Please, stop," she begged quietly as she turned away to hide her embarrassment.

"Why does this make you so uncomfortable?"

"It's… it's not appropriate."

"Hmm, because you haven't dug your nails down my back?"

Her breath shuddered as she attempted to collect herself. He pulled her against his firm chest. "Dracke—"

"Are you all right?" he asked.

"Yes," she answered quietly.

"Why does this bother you so?" She trembled against him, and he wished he could ease her nerves.

"He… he didn't mean to."

Dracke suddenly turned serious. "What are you talking about? Did someone hurt you?"

"It doesn't matter. He—" She pulled away, regretting the words she was about to utter. "Never mind."

He brought his hand to her chin and gently raised her face until he met her gaze. "Who did this to you?"

Her eyes closed to hide the forming tears. "Can we get back to work?"

Knowing he wouldn't get any more out of her, he removed his hand. Neither spoke as she continued to catalog. Dracke sat beside her and worked as well, glancing at her from time to time.

What did she mean? Did someone hurt her? She is innocent. I find myself—

"Dracke, can we get a snack?"

Her voice pulled him from his thoughts. "Follow me." He shook his head to clear it as he led her to the kitchen. He set up a plate with strawberries, grapes, and nuts.

"Where do you get this?" she asked as she enjoyed the fruit.

"From the garden. It's the magic around my land. As you see, even the roses grow with no problem."

"It's amazing." She smiled at him, blushing in surprise when he returned her smile. Biting into a particularly juicy strawberry, she giggled, and the red juice glided down her chin. She reached for a napkin. The sweet, sticky liquid dripped down, and Dracke could no longer resist.

He licked it from her neck before sinking his fangs into her throat. The strawberry fell from her hand as she stood in shock, her breath shaky as her heart pounded in her chest. He pulled back, lust and shame reflecting in his eyes.

She looked at him for a moment, speechless, before she slapped him hard across the face. "You are disgusting!" she cried out. "Why would you do that?"

"I—" He shook his head. "I couldn't stop myself. I needed your blood, needed you, *draga mea*."

"Go to hell," she yelled as she ran from the room.

Dracke wiped his face, angry with himself for what he did. Part of him wanted to go after her, to beg her forgiveness, but he decided it was best to give her space.

In the shower, Mina scrubbed herself over and over as the shame tore through her. *How dare he? He had no right!* Her eyes closed, and she thought of his tongue flicking on her neck. He raised his head, gazing at her intently before his lips were on hers, his kiss greedy. His hands gripped her arms while his tongue explored her mouth.

Her breath caught in her throat when his fangs gently scraped along her lips. Then she shuddered as his hand caressed her hip before moving lower. His fingers were between her thighs, but her back hit the shower wall, pulling her from the moment.

Her core heated, aching to be touched again. She shut off the water, dried, then wrapped a towel around herself and stepped into her chamber, only to find Dracke waiting for her.

"What are you doing in here?" she demanded.

"I wanted to be sure you are all right. I need blood to live, and I can usually control my urges. This time—"

She turned away. "Please, go," she begged softly.

"I'm sorry."

"You… you had no right to do that. I am not your dinner."

"I am sorry for that as well."

Her head snapped in his direction. "Then what was your first apology for?"

He cleared his throat. "Apparently, since we have fed from each other, it has created a… legatura between us." He watched her face scrunch in confusion. "A connection. I imagined I was kissing you, and—"

"You caused that?"

"Yes."

She braced herself against the wall as her face flushed from the blood rushing through her. "Do you see me that way?"

"I cannot. You are too pure for me," he said sincerely. He looked up when she let out a scoff in response. "What is it?"

"I am not what you think I am."

"And what do I think you are?"

"Someone who will give whatever is necessary to help, that I am selfless and honorable."

"And what are you?"

"At the moment, I am your prisoner, which is all you need to know."

"Mina—"

"I need time to myself after what you did to me." She sighed in relief when he vaolmersed from the room. Dressed in her nightgown, she sat on the bed, contemplating the night's events.

Dracke paced in the parlor, his brow furrowed while his anger flared over what he did. To violate both her mind and her body in such a way, knowing she had done nothing to deserve either.

"Master, I am sorry to bother you."

"Is there a problem?" he demanded, turning to Celine.

She swallowed hard. "It's just, Madam Mina—"

"What about her?" he asked as he stalked towards her.

"She is crying and sent me away. I am worried."

Dracke stopped in his tracks and sighed. "I… I fed from her."

"What?"

"I didn't mean to. I will try again to apologize." He vaolmersed to the hallway, appearing outside Mina's chamber, hoping to earn even a nugget of grace. He knocked softly. "Mina, will you speak with me?"

Upon hearing no response, he walked inside to find her asleep on the bed, tears still wet upon her cheeks. He draped a blanket over her and returned to his parlor. Celine had refilled his goblet, and he lifted it to his lips, grimacing at the blood which was nowhere near as sweet as what he'd enjoyed in the kitchen.

Mina walked into the library the next night and began to catalog, not bothering to look up when Dracke appeared. "How are you?" he asked, knowing better than to expect an actual response.

She said nothing, so he sat beside her and placed his hand on her shoulder. Immediately, she stood and shelved a few books then gathered some more. When she came to sit back down, she moved her chair away from him before she continued to work.

Dracke vaolmersed to the kitchen and returned with a plate, setting it beside her books. She shoved it away and continued to write.

"Will you at least eat?"

"Why?" she asked, not looking up from the book in her hand.

"Because you need to."

"Oh, right. I eat so you can."

"Mina, please. It was an accident."

She scoffed. "So your fangs 'accidentally' fell into my neck?" she asked, staring at him with flames in her eyes.

"Mina—"

"I'll eat your food if you'll leave me alone."

When he vaolmersed from the room, she picked up the plate and ate every bite before she resumed cataloging. The night wore on slowly with her meticulous work. She yawned and realized her eyes were watering from exhaustion. After shelving a few books, she picked up her dish and went into the kitchen. She placed it in the sink and started to turn when thoughts of Dracke ran through her mind.

Her back bumped against the counter as she imagined his fangs penetrating her skin, her heart speeding up as his tongue brushed along her neck.

"Madam Mina, do you need anything?"

Mina's eyes flew open, and she gave Yvette a small smile as she tried to hide her embarrassment. "I'm fine, thank you," she said as she hurried from the room.

The next few nights passed in a similar manner, with Mina eating and working in the library. One night, Dracke decided he'd had enough. He appeared beside her, drew her to him, and vaolmersed them into the dining room. He pulled out the chair and sat her down before sitting on the edge of the table.

"We need to talk."

"Please do," she said, refusing to look at him.

"How can I make this right?"

She shook her head. "Can you go back in time?"

"No."

"Then there's nothing you can do."

"Master—" Celine froze when Dracke held up his hand, gesturing her to stop.

"Mina, work with me."

Celine cleared her throat. "I'm sorry, but—"

Dracke stood up and faced her. "What is so important?" he snapped.

"There is a constable at your door asking about Madam Mina."

"No," Mina whispered.

Dracke looked at her in confusion, then turned his attention back to Celine. "What does he want?"

"To speak with the both of you," Celine answered.

Dracke took Mina's arm and gently pulled her from her chair, holding her to him as he escorted her to the grand foyer. Mina stopped in her tracks, and Dracke nearly fell with her when she did.

"What do you want?" Dracke asked, looking over the stranger who was a bit shorter than him. His hair was sun-kissed and his face clean-shaven, while his clothes were more refined than what Dracke expected.

"Apologies. I am Constable Gustave of Lyndon, and I come on behalf of monsieur Renfield, on behalf of his daughter."

Mina stepped forward. "What about me?"

He cleared his throat. "I apologize, but your father came to me saying… well, saying you are being held here against your will. Is this true?"

She turned to Dracke before letting out a small laugh and smiling at Gustave. "Don't be absurd. He is mistaken, as I am here voluntarily."

"Then you will have no problem coming home for the night to reassure your father and your sisters?"

Mina swallowed hard, taking Dracke's hand and leading him away for privacy, glancing back at Gustave. "You want me to forgive you? Let me return for the night so I may assure my family I am well. I will return before sunrise, I swear."

His jaw clenched at the thought of her leaving. "I am not happy with this agreement, but for tonight, I will allow it."

"Thank you."

"Know this," he said as he gripped her arm. "If you fail to return by sunrise, I will come for you myself."

Her eyes went wide. "You can leave?"

"I came to you in the woods."

"No, I mean, these lands. You can leave?"

"I can."

"Then why have you not left before?"

"I did not wish for anyone to see me. Now remember this, if I have to come for you, you will spend your remaining days locked away in the dungeon. Is that clear?"

"Yes, Dracke. Thank you."

He flinched at her gratitude, quickly releasing her arm. "Of course," was all he could say.

Mina looked at Gustave. "I will return to Lyndon shortly."

"I am to escort you."

Dracke glanced down when Mina tensed against him, her hand gripping his tightly. "I can ride just fine," she insisted.

"It is dark out, and there are wolves in the forest."

"Very well," Mina relented.

She slipped on her cloak and walked outside with Gustave. Their horses were brought out, and they said nothing as they mounted.

Chapter 7

The Sun

s soon as they arrived at her father's manor, the door swung open, and Marius burst down the stairs. He pulled her off her horse and held her tightly, kissing her forehead and cheeks in relief at the sight of her.

"I can't believe you're really here," he exclaimed in joy.

"Father, you worry too much. I am fine," Mina said as she stepped back, letting him look her over to see for himself.

"How? I left you with a monster."

"He is not a monster!" She couldn't believe she was so quick to defend him, but if it assured her father, then it was a good thing.

"Mina, that thing was a beast!" Gustave said. "How could you see him as anything else? He was disgusting."

Before Mina could respond, Marius laced his arm with hers. "Well, let's get you inside. Your sisters are eager to see you."

I'm sure, Mina thought as he led her up the steps. In the foyer, her sisters approached her. Elise's eyes went wide when Mina removed her cloak. She ran up to her, but instead of embracing her, took the fabric of her gown into her hands.

"Wherever did you get this?" she demanded.

"Prince Dracke provides my clothing," Mina answered.

"This alone is worth more than my entire closet!" Elise pouted. She turned to Marius. "Why does she get to stay with a prince?"

"She is not there willingly," Marius pointed out.

"And he is more monster than prince," Gustave added.

Mina took a breath while thinking over her words. "Let me make this clear. I am helping Dracke with his library, and I am there of my own free will." She hoped her voice sounded more confident than she felt, for she needed them to believe her.

"Bells, you traded yourself for me," Marius said.

She paused for a moment before she responded. "Yes, I did. He then asked me to help him catalog books, which I am. You know I have needed something to… to fill the time." Mina was surprised when Marie approached her and hugged her. "Sister?"

"We have been worried about you."

"Thank you, but I am fine."

Marie studied her eyes for a moment. "You look well for a change."

Mina laughed softly. "Thanks." Marie and Elise exchanged a glance. "What?"

"You're laughing again," Marie said.

"See? I told you, I'm fine."

"Well, we have your room made up," Marius said as he took her arm.

"Oh, I am not staying. I promised Dracke I would be back by sunrise."

"You're on a first-name basis with the prince?" Elise asked in shock.

"Yes, at his insistence."

"Well, we'll see how the night goes." Marius led her into the parlor, where Delphine brought in honey tea and lemon scones. "What is it like there? Do you have to sleep in the cell?"

"No. I have a beautiful bedchamber, and I am treated well. I assure you, I am happy there." She turned to Gustave when he scoffed, not realizing he had followed behind them. "Why are you still here?" she demanded.

"Because I desire to speak with you."

Mina looked at her father, who gave her a small nod. She sighed and stood up, walking slowly to Gustave. They stood by the window, watching the snow as it fell.

"How are you?" he asked softly while caressing her cheek.

She stepped back. "Do not touch me," she said through clenched teeth.

He raised his hand in a peaceful gesture before lowering it to his side. "Seriously, how are you?"

"I'm fine."

"I want to explain what happened."

"What is there to explain? You got drunk, kissed me and groped me, ripped off my…" She shook her head. "You then played it all off as a drunken prank."

"I'm sorry that's how you see it," he said with a scoff.

She glared at him as anger rose in her chest. "That is not an apology, not even a pathetic attempt at one."

"I was drunk, and you were so beautiful in the candlelight. I couldn't help myself." Mina rolled her eyes, but he continued. "It didn't mean anything. Can't you let this go already?"

"No, because what you did," she said with a breaking voice, "was more than I can bear. I told you no, told you to stop, and you wouldn't listen to me."

"You are overreacting to a simple kiss."

Her hands gripped the fabric of her gown as she tried to hold back her tears. "No, it was worse. You were so drunk, you do not even remember."

"I was hurting—"

"We all were," she murmured.

"What can I do?"

"Leave now. Let me have this time with my family. If I am lucky, I will never see you again."

"Fine," he huffed then quickly left the room.

"Are you all right?" When she didn't answer, Marius walked to her. "Bells?"

"I'm fine," she said, wiping away unshed tears. He placed his hand on her shoulder, and she looked at him. "Why did you send him?"

"To check on you."

"No, why send *him*. Why not come yourself?"

"I could tell the prince does not care for me. I figured if I came and asked for you, he would slam the door in my face. I thought sending someone with authority would help. What happened? You and Gustave used to be inseparable. Your mother and I thought one day the two of you would get—"

"No. He was my friend, but he made a mistake. I cannot forgive him."

"I'm sure it wasn't that bad. Gustave has been like the son I never had." He regretted it when her eyes watered again. "Bells, what happened?"

"I won't discuss it."

"Honey, did he—"

"No."

"Then what?"

"Please, can we finish our tea and speak of more pleasant things? I don't have much time here."

"Very well."

Once they seated themselves, she lifted her tea, grimacing because it was cold, but making herself finish it. "How is everyone doing?" she asked.

"We are all well. I didn't tell your sisters what the prince looked like, for I didn't want them to be afraid for you."

"Thank you." Her scone crumbled, and she laughed as her hand swept away the crumbs.

"You seem different."

"In a good way?"

"Surprisingly, yes." He sighed. "The ball is tomorrow night. I don't suppose the prince will let you attend?"

"It's not like that. Honestly, I have no interest to go."

"Why not?"

She brushed the question aside. The clock ticked on as they spent the evening discussing her work in the library and the room she was now staying in. Throughout the night, she reassured him often she was perfectly safe with the prince. She had another peppermint tea while Marius drank coffee.

She looked up when the bells chimed five times. "I need to get ready to return since it is an hour's ride."

She stood, and Marius gripped her arm. "You are not returning to him. I've lost your mother. I will not lose you, too."

She gave him a sympathetic smile. "Father, you aren't losing me. I will return soon, I promise." She started to pull away, but his grip tightened. "Please," she tried.

He sat her back down. "This is the end of this discussion. You will stay with me. I can't—" His voice cracked. He cleared his throat. "I can't lose you, Bells."

"You cannot keep me here."

"I must. I will face him now that I am back to my strength if need be."

She fidgeted in her seat as she worried about Dracke's reaction. How could she tell her father, since she had spent the night convincing him she wasn't a prisoner?

"Father, please, I need to return," she pled softly.

"Stay here for a moment."

Reluctantly, she nodded. "I will."

He left the room, shutting the door behind him. She picked up another scone, not hungry but needing to do something to help ease her stomach. After some time, her father still had not returned. She went to the door, only to find it locked.

"No," she murmured in fear. She went to the window, trying desperately to get it open. It was frozen in place, and she pulled again on the window to no avail. She returned to the door, pounding her fists, and crying out for her father.

Marius opened the door, causing her to step back. "What is wrong?" he demanded.

"You locked me in here!" she yelled, her eyes going wide when the bells chimed again. "Oh, no." She looked out the window. The sun was starting to rise. She turned back to Marius. "Please, let me go." She stepped forward, but he blocked her path. "Father—"

A thunderous crash exploded inside the house. "Where are you?" Dracke called out.

Marius turned, ready to stop him, but Dracke easily shoved him aside. He grabbed Mina's wrist and yanked her to him.

"Dracke, please wait—" she started to explain, but he vaolmersed them into the dungeon. "No, please!" She watched in horror when he vanished without a word. She sat on the floor, pulling her knees to her chest, and sobbing into her gown.

Mina came to, shivering from the cold as her gown offered her little protection. She slowly sat up and focused on the tiny cell, trying to keep her panic at bay. Dracke appeared before her, setting down a tray with bread and water.

"Dracke, please," she begged, watching in despair when he vanished. Her anger boiled over when she picked up the plate, and she screamed in fury as she slammed it into the wall. She huddled in the corner, attempting to get warm while telling herself her tears would do her no good.

Dracke appeared with her next meal, and he saw the mess on the floor. He turned to Mina, ready to scold her. Instead, his heart dropped when he saw her.

"Mina?" He stepped closer after she didn't look up. "Mina?" he tried again. Worry flooded through him, and he knelt beside her, putting his hand on hers. She was cold to the touch and unresponsive.

He scooped her into his arms and vaolmersed her into his parlor, sitting with her on his lap in front of the fire. He stroked her hair and spoke softly, reassuring her she was safe.

She began to warm and peered at him. "Dracke?"

"I'm right here. What happened?"

"I don't know. I told my father I had to leave, but he locked me in the parlor and refused to let me go."

"Wait, what?"

"I heard the bells and told my father I had to leave. He tricked me. Then you showed up and…" She looked away as she wiped her tears. "I didn't have a chance."

"I've never had a prisoner react to the cells the way you do. Why is that?"

"I'm claustrophobic," she admitted.

He let out a gasp. "You said you didn't like small spaces, but I had no idea you were so afraid. Why didn't you tell me this?"

"Because it's embarrassing."

"No, it is not. I was angry you didn't return, and I wasn't thinking. I never meant to hurt you."

"Yes, you did. You were punishing me for breaking my promise."

"I thought because of what I did, you never wanted to set foot here again."

"I am still angry with you, but I promised you I would return, and I had every intention of keeping that promise." She pulled away from him. "I need to clean up." He stood with her and tried to take her hand, but she jerked it away. "You do not have the right to touch me again."

"Mina—"

She ran upstairs to her chamber and slammed the door. She tore the dress away as she ran into the washroom, ready to warm up under the hot water. Her stomach filled with dread at the thought of being back in the cell.

Dracke paced in the parlor, unsure of how to make things right with Mina. His thoughts were muddled, as he knew he could not tell her the truth. *She certainly lives up to her name. She is the most beautiful creature I have ever seen.* He shook his head. *Think! How can I make this right?*

He remembered catching Marius with the rose, saying it was for his youngest daughter. Dracke went outside and gathered a dozen of the most beautiful roses in the garden. He put them in a vase, then took them to her room and knocked softly.

"Mina, I have something for you." He waited a minute, then went inside when she didn't respond. Walking in, he heard the water and realized she was in the shower.

He set the flowers on her nightstand, then vaolmersed into the kitchen. A bowl of fruit sat on the counter, and he made up a small plate, adding chocolate. He returned to her room, placing it beside the flowers. Satisfied, he vaolmersed to his parlor to give her privacy.

Mina tightened her robe as she walked into her chamber. She smiled at the roses and rushed to smell them. Then she saw the plate of fruit, including strawberries, and her stomach churned. The thought of his fangs sinking into her throat was more than she could bear. She tossed the plate into the bin before going to the window nook and looking out, her face flushed with anger.

Mina went into the library, thankful she had not seen Dracke for the past few nights. Her plate would appear, she would eat, then she would catalog. She rather enjoyed the routine. Tonight, a nervous laugh escaped her when the plate disappeared. Her nerves were more on edge than usual, though she didn't know why.

Ready to start a new stack, she went to shelve the books in her hand, but a chill ran up her spine. She realized she was not alone in the room, so she took a step back, planting herself firmly against the bookshelf as she scanned for movement. Seeing none, her body eased. She turned to place the books on the shelf. Dracke appeared directly before her.

She screamed and clutched the books to her chest. "What do you want?" she demanded.

"I could hear your heart racing all the way in my parlor, and I was worried. Are you all right?"

"I'm fine," she said as she shoved the books onto the shelf and brushed past him. She sighed when he sat beside her, kicking his feet up onto the table.

"So, what happened?"

"I… it was nothing. I scared myself. I'm all right now, so I don't need you here."

He scoffed. "Are you dismissing me?"

Her breath sucked in as she opened the book, copying the relevant numbers into the catalog. "Of course not. I was merely—" She sighed when he vanished. "I hate when you do that," she scolded the empty room.

The night wore on, but she kept her focus, trying not to think of Dracke or what he did to her. She stretched and stood up, smiling when she saw the sun start to rise. It surprised her how well she had adjusted to sleeping during the day.

Daytime. Why didn't I think of this sooner? Laughing at the thought, she shook her head.

Mina sat in the nook. She had awakened at midnight and couldn't fall back to sleep. For her plan to work, she would need to sleep all night. She gathered her cloak and rushed outside, the chilly air gusting around her.

The snow blew by as she walked briskly through the garden. She ignored the biting cold as the exhaustion crept in and continued for nearly an hour, until she could barely keep her eyes open.

Mina awoke to see the first rays of sun beaming into her chamber. She dressed and went downstairs to the kitchen to fix herself breakfast. Celine walked in.

"Madam Mina, are you all right?"

"I'm fine," she said as she took a sip of her tea.

"You slept all night."

"Yes."

Celine shook her head, clearly confused. "Can I help with anything?"

"Not at the moment. Would you like some breakfast?"

Taken aback, Celine quickly collected herself. "Madam, we are here to serve you, not the other way around."

Mina laughed. "It's just some eggs and toast."

"I will be turning in now, but thank you."

Mina finished her breakfast and set her dishes in the sink before going to the library. She opened the curtains, relishing in the little warmth the sun provided.

"Oh, I've missed this."

She gathered a few books and sat at the table, humming as she worked through the day. Pausing only for a quick lunch, she smiled at her own ingenuity.

Don't have to worry about Dracke during the day. For some reason, he hates the sun. Works for me.

Once the day turned to evening, she made a small dinner, then turned in.

Mina smiled and stretched, ready to fall back to sleep when she realized she wasn't alone in the room. She sat up to find Dracke looking at her.

"Do you need something?" she asked as she clutched the blanket to her chest.

"I wanted to make sure you're okay."

"I'm tired, but fine." She yawned to make her point before lying back down. "Goodnight," she said as she settled under the blanket and nestled her head onto the pillow.

"No, we have a library to catalog."

"I did thirty-two books today. I need to rest."

"Today?" he asked, his eyebrow arched.

"Mm-hmm." For a second time, she yawned in the hopes he would take the hint.

He sighed. "I understand you are upset with me, but to purposefully avoid me? Am I really so bad?"

"I mean, you drank from me," *while licking my neck,* "then you threw me into your dungeon. What do you think?"

"What I think is you are being childish. Why not talk to me?"

"Oh, you mean like when you were stalking me in the library?"

"How did you—"

"It doesn't matter," she cut him off. "I thought you were giving me space. During the day, I don't have to worry about you, do I?"

"Aww, you worry about me?" he teased.

"That is not what I mean!" she snapped.

"But you'll miss our sparkling conversations."

She sat up with fire flickering in her eyes. "There isn't one thing I miss about you."

"Fine, I'll leave you in peace." With that, he vanished.

Her head hit the pillow, and she prayed the rest of her night would be uneventful.

Running through the woods, the only sound around her is her quickening breath as the cold stings her eyes and cheeks. The beast is behind her, his breath nipping at her heels as he gains on her. She trips on a root, and the creature pounces on her.

Mina awoke, screaming, and falling. Dracke appeared beside her, grabbed her, and placed her back onto the bed.

"Are you hurt?" he asked.

She shook her head. "It was a nightmare. I'm okay," she said through ragged breaths.

He sat on the edge of the bed, wiping her tears before pulling her against his torso. Her hand laid on his chest to push him away when her body went tense at the realization she may be right about him. She looked at Dracke, her lip quivering.

"Are you all right?"

She pulled away. "I'm fine. Thank you for checking on me. You can go now." Her frustration grew when he didn't move. "What are you waiting for?"

"You, Mina."

"What?"

He cleared his throat. "I am waiting to be sure you really are all right," he said as he stood up.

"I'm fine," she replied as she rolled away from him, pulling the blanket up to her chin.

"Very well." He vaolmersed into his parlor, bending down to retrieve his dropped goblet. Celine immediately came over to clean up the mess. He refilled it as he watched her.

"Is Madam Mina all right?" she inquired.

"She's fine. Just a nightmare."

"Hmm, not her first."

"What?"

"Apologies," Celine said as she stood up and walked towards the door.

"Celine?"

She took a breath before she faced him. "You told me to stay close and keep an eye on her. Sometimes she whimpers and cries out before waking up."

"Does she say anything in her sleep?"

"It's not my place, master."

"Tell me," he commanded.

Celine looked down for a moment. "She says, 'no, stop.' Then she cries."

"Is that all?"

"Sometimes she'll take a shower."

"And?"

"Even if she had one right before bed."

He didn't mean to. "What has she been through?" he asked softly.

"I don't know, master. Oh," she said when she realized he wasn't asking her. "I will get these taken care of." She took the dirty rags to the laundry.

Was it Gustave? It's obvious she can't stand to be around him. Hmm, but then she didn't like talking about being a governess, either. I will find out.

He went to the library, shutting every shutter, then locking them into place before closing the curtains. Ready to speak with Mina, he went to his room, climbed into his coffin, and fell asleep.

The lid rose slowly as he was reluctant to leave, knowing the sun was up. He winced at the few rays of sunlight streaming into his chamber, grateful they did not reach him. He vaolmersed into the library, sat at the table, and waited patiently for her. When she walked in a few minutes later, he smiled at her as he stood.

She stopped at the sight of him, then continued past him and began to gather books. Her breath caught in her throat when he appeared directly behind her.

"Did you sleep better?" he asked.

"Yes," she responded, her voice sending a chill through him. She walked around him, then sat down and began making notes.

"Was it Gustave?"

Her body tensed, and she froze, her quill still by her face, visibly shaking in her hand. "No."

"Mina, your heart is racing, and I can smell your fear."

The quill fell on the table as she jumped to her feet to face him. "What do you want?" she demanded.

"Nothing. I thought we could catalog together. I've missed… our time together."

She went to the window and yanked open the curtain, only to discover the locked shutters. "You did this?"

"I have… issues with the sun."

"I didn't switch to days to avoid you, despite what you might think. I missed seeing the sun, what little you have of it here. I need it."

"Feel free to step out any time."

"You know what? I will." She left the library and ran out the door, knowing he would not follow. It was snowing with a few clouds dotting the sky, but the sun was out. She hadn't grabbed a cloak, and she shivered as she walked around the garden, still in shock at the bright red and pink roses contrasting against the white snow. Celine approached her, grasping a fur cloak in her hands.

"Madam Mina, please put this on," she insisted, wrapping it around Mina's shoulders.

"Thank you."

"Master has requested you not stay out too long, as he worries about you."

"I'm sure," Mina blurted out.

"Madam, I am serious."

Mina thought over her words. "I apologize. Thank you. Tell him I will return shortly."

She ventured farther from the manor and cut through the woods when suddenly, she heard labored breathing. Thinking of her nightmare, she quietly made her way back towards the chateau. She froze when the sound was directly behind her.

Instinct kicked in, and she ran as fast as she could, not daring to look for fear of what she would see. Nearly to the chateau, the beast pounced on her. She managed to roll onto her back, trying to kick off the black, hairless dog. She was about to scream when it began to lick her face.

Frozen in fear and shock, she watched him back up and wag his small tail while he studied her. He had black skin and red eyes, with a dark smoke emanating from him. His eyes stayed on her as he walked around her.

"G…good boy," she managed, her voice shaking. He approached her and lowered his head. Her hand shook as she reached out, taking a chance, and petting him. Surprisingly, he nuzzled his face in her palm. "That… that's a good boy."

She stood up slowly, watching him as she made her way to the chateau and rushed inside. As soon as the door shut behind her, she locked it, and leaned against it as her heart beat in her ears. She went to the sink, poured a glass of water, and drank it down in one gulp. She set the cup down before returning to the library.

"Are you all right?" Dracke asked.

"What was that thing?"

"Ah, I gather you've met Duke."

"I beg your pardon?"

"He is… was my hunting dog before the," he cleared his throat, "change occurred."

"The change?"

"We don't speak of it. He didn't hurt you, did he?"

"He scared me, but I'm all right."

"I'm glad. The shutters are unlocked. I'll retire for the day and leave you in peace."

"You… you could stay. If you want to, I mean," she said as her eyes locked with his.

"For today."

"Thank you." Mina looked at him for a moment. "Are you all right?"

"Fine," he murmured.

"Dracke?"

"It's a little… difficult. For me to be up during the day, I mean."

Mina started to ask but instead resumed cataloging. They worked for a while, and Celine brought in a tray with fruit and chocolate. Mina was relieved to see there were no strawberries. Celine handed Dracke a goblet, and Mina enjoyed the red grapes while he sipped his drink.

"What?" she asked when she caught him staring.

"Apologies. I miss food."

She took a chance. "Why can't you eat?"

He stood up, his hand clenching as he turned away. "I am weary. I think I will retire for the day."

"Dracke, you don't have to go. I'm sorry." She reached for him, but he vanished before her. She sat back down, ignoring the rest of the fruit, and working instead.

Once she could barely keep her eyes open, she went upstairs and cleaned up before lying in bed. Confused about her feelings for Dracke, she stared at the ceiling as she thought about him. She knew there was something that made her pity him, but part of her was still angry and disgusted by his treatment of her.

Chapter 8

The Week

racke sighed as he drank the thick, coppery substance from his goblet, cringing at the bitter taste. The strawberry juice he licked from Mina's neck had awakened his desire to eat real food. He hadn't missed it in a while, but now cravings consumed him.

"I have everything set up in the library." Mina's voice pulled him from his thoughts. He glanced at her but quickly averted his gaze. "Will you work with me tonight?" she asked with a yawn.

"I have other affairs to attend to, I'm afraid."

She approached him. "Please, Dracke. I'm sorry I asked. I'll never bring it up—" Before she could reach for him, he vanished, and her hand grasped at air. Her shoulders sagged as she made her way to the library.

Unable to focus, her eyelids heavy, she sat in the chair and stared at the wall as she tried to assess her feelings. *I even changed my schedule back to talk to him. He won't hear me out? Why did I even bother?*

She forced herself to focus and catalog. After a few hours, Celine brought in a tray and left without a word. Mina worked until hunger finally hit her. She lifted the lid but quickly slammed it down. Picking up the tray, she practically ran into the kitchen and let it clatter onto the counter, startling Celine and Yvette.

"Madam Mina, what's wrong?" Celine asked.

"What is this?" Mina demanded, lifting the lid.

Celine shook her head. "It's tomato soup. Is something wrong with it?"

"I don't want it!" Mina shouted.

"My apologies. I thought you would enjoy it," Yvette said, glancing nervously at Celine.

Dracke appeared. "What is going on?"

"I don't appreciate your sick sense of humor."

"Mina, whatever do you mean?"

"Don't play dumb. Tomato soup, really?"

Dracke sighed before he took her hand. "I assure you, I have nothing to do with selecting your menu."

She stared at him in disbelief, but the confusion in his eyes told her he wasn't lying. Her face reddened as she pulled away. Dracke gestured for his help to leave, which they quickly did.

"I'm sorry," Mina said softly, hugging herself. "I... it was an overreaction."

"An understandable one after what I did to you. I can't say I blame you for hating me."

"I don't... I don't hate you," she admitted. "I'm confused about my feelings, though. Are you my warden? My enemy? I don't know."

"Mina, it's true I started out as your enemy. And we have both made mistakes. I tried to make it up to you with fruits and flowers in your room."

"I couldn't stand the sight of the strawberries."

"What?"

"I threw them away," she admitted, swallowing hard.

Dracke appeared before her, tilting her chin so their eyes met. "I never wanted to hurt you. I am sorry. Can you ever forgive me?"

She brought her hand up to remove his but instead gripped his wrist as she looked at him. A spark flew between them, and neither could move for a moment. Until he leaned down, his lips an inch from her own.

"Mina, please."

Her eyelids fluttered as she pulled away and ran upstairs. Chest heaving and heart pounding, she went into the washroom, quickly undressing as she stepped inside the shower.

She let her fingertips trace her lips as she imagined his mouth crashing on hers. His hand explored her neck, then down to her chest, cupping her gently as the water rained down on them both. Her core ached for him.

"Is this what you want?" he whispered.

Mina debated but realized it was all in her head. "Yes," she responded. "I can't take much more of this."

"More of what?"

"You, teasing me. Your tongue, your hands. I need you."

"What do you need me to do?"

"Dracke, please," she begged. His fangs sank into her throat, and her blood dripped down the shower drain. Her breath caught when she remembered he could feel and see this, that he may even be causing it. "Stop!" she cried out, falling to her knees. She brought her hand to her neck, relieved to find there was no blood, no wounds, nothing at all.

She quickly dried and dressed, then started packing a bag. Dracke vaolmersed beside her.

"What are you doing?" he demanded.

"I can't... I can't do this. What you do to me, what you are trying to make me feel..." She shook her head. "Why are you toying with me like this?"

"Mina—"

"I have to go."

"Where are you going?"

"Away from here. Away from you!"

"Wait."

She stopped packing and looked at him. "Why?"

He sighed. "If you wish to go, I will not stop you."

The clothes fell from her hands as disbelief washed over her face. "But the arrangement? That I stay here in place of my father?"

"You've paid for his crime."

"You would let me go?"

"I do not admit this lightly. It would break my heart to do so, as you are the first friend I have had in decades, but yes, you are free to go."

His words sank in, and after a moment's pause, she spoke up. "Let me return home for a week to reassure my family all is well. After the way you took me from there, I am sure they are worried sick. Then I will return."

"Why would you come back?"

"Because you need me," Mina said, turning away as she tried to decipher what her heart genuinely wanted. "You need my help. Your books, I mean."

"One week, then you'll return to me?"

"I promise."

"If you will wait to leave until in the morning, I will agree."

"Why not transport me there now?"

"I have a feeling they may be waiting for me after what happened last time I was there."

"I didn't think of that."

"I will arrange for a coach to see you safely home."

"Thank you." She walked up and placed her hand on his arm. "This means a lot to me."

He swallowed hard. "I am glad, but you still need to eat."

"Dracke—" He pulled her to him and vaolmersed her into the kitchen. "Really?" she asked with a laugh.

He gave her a smile in return. He sat her at the table, then heated up stew and bread. "Why don't you drink wine?" he asked as he reached for a bowl.

"I have seen the vile things it makes people do, and I have no interest in feeling or behaving that way."

"I understand." He set the meal down. "I haven't had wine in a very long time. I do miss the flavor." He sat across from her. "We have such exotic, expensive wines on hand. My cellar is full of them."

"Why don't you drink it?" she asked, blowing on her spoonful of stew.

"Mina, do you not know what I am?" His eyes widened when she shook her head. "I am a vampyr."

She swallowed hard. "I have heard of it, but I don't really know what it is. Can you explain?"

"A vampyr is an immortal creature. I was… forced into this. I must drink the blood of others to survive."

"Why were you forced?"

"All I can answer is it happened on my twentieth birthday as a punishment."

"I'm sorry."

"Whatever for?"

"That you were turned into this. Regardless of what you've done, no one deserves this."

"I… Thank you."

"I will turn in since I am travelling in the morning."

"Of course. Will I see you before you leave?"

"Yes. I will come to your room if it is all right?"

"For this one time, I'll allow it."

"Thank you." She stood and surprised him when she kissed his cheek. "I'll see you then."

Her heart pounded with excitement at the prospect of seeing her family, though worry nagged at her, too. She thought of the time she returned home following her unspeakable loss. When her throat swelled, she quickly pushed it away and focused on seeing her father again.

She knew it was he, above everyone else, she would have to reassure. Remembering what happened last time, she worried he would not let her leave again. Still, she had to go. She would show him she was fine and not living with a beast.

Who am I kidding? He is terrified of Dracke, terrified of what he will do to me. I will show him he has no reason to be afraid. The only problem is, can I believe that myself?

Realizing it was all out of her hands, she crawled into bed, saying a silent prayer for the week to be one of happy reunions, good times with her family, and for nothing to go wrong.

Mina knocked softly. "I'm getting ready to leave."

"Come in."

She opened the door and stepped inside, her eyes adjusting to the dark. A few candles lit the room. "Dracke?" She nearly screamed when he stepped in front of her.

"Apologies, Mina. I did not intend to frighten you."

"Quite all right," she murmured.

He took her hand and kissed her palm reverently. "Before you go, I want to make sure you truly are all right."

"I am, really. I'm excited to see my father and assure him I am safe here."

"Very well. I will see you in one week. I have hired a coach that will drop you off, then return to pick you up."

"Thank you." She gasped softly when he kissed her hand again.

"I have a gift for you." He handed her a small velvet pouch.

Mina opened it to find a ruby necklace. "Dracke, I can't."

"I insist, for all of your hard work in the library. Be safe, *draga mea.*"

"Thank you."

She went to her room, slipping on her cloak and gloves before going downstairs to find Celine had the coach ready for her. Mina climbed in, ready to see her family. The snow-laden trees swept by as the carriage made its way. Bits of red and blue stuck out from the snow, as cardinals and blue jays dug for worms.

The ride was smooth, and she was surprised at how quickly they arrived. Before she could stand, her father swung open the door. He pulled her from her seat, lifted her from the coach, and squeezed her tightly in his arms.

"Oh, Bells! I've been so worried."

"Father, I'm okay. As you can see for yourself."

He stood her on her feet and circled her as he looked her over. "Hmm, so you are."

"Dracke was angry, thinking I had broken my promise to him, but he did not hurt me."

"Is that why you're here? To show me you're okay?"

"And to stay for the week, if you'll—"

"Laurent, get her things inside! Then check to be sure everything is ready for our celebration tonight," Marius called out, pulling Mina close to him and holding her as though he would never let go.

Inside the manor, he helped remove her cloak. "What are we celebrating?" she asked.

"You'll hear soon enough," he said with a smile.

Marie and Elise ran into the foyer, curious as to what all of the fuss was about. Elise looked at Mina, unable to hide her jealousy at the fine gown and jewels she was wearing. Refusing to embrace her, Elise instead ran from the room. Marie approached Mina and took her hand.

"Sister, how are you?"

"I am well," Mina answered. "How are the two of you?"

"We are fine. Come in, and I'll tell you all about the ball."

Mina smiled at the thought of discussing something normal, something… human. They went into the parlor and sat while Delphine served them tea and scones.

"Jonathan and I are engaged," Marie said with a smile.

"Congratulations!" Mina hugged her tightly, causing her to nearly drop the scone in her hand. "Marie and Jonathan Harker. It sounds wonderful."

"Thank you."

"And Elise?"

Marie shook her head. "Sir Arthur arrived at the ball with Lucille Westenra on his arm. Elise is devastated."

"I am sorry to hear that."

"Did I hear right, you are staying for a week?"

"Yes."

"What is the situation with you and the prince? Do you live there now, or is it temporary while you help him with his library?"

Mina was taken aback by Marie's sudden curiosity. "I… I'm not sure myself. Why are you asking this?"

"He lavishes fancy gowns and decadent jewels upon you. I thought perhaps you were courting."

"No, we are friends."

Marie chuckled. "I am not sure it is possible for a man and woman to be just friends."

"With us, anything is possible. I would like to get a shower and rest."

"Of course. Take a nap while we finish setting everything up. We are celebrating my engagement tonight, but I have a feeling all eyes will be on you," Marie said with a hint of jealousy.

"I don't have to go," Mina replied.

"No, I want you there."

Mina gave her a small smile before retiring to her chamber. She looked at the lavender and silver duvet, her small vanity, and the plush white rug on the floor. She had not realized how much she missed everything until now.

She took a shower then slipped into a nightgown, thinking of Dracke as she pulled the blanket to her chin. Not even gone for a day, but she missed him already and wondered if he missed her as well.

Marie walked in and opened the curtains, letting in what little evening light remained. "Are you ready for dinner?"

Mina stayed under the covers. "Depends. Who all is here?"

Marie laughed. "As we thought, everyone."

"Truly?" Mina asked as she sat up.

"Yes. Father had the good wine brought in." Her smile dropped when she noticed Mina lost her color. "What's wrong?"

"Nothing. I must still be a little worn out from travel. I'll get dressed." She glanced at the gold and white chest in front of her closet. "What is that?"

"It was on your coach. The driver insisted it is yours."

"I've never seen it." Mina jumped to her feet and rushed to the chest. Opening it, she found more luxurious gowns and pouches full of fine jewelry. She smiled at Marie. "Dracke must've packed this for me."

"Just friends?" she quipped with a spark in her eyes.

"I'll get dressed and be down shortly."

Mina waited until Marie was gone, then decided on a silver ball gown with a tight bodice, white stars embroidered along the skirt, and silver shoes. She looked through the jewelry and put on a necklace with a diamond star. Checking her reflection in the mirror, she tried not to think of the small fortune she was wearing.

No wonder Marie doesn't believe we are just friends, not when he lavishes such gifts upon me. Shaking her head, she went downstairs. Elise visibly trembled with envy at the sight of her.

"Wherever did you get this?" she asked through clenched teeth.

"It was a gift from a friend," Mina replied in a soft tone, trying to appease her. She glanced over when Marie chuckled before walking behind Elise.

"Yes, apparently she and the prince are very good… friends."

"Hmm, so what favor did you do for him to be so richly rewarded?" Elise asked with a smug smile.

Mina immediately stared at the floor. "I have been helping him with his library is all."

"Yet you wear a gown worth more than what father makes in a month. You must do *something* to earn it."

"Elise, enough," Marius commanded as he walked in.

Her face reddened, as she had been unaware he was listening in. "Apologies, Father."

He sighed. "Bells is only here for the week. Can the three of you get along while she is here?"

"We will," Elise assured him.

"Good. Everything is set up for dinner. Come, let us dine and celebrate."

They walked into the small ballroom crowded with guests excited to not only celebrate Marie's engagement but the return of Marius's daughter, as well.

Mina hugged the wall, trying to avoid gaining anyone's attention. She found a seat in a back corner and kept to herself. A curse slipped from her lips when Gustave approached her. She tried to get up and leave but was unable to before he reached her.

"Evening, Mina. I am glad to see you are well."

"Thank you," she responded coolly, praying someone would come speak with her or pull him away.

He sat beside her. "Would you like a drink?"

"I don't drink wine," she reminded him.

"Neither do I."

The goblet in his hand contradicted this confession, and she could smell the hint of wine on his breath. "Oh, really?"

"Not anymore. Not since the night I..." He looked down for a moment. "I am sorry, and I am trying to do better. Will you ever forgive me?"

"Why should I?"

He took her hand, softly kissing between her knuckles. "Because you are the most beautiful woman in this kingdom. No one could blame me for trying to lay my claim to you, could they?"

"Do you know what all you did?" she asked quietly.

"I mean, I kissed you."

"And?"

His eyes grew wide. "What else did I do?"

She scoffed. "You hurt me."

"What? How?" he asked, panic rising in his voice.

"Well, I guess that is a fair punishment for you. I will never tell you the extent of the damage you inflicted upon me. You can spend the rest of your miserable life wondering what you did and fearing the worst." She stood and tried to flee from the ballroom. Someone grabbed her elbow, and she was brought into a small circle by her father.

"Bells, you remember my partners."

"Of course," she said with a smile. "Messieurs Louis and Mont. How are you?" she asked, taking slow breaths to calm her racing heart.

They made polite conversation until the food was served. Everyone took their seat, and once each plate had been set, her father stood and gathered their attention.

"Good evening. We are here tonight for two reasons. We are celebrating the engagement of my daughter, Marie, to Jonathan Harker." He paused as a few people clapped. "We are also celebrating the return of my daughter, Bellamina, who has been… away. Thank you, all of you, for coming tonight."

Mina could only stare at her plate, ignoring Gustave's fiery gaze, who sat directly across from her. She knew he wondered what he did to her while in his drunken state. Her stomach turned, but she made herself eat a few bites to appease her father. Once he left to discuss business matters, she quietly left the ballroom and went into the parlor. She sat in front of the fire, wondering how Dracke was doing.

Why do I miss him? He was cruel to me… but I yearn to be in his arms. When we touched, there was a spark. I saw it on his face. He felt it, too. So why push me away now? Why violate my mind and make me… I don't even know! Was he trying to seduce me? To make me angry? She gasped in realization. *Or did I cause it, thinking of him like that? Was it my fault this time?*

"This is unfair," an angry voice declared behind her.

Mina looked over her shoulder to see Gustave. Immediately, she jumped to her feet and faced him. "What is?"

"Torturing me so. Please, Mina, tell me what I did?" His words slurred, and he leaned against the doorway for support.

"Liar! You are drunk," she hissed in disapproval.

"I can't help but enjoy a drink from time to time. You should, too. Learn to loosen up! A rare creature like you should enjoy the finer things in life, such as myself," he claimed, as he stalked across the room to her.

As he approached, she flinched in fear. "Please, stay back."

He gripped her wrist tightly and pulled her to him. "At least tell me what I did!"

Diffusing the situation was the best solution she could come up with. She gave him a gentle smile and used a soft tone. "Dear Gustave, it is all right. Why don't we get some tea, and we can talk? How does that sound?"

He slapped her across the face. "Tell me right now!" he demanded as he shoved her to the ground.

"Gustave, please—" she begged as she attempted to stand. His hand clamped on her shoulder, keeping her firmly on her knees.

"Hmm, I like you in this position." His other hand reached for his belt. "Perhaps we can enjoy ourselves tonight."

Mina looked around the room, trying to find a weapon, a distraction, anything to stop him. "Please, don't." Her body trembled, and she froze in fear when his belt ripped away. He gripped her neck, pulling her face towards him. She turned and bit down hard on his arm until she drew blood.

"You'll pay for that!" He grabbed her again, forcing her face mere inches from his crotch. "I should've done this sooner," he said with a smile.

A dark shadow overtook him, and Dracke threw him against the wall. "Touch her again, and I will not hesitate to kill you."

Gustave charged, but Dracke easily ducked away from his fist, grabbing his arm, and flinging him to the ground. Dracke knelt over him, his dagger at his throat. Without looking at Mina, he made his offer. "Say the word, my dearest Mina, and I will kill him."

Mina stood, still shaking while trying to form a comprehensible sentence. "Please, don't," she managed softly. "He's drunk."

"That does not give him the right to touch you."

"I never said it did," she explained as her breathing slowly returned to normal. "But he doesn't deserve to die. He needs to sleep it off somewhere."

"I will take care of him."

Before Mina could say another word, Dracke lifted Gustave and vaolmersed from the manor. She ran to her bedroom. Her dress fell to the floor as she rushed into the shower, weeping and trembling in fear under the water.

"Are you all right?"

Mina froze for a moment until she realized who was speaking. "Marie? Oh, um, I don't feel well. Would you please give my apologies?"

"I will. Do you need anything?"

"No, thank you." She turned the water off and heard Marie leave the room.

Quickly drying and changing into a nightgown, she shook her head as she thought of how Gustave behaved. She knew he would not let this go, and her stomach was heavy with dread at the thought of seeing him again. She considered riding her horse back to Dracke's and never returning.

Dracke thinks he is a monster, but truly if anyone is, it is Gustave. He was hurting? So was I! We both lost Colin, and… What did Dracke do with him? Please, please don't hurt Gustave. No matter what he has done to me, leave him be…

Her head hit the pillow, and she was out until the next morning.

Chapter 9

The Truth

ells?" Marius said. Her eyes flew open when her father put his hand on her forehead. Mina stayed in bed, facing away from him. The night before, she left the party without saying a word. When he realized she was gone, he became concerned, sending Marie to check on her. Marie said she was not feeling well, but Marius thought there was more to her story.

"Morning," she said, remaining on her side.

"Marie told me you were ill last night. You don't feel warm. Are you all right?" He glanced down at the dress still on the floor, surprised she would be careless with something so valuable.

"I'm better now, yes."

"Hmm, all right. Breakfast will be ready shortly." He scooped up the gown, inspecting it on his way out.

Mina dressed in a pale blue gown with matching shoes and sapphire jewelry. When she looked in the mirror, she was shocked to see a bruise on her cheek. She slipped from the room and went to Elise's, grateful she wasn't there. Mina saw the array of makeup on the vanity, and she quickly applied some so the bruise was no longer visible.

She went downstairs, and everything crashed inside her when she saw Gustave sitting at the table. Her smile, her heart, and her stomach all fell. She turned, but before she could break for upstairs, her father laced his arm with hers and escorted her to the table. She was trapped and had to pretend everything was fine. Everyone was quiet while the food was set up.

"Thank you for having me, Marius," Gustave said, breaking the silence. "I am always happy to spend time with you and your beautiful daughters."

"Of course, son! You are always welcome here."

When Gustave adjusted himself in his seat, he grimaced in pain and shot Mina an angry look. Mina was the only one to notice.

She turned her attention to Marie. "Have you and Jonathan set a date?" Knowing this would turn the entire conversation to the upcoming nuptials.

"We are planning for some time in late spring." She spoke of a few possible musicians she wanted, and whether she would have an afternoon or evening wedding.

Mina ignored Elise, seeing her usual pout. "What are you doing today?" she asked Marie.

"Elise and I are going shopping for my wedding gown. Would you like to join us?"

"That sounds nice."

Elise snorted, nearly spilling her coffee. "You've never liked shopping."

"Maybe it's because I want to spend time with the two of you," Mina shot back.

Elise quickly straightened up at her sharp tone. "Of course."

Once the empty dishes were cleared away, she stood to follow her sisters. Marius cleared his throat.

"Bells, would you stay for a moment?"

Mina gave Marie an apologetic look. "Go ahead. I'll meet you at the dress shop shortly." She turned her attention to Marius and Gustave. "Yes, Father?"

"I think it's time to address the elephant in the room."

"What do you mean?" Mina asked.

"You and Gustave. You are of age, and he has asked for your hand."

Her throat tightened at the thought of marrying him. "What did you say?" she asked as her heart thumped in her eardrums.

"I told him he has my blessing, but the final decision is of course yours to make."

Gustave sat up straight, shooting her a charming smile. Mina shook her head. "I have nothing to say to him," she answered, leaving the room and catching up to her sisters.

Mina made herself focus on the beautiful gowns Marie tried on. If she lost herself for even a moment, she was with Gustave again. She wasn't ready to face that. She smiled at Marie, telling her how lovely she looked.

Marie finally settled on one with long sleeves, a tight bodice which accentuated her curves and bust, and lace covering a white satin skirt. The train was nearly twenty feet long.

"Does our father know how much you are spending?" Elise asked when she saw the price.

"He told me to get whatever my heart desired."

Elise rolled her eyes. "Typical." She glanced at Mina and smiled. "What about you, precious *Bells*? Thinking of marrying your prince?"

Her eyes went wide, and her face flushed. "I told you, we're just friends," she murmured.

Elise's hand went to the sapphire pendant resting on Mina's chest. "So, a 'friend' gives you jewels like these?"

They were interrupted when Marie walked in between them. "I'm ready for lunch."

Mina held the cool sapphire in her hand and avoided looking at Elise. "Could we go to the tea house? I've missed it."

"That sounds good," Marie said, linking arms with her sisters and walking across the town square. Mina felt guilty about what she wore when she saw the beggars in the streets, holding out their plates and asking for coin.

Marie chose a table in the corner, and they took their seats. Once it was set with sandwiches, sweets, sauces, and a variety of tea, Marie sipped hers first.

"Hmm, honey and chamomile. Always a good choice."

"Boring," Elise said. "I enjoy my tea with a little spice."

"You like everything with a little spice," Mina said under her breath.

"What was that? What are you insinuating?"

Mina immediately sat up straight. "Nothing."

"Speaking of spice, did you hear about Lady Elizabet and Lord Byron's brother? Apparently, a scullery maid caught them in the dining room together," Elise said with a shy smile.

"Everyone already knew," Marie said.

"Except Lord Byron."

Elise and Marie giggled. Elise's giggle turned into a scowl when Mina frowned. "What is your problem?"

"Nothing. Just, is this what you do all day? Sit around, and talk about other people?"

"Why, what exactly do you do?"

"I told you, I catalog books—"

Elise let out an exaggerated yawn. "Hmm, yes. So exciting."

Finally, Mina had enough. Her hand clasped her sapphire pendant. "As you said, I am well paid for my work."

Elise cleared her throat, taking a bite of her scone. "Baubles compared to what my own suitor will lavish on me."

Mina sighed. "I told you, he is not a suitor but a friend." She reached for the butter when her sleeve rode up, and Marie grabbed her arm.

"Did he do this?" she asked, turning Mina's arm so Elise could see the bruise.

"No," Mina said, yanking her arm free of Marie's grasp. "Dracke has not hurt me." Mina knew this was not exactly the truth, but she had to reassure her family she was safe with him.

"Then how—"

"I tripped last night, when I was sick." Mina finished her tea. "I am going for a walk. The fresh air will do me some good."

"No," Marie said, taking her hand. "Please, tell me what happened. Who did that to you?"

Mina glimpsed at Elise before meeting Marie's gaze. "It was Gustave. He was drunk and—"

"He would never," Elise said through clenched teeth. "He is nothing but a gentleman, and he certainly would have no reason to touch someone like you."

Marie and Mina exchanged a curious glance. Marie turned her attention to Elise. "Oh, really? Go on, sister. Why not?"

Elise shifted in her seat. "Only because he—"

"Do you ladies need anything else?"

Marie ignored Elise's pout as she turned to face the owner. "No, thank you. We are almost finished. Everything was delicious today."

"Thank you."

Mina pulled away and stood up. "I need fresh air. I will see you at home later."

As she exited the shop, she pulled her cloak tighter when the bitterly cold wind hit her. The clouds were thick, making it nearly dark as night. She walked towards the manor when she ventured to the woods. The creek trickled by, parts of it covered with a thin layer of ice as the snow continued to fall.

"You dare to refuse my hand in marriage?"

Mina's body tensed at the sound of Gustave's voice. She turned to face him. "I didn't refuse."

He scoffed. "Not outright." In a flash, he was on her, his hand gripping her chin and forcing her to look at him.

"I just needed some time to think, is all."

"Don't lie to me."

"Gustave—"

"I see how you are dressed. I know it comes from your precious prince. You would choose a monster over me?"

Mina stepped back and scowled. "It is you who are the monster!"

His hand grabbed her neck in a flash. "Listen here, little miss perfect." The warmth of his breath caressed her ear as his grip tightened. "I always get what I want. And if I can't have you, I will go after the next best thing."

"What do you mean?" she choked out when his hand released her.

"Oh, that's for me to know. So answer me here and now, will you become my wife?"

She spat at him, and he tackled her. He grew concerned when she wasn't moving, then saw the blood under her head as it seeped into the ground. He quickly stood and ran from the woods.

Mina opened her eyes and groaned, blinded by the light. "Where am I?"

"You're safe now."

"Father?"

"It's okay. You tripped in the woods and were knocked unconscious. What were you doing out there by yourself?"

Mina glanced about to see it was just the two of them in her room. "I needed some air."

"So you went into the woods?"

"Father, please. You worry too much."

"You could've bled to death out there! If anything, it seems I do not worry enough."

"Who cleaned me up?"

"Marie, of course. She was worried sick when he brought you in with blood matted on the back of your head."

"He? Who brought me in?"

"Dracke, though I did not recognize him at first. He wore a thick cloak and did not stay long."

Mina brought her hand to the back of her head, surprised there was no wound. "I'm not hurt?"

"He said he… healed you in the woods. He could barely stand. I actually offered him to rest in my parlor, but he insisted on returning to Parysse. What happened out there?"

"I'm tired, and I'm hungry," she said, ignoring his question. She was not ready to deal with it yet.

"Dinner will be brought up shortly."

Mina sighed as she slipped away from the bed. "I'm fine, see?" she said as she twirled in front of him. "I'll get dressed and be down." She walked towards her chest when she stopped, catching her father before he made it to the door. "Gustave isn't joining us, is he?"

"No, he had other plans tonight." Marius started to ask about earlier when he mentioned Gustave asking for her hand, but he thought better of it while she was recovering.

Mina changed into a gown and a diamond necklace. She joined her family in the dining room. Dinner was served, and she caught Elise staring at her.

"Do you need something?" Mina asked.

"Is that… are those diamonds around your neck?"

Mina gingerly ran her fingertips along the pendant she wore. "They are."

"Did you pack these things to intentionally make me jealous?"

"No, as I did not pack them at all. Dracke packed the chest for me."

Elise's mouth fell open. "Just friends, right," she muttered.

"What does the prince look like?" Marie asked.

Mina glanced at her father when he choked on his drink. "He is tall, lean, with long black hair, and piercing eyes."

"Is he handsome?" Elise teased.

"Well, art is subjective," Mina blurted out.

Elise giggled furiously as Mina blushed. "Really?" she snarked.

"It's… I—" Mina became too flustered to speak.

"I am glad I found the perfect gown. With that out of the way, I can begin to plan everything else around it," Marie said to break the tension in the room. She continued to talk about the things she wanted for the ceremony and the reception.

Once dinner was finished, Marie and Elise excused themselves and left. Mina started to stand.

"Bells, could we have a moment?" Marius asked.

"Of course," she said as she remained seated. "Is everything all right?"

"I'm worried."

"About the wedding? It's not for—"

"No, Mina. About you."

"What about me?"

"You and the prince seem awfully close."

"As I've said, he is a good friend."

Marius sighed. "Still, I worry. With your tumble in the woods today, perhaps it is best if you stay in the manor."

"For the rest of the week?" Mina asked.

"No."

"What exactly are you saying?"

"I think it's best if perhaps you did not return to Parysse."

"Father, I had really hoped we would not have this conversation. He let me come home because I promised him I would return."

"Let you?"

She took a drink, her throat suddenly parched. "That is, uh, I mean only what I said, I did promise him I would return. I am not his prisoner, and I am helping him with—"

"You know what he is, right?"

"I do."

"Yet you care for him?"

Mina blushed. "I don't really know how I feel," she answered honestly. "However, it is not your place to ask."

"Bells, I am your father, and I have every right to be sure my child is safe and all right."

She scoffed. "I am not a child, and I am fine. If you are so worried about me, why do you let Gustave come into this house?"

"Tell me why I shouldn't."

"He…" She turned away. "It doesn't matter. I won't be here much longer."

"Do you love the prince? Is that why you refused Gustave's hand?"

"Why would you think that?"

"Hmm, no denial. Interesting. The way you speak of him, the things he has given you. It makes me wonder. You are more than friends, aren't you?"

"I assure you, we are not."

"Then prove it to me. Stay here."

"Why? So Elise can gloat about another failure? So Gustave can—" She shook her head. "No, I have no interest in staying here. It was bad enough the last time I returned."

"When you stayed for the night?"

"No, after…" she wiped her tears, "after losing Colin. I never spoke up." She looked at him and swallowed hard. "But Elise tormented me relentlessly and was even downright cruel."

"Oh, Bells." He stood and pulled her tightly into his arms. "I am so sorry. Why did you not tell me?"

"I didn't want to widen the rift already growing in this house, and because she wasn't entirely wrong. I couldn't save him…"

"No one could. It was not your fault. Now, about you staying here?"

"I will return to him at the end of the week like I promised. Do not ask me again."

"Very well." He sulked from the room.

She sat in the chair by the fireplace, closing her eyes, and thinking of her last day at the Blanc Estate.

The doctor shook his head, standing beside the bed. In it was a young boy, pale and shaking. "I'm sorry, but I'm afraid there is nothing else we can do. The medicine has not worked, nor the blood transfusions."

"Please," the mother begged softly as her tears streamed down. "You must save our child. We cannot lose him."

"My sincerest of apologies, but all hope is lost. The best you can do now is to prepare his soul for the afterlife."

"No!" the mother cried out, crumbling into her husband's arms. Mina stood back, watching it all unfold. The husband thanked the doctor on his way out. He turned to Mina.

"Please, stay with us?"

"I will, Monsieur Blanc. I promise."

She approached the boy, knowing she shouldn't touch him, as he was dying of the plague which only infected the young. Still, the doctor instructed them to avoid all contact just in case. Watching him tremble as he continued to grow paler, she could stay back no longer.

"What are you doing?" the mother asked when Mina sat beside him, taking his hand.

"I will not leave him alone."

The father gasped, looking at his wife. "Thank you, Mina."

"I have no children while you have three others. I will bring him what comfort I can."

"Risking yourself—"

"I care not," she admitted, stroking his hair. "He has been like a son to me, and I will not abandon him now."

The mother cried harder into her husband's chest. He stepped closer, watching his son's ragged breathing. "It's near the end, isn't it?"

Mina nodded, wiping her own tears. "Yes, his heart is slowing down." A strangled sob escaped Madam Blanc. One hand holding the boy's, Mina laid her other upon his chest, listening and watching. When the death rattle escaped his lips, she hung her head, collecting herself before looking at his parents. "Colin is gone."

His mother fell to her knees, screaming and clutching her chest. His father knelt with her, holding her as she sobbed. Mina pulled up the sheet, covering Colin to his chin.

"Mina," the father tried, clearing his throat as they stood. "Will you stay with him while I get her settled with our children and send for the priest?"

"Of course."

They left the room. Mina continued to hold his hand, cold and limp in her own, as she wept.

Dracke gasped as the pen slipped and landed with a clatter on his desk. He clutched his head as unshed tears formed in his eyes.

"So that is why she did not wish to speak of her days as a governess." He drew in a quick, shaky breath. Celine walked in with a fresh bottle and set it beside him. "Thank you, Celine. I…" He met her gaze. "I don't think I've ever properly thanked you."

"Whatever for?"

He nodded to the bottle. "Keeping me alive."

"It's what anyone would do."

He scoffed. "No, they wouldn't."

She turned to leave but stayed for a moment. "Master, why did you let Mina leave?"

"What do you mean?"

"The curse—"

"Yes, I am well aware. However, after what I have done to her, I could not deny her that which her heart desired. I owed her some small reprieve for the pain I have caused her."

"What about our pain?" Celine asked quietly, looking out the window.

"I am sorry. I have researched through nearly every book, and still, I am no closer to breaking the curse. Is something the matter?"

"It's just… I was with you and know what will become of us. The others do not. They simply know there is a curse and not to leave the grounds. I feel as if they should be informed of what is coming so they might have a chance at saying their goodbyes."

His shoulders sagged. "I know, but I am afraid they would try to leave, not understanding that to do so would only escalate their timeline." He glanced outside at the statue by the gate, shaking his head. "Foolish man," he muttered.

"Please, do not speak so harshly of my husband. This was my fault, as I told him about the curse. Even knowing, he tried to flee."

"For now, we will not say anything. Agreed?"

"Yes, master. Are you all right?"

"I am." He continued to write. Once finished, he looked at the paper, his farewell letter to Mina should the curse consume them all.

Mina stepped out of the shower, wiping her eyes yet again and wondering why the memory was suddenly so powerful. Focused on getting ready for bed, she jumped when someone knocked on the door.

"You have a visitor," Marie said from the other side.

Mina dressed and went to the door, seeing the concern on her sister's face. "Who?"

Marie took her hand and led her through the hallway without a word. They went downstairs and into the parlor. Mina's eyes went wide.

"Prince Alain, what are you doing here?" She bowed, elbowing Marie to do the same.

"Could we speak in private?" he asked.

"I will leave you in peace." Marie gave Mina a confused look before exiting the room.

Mina approached the young prince. "Is something the matter?"

"Is it true? Are you staying under the care of Prince Dracke?"

"I am," Mina answered.

"This disturbs me to learn. Why are you staying with him?"

"He is a friend, and I am helping him."

"I don't like it."

"Your Highness?"

"When Marius found the documents relating to the prince, it sent my father reeling for more information. He has scoured through countless books and scrolls. Tell me, what do you know about Dracke?"

"Not much, as he is very private."

"Is it true that he is a vampyr?"

Her breath sucked in as she considered carefully how to answer. "Yes, but he does not hurt innocents."

"That isn't true."

"What do you mean?"

Alain gestured for her to sit with him on the sofa, telling her of the history he and his father had learned. "Does this surprise you?"

"I saw a little of this history in the books in his library, but I had no idea he was the one to inflict such horror on those people."

"So you will not return to him now?"

Mina realized this was a ploy from Alain and her father to keep her away from Dracke. "I will think on it," she answered.

"I worry about you."

She smiled at Alain. "Thank you."

He looked at her for a moment, seeing the sorrow in her eyes. "You were thinking about Colin again, weren't you?" She nodded, and her head went down. "I think of him every day. I miss when we would read together in his mother's garden."

"Me, too."

"I need to return. Even though it seems the blood plague has been quelled, my father insists on keeping me in the palace to be safe."

"As well he should," Mina offered with a sincere smile. "Would you like me to escort you back?"

"No, I have two guards outside."

"Thank you for coming to see me. If your father will allow it, I will visit you soon."

"I would like that." He hugged her tightly. "I miss you."

"I miss you, too." As she watched him leave, she thought about what he had told her. Marie ran in.

"Another prince? What did he want?"

"Checking on me since he learned where I am now residing."

Marie nodded, waiting for more information. Her eyes dulled when she realized would get nothing else. "I see."

"I am quite tired now."

"You had an exhausting day. Get some sleep."

"You, too." Mina went upstairs and slipped into her nightgown. Exhaustion crept in, and she fell immediately to sleep.

"Mina?"

"Dracke, what's happening?" She was lying on the ground with Dracke leaning over her, his shirt covered in blood. "You're hurt!" she cried out.

He grimaced before putting on a calm face. "I'm fine." He took her hand. "I'm here, Mina. I'm with you until the end."

"I don't understand. What—" She sat up when he disappeared. She got to her feet, running around in the dark, and calling frantically for him. "Dracke! Dracke, where are you? Please, don't leave me alone."

Chapter 10

The Trick

ina walked downstairs but stopped abruptly on the last step when Elise giggled at her. "What?" Mina asked as she looked down, worried something was wrong with her outfit. Nothing appeared out of place.

"Oh, Dracke!" Elise called out, laughing harder.

"It was a nightmare!" Mina yelled, rushing to her. "Shut your mouth about things that do not involve you."

Elise went silent, staring at Mina with wide eyes. "I… okay. I'm sorry."

Mina turned away and went into the kitchen, filled a glass with water, and quickly drank it with a trembling hand. Elise walked in behind her.

"What has happened to you?" she asked.

Mina sighed as she placed the glass in the sink. "What do you mean?"

"You have never come after me like that before. I should be angry, but honestly, I find myself worried about you."

"I had a nightmare. Dracke was dying, and I couldn't help him."

"Like Colin all over again?"

"I don't want to talk about it," Mina snapped.

"I was just asking. Sheesh!" She turned on her heel and left the kitchen.

Mina's hand gripped the counter as she pushed down the memories. She joined her family in the dining room, saying nothing as they talked and ate. Her stomach churned at the thought of eating, and she politely excused herself. She slipped on her cloak. The chilly air hit her as soon as she stepped outside, but she enjoyed her walk. Her father approached her as she neared the manor.

"I have been called to the Ciel Palace. Would you like to accompany me?"

"And how long will we be gone?"

Marius sighed. "Mina, this isn't a trick to make you stay here. I thought you would like to see Alain again."

That's how you're going to play it when you know for a fact he was just here? Mina realized she didn't really have a choice. She could politely decline, but in doing so, her father would see her distrust of him. "Yes, that is fine. I will go with you."

They stepped into the coach, where Marius surprised her by reading documents instead of continuing his debate about making her stay. She enjoyed the quiet ride as the snow and trees flew past. At the gate, she grasped her father's hand in her own. He looked down but said nothing, and she sighed in relief when they were on the isle.

"Don't like the travel?" he asked.

"No. It's as bad as being vaolmersed."

"What?"

"Nothing."

Dracke sat at the table, swirling his goblet as he stared at the empty chair. Perhaps it had been a mistake to offer her freedom. She promised to come back, but would she? After all, a beast such as himself certainly didn't deserve to have her. He knew this in his heart.

He would give anything to break the curse, but more than that, he would give anything to be loved. Celine cared for him, and he knew his mother had loved him, but to be loved for body and soul, to have a woman crave him the way he craved her, to have her life intertwined with his, was what he longed for the most.

Mina could be that woman and give him a future. His shoulders sagged. He could not tell her about the curse, nor could he explain why they were connected, to do either would be to take away her choice. He wanted her to love him because it was what she wanted. She was compassionate and giving, and he knew if he could tell her about the curse, she would do whatever was necessary to free him from it. He had never craved love until he tasted hers.

"Draga mea, my dearest. I miss you," he said as he drank the last sip.

Marius and Mina walked inside the palace and were instantly greeted by Alain. He rushed to her and hugged her.

"Your Highness," she said with a bow.

He took her hand, then looked at Marius. "Are you here to see my father?"

"We are," Marius answered as he removed his coat.

Alain led them through the castle and into his father's office. Willam stood up at the sight of them.

"Your Majesty," Mina said while she and her father bowed.

"Welcome, Marius. What brings you here?"

Mina turned to her father, her brow furrowed. "You said you were called—"

"I need your help," Marius said to Willam, ignoring Mina.

"Of course."

"I need Mina to stay here under your protection."

Her eyes widened, as she realized she had walked into a trap. "Father, please—"

Marius held up his hand to silence her. "I implore you, Your Majesty."

"Alain can always use an additional governess. I know he misses reading with her," Willam said.

"Majesty, please. I cannot stay." Her body shook as panic rose in her chest.

Willam gestured Marius over, and Mina watched as they spoke quietly in the corner. Alain glanced at her.

"I'm sorry."

"You knew about this, didn't you?" she asked, trying to keep her voice calm.

He hung his head in shame. "Yes," he admitted.

"Why would you do this to me?"

"Because of how dangerous Prince Dracke is."

"He is not a threat to me. I… I care for him greatly."

"But you're not in danger?"

"Not from him," she said with a scoff.

"Then who—"

They looked up when Marius and Willam returned. "Mina, you will stay here as governess to Alain," her father announced. "It's all been arranged."

"My apologies, Majesty, but I have a duty to fulfill. I promised Prince Dracke I would return."

"I will send a courier with a message."

"Majesty, please—"

"Do not argue with your king," Marius snapped, his skin flushing because she dared to disobey Willam. "You leave me no choice. I will not lose you again."

"Father, I made the choice to stay with him, and in doing so, I saved your life. Please, you cannot leave me here." Her eyes glistened.

"I am sorry." He turned to Willam. "Thank you for your help." He bowed and started for the door.

"I will return to Dracke," Mina declared with defiance. "You cannot keep me here!"

"Good luck," Marius said as he spun on his heel. "The gate is closed to you."

With her jaw clenched, Mina stepped forward. "Then I will jump!"

Taking a deep breath, Marius approached her and took her hands. "Please, Bells, stay here and be safe." He kissed her forehead.

"No. I do not wish to defy you, but I made a promise, and I will not break it. Not again."

"I am sorry," was all he said as he turned and left.

Mina turned to the king and fell on one knee before him. "Majesty, please, I humbly beg for your help. I know you understand the importance of a promise."

"Yes, and when your father came under my service, I promised him I would do whatever was necessary to protect him and his family, should he ever need me."

"I am safe with Dracke," she said as she stood. "Please, let me return to him."

"I cannot. Come, Alain will show you to your new quarters."

Mina buried her face in her hands, and Willam turned away, clearly uncomfortable around a crying woman.

Alain stepped forward and hugged her. "Mina, everything will be all right. Don't worry."

She wiped away her tears and followed him to her room. It was small and painted light blue with white furniture and accents.

"Thank you," she said, smiling at Alain. "You know my desire to leave is nothing against you."

"I do. And I am sorry I believed them when they told me you were in danger. I… I told my father I had to have you as my governess."

"This was your doing?" Mina asked with a hitch in her breath.

"Yes. I'm sorry. I thought I was protecting you from Dracke."

"Alain, I appreciate that you care so for me, but I assure you, I am safe with him. I help him in his library. That is all. I am not in danger."

"And now I know, I'm going to help you escape."

"Alain—"

He shot her a smile and a wink before he left the room. She sat on the edge of the bed, pondering what would happen when Dracke realized she wasn't coming back to him.

Surely, he would not attack my family out of revenge? The thought terrified her. *No. Of course, he wouldn't. He…* She shook her head, wiping more tears as they trickled out. When she glanced around the room, she noticed the writing desk in the corner. She walked to it, relieved to see it stocked with everything she would need. She sat down and wrote Dracke a letter.

Chapter 11

The Confession

racke paced the parlor, angry his coach returned with only a sheet of paper. *She's gone.* Two words, and his heart had shattered. Two words, and his world was empty. He fell to his knees, crumpling the note in his hand and crying in rage. He collected himself and wondered where she could be.

He vaolmersed near the village, not wanting to appear inside the manor lest they had traps waiting for him. Watching until the streets were empty, he went up the steps and knocked, doing his best to keep his fury at bay. The door opened to a young woman.

Shocked by his appearance, she lowered her gaze. "Welcome to Renfield Estate. How may I help you?"

"Tell Marius Prince Dracke requests an audience with him at once."

She gestured him inside. "Please, wait here while I get him," she instructed.

His hand clenched and unclenched as he paced the foyer, waiting for Marius to appear. When he walked in, he seemed unmoved.

"Welcome."

"Save it," Dracke snapped, stepping towards Marius. "Where is she?"

"She is safe."

"Did she ask for this?"

"No. In fact, she fought me every step of the way, fighting tooth and nail to return to you. Are you proud of the hold you have over her? Is that why you're here now, to gloat?"

"I am here for her!"

"Well, you will never find her."

Dracke appeared before him, his eyes glowing red as he met Marius's gaze. "Look at me," he commanded. "You will tell me where Mina is."

Marius squirmed, struggling to fight the urge to give in to his control. "No," he managed.

Dracke grabbed him and pulled him closer. "Tell me," he commanded again.

"She… she's in the Ciel Palace."

"It still exists? I thought it was destroyed," he said to himself. "I will go there at once."

"You can't. The only way there is through a magic gate which has powerful wards. You'll never be allowed to pass."

"You will take me there."

"No."

A gasp drew their attention, and they looked to see Elise had walked into the room. Dracke stared at her as he spoke to Marius. "Take me there now, or she will take Mina's place."

Marius shook his head. "You can't! You have no authority here."

Dracke laughed. "How little you truly know. I freed you in exchange for your daughter. That was the bargain. Now decide, Elise or Mina."

Marius glanced at Elise. "I'm sorry."

"Father—"

"Run!" he cried out as he swung at Dracke, who didn't budge an inch when Marius's fist made contact with his chin. He then grabbed Marius by the shoulders and tossed him to the floor. Elise froze in fear as Dracke stormed to her and grabbed her arms.

"Father!" she called out.

Marius jumped to his feet. "Please, don't take her!"

"Then give me Mina."

"I… I can't. Please, leave my daughter alone!" He raced for them, only to watch them disappear into thin air. "No!"

Mina walked with Alain towards the dining hall when they heard a ruckus and loud yelling. They followed the sound and found her father calling out for help.

"What's wrong?" Mina asked as she took his arm.

"Dracke took her!"

Mina brought her hand up and caressed his face, speaking in a soft tone to soothe him. "Father, please, calm down, and tell us what has transpired."

"Dracke came looking for you. When I wouldn't return you, he took Elise."

Willam approached. "Marius?"

He bowed. "I apologize, Your Majesty. In my heartache, I was not myself."

"What is going on?"

"I need to leave," Mina explained. "Dracke has taken my sister in my stead. I need to make sure she is all right. Please, let me go."

Willam looked at Marius. "This is your family and as such, it is your decision."

"Do I sacrifice one for the other?"

"Father, please. It is not a sacrifice. I want to be there. I really do. Please, take me to him."

Reluctantly, Marius nodded to Willam. "Release her."

"At once."

Marius took her arm and escorted her from the palace. On the way, Mina said a quiet prayer for her sister to be all right.

Before the coach had fully stopped, Mina swung open the door and jumped out, running inside as fast as she could.

"Dracke!" she called out. "Dracke, please, I'm here!"

He appeared. "Mina."

"I'm here," she said softly as her hand went to his chest. "Please, where is my sister?"

"She is sleeping, safe and sound. I assure you."

"Why did you take her?"

Marius ran in. Dracke glanced at him, then returned his full attention to Mina. "To find you, of course."

"Why? You said I was free to pursue my own path."

"I did, but once you were gone, I realized how empty my life is without you. Do you not understand how important you are to me? I would cross oceans of time to find you."

"Dracke—"

He fell to his knees, clasping her hand against his chest. "I am intoxicated by your smile, condemned by your eyes, and brought to my knees by your touch."

Mina's breath shuddered. Her face flushed, and she couldn't believe what she was hearing. "Dracke, please. I… I thought we were friends."

"We are, but I want more." He stood up, keeping her gaze as his hand swept along her jaw and neck. "I want to know every piece of you, every inch, every scar. I want to breathe you in and never let you go."

"Let my father and Elise leave, then you and I will talk."

"Do you think I would hurt her if you told me here and now you do not feel the same?"

"No," she responded honestly. "I want them to get home safe and sound, please."

"Fine." He disappeared and reappeared a moment later with a very confused Elise. She backed away from him and ran to her father. "She is unharmed, as you can see." He waved them out.

Mina ran to them and gave them each a hug. "Please, be safe," she said.

"Bells, come home with us."

"No. This is where I am meant to be. I will see you again, I promise you." She watched as Marius quickly took Elise from the room. She then approached Dracke, looking into his eyes. "Why would you say those things in front of my father? Did you mean what you said, or was it for show?"

"What do you think?"

"I don't know." She stepped back as his words replayed in her mind. "I can't, Dracke. I need time to think about this."

"Mina—"

She ran upstairs and locked herself in her washroom, starting the shower and trembling. *Could I ever love him? Is it possible? I have missed him while I was with my family. He defended me and saved me, but I still haven't forgiven him for feeding from me nor for throwing me into the dungeon.*

All thought slipped away as she was suddenly back in the kitchen with strawberry juice flowing down her mouth. Only, this time, she was completely undressed as she stood before Dracke. His tongue continued from her neck down to her chest. Mina started to push away the images, but her body ached for his touch.

Her senses let loose, and she let him do whatever he wanted. His mouth wrapped around her nipple as his hand caressed down her stomach. Her legs spread, and his fingers explored her as his tongue teased her chest. He pushed her gently against the wall while kneeling in front of her. His fangs punctured her thigh, and she cried out as lightning rocked her body.

Her mind shattered as she was completely under his control. When his tongue pushed inside, her thighs tightened, and all thought ceased to exist. Pleasure rushing through her core was the only thing her body could focus on. When his finger joined his tongue, she collapsed on him, her body spent as she drowned in the waves of pleasure.

Mina hit the shower floor, cried out in pain, and realized she was alone. It had all been in her head. Dazed, she sat up and felt around her throat and thighs, grateful to find no blood. She finished washing herself, turning down the temperature as her body was heated from the experience.

She used the lavender soap, letting the scent flood her senses and lure her into deep relaxation. The effect was immediate after what she had just experienced. Exhaustion swept through her, so she hurried and dried off, changed into a nightgown, and collapsed into bed, one thought racing through her mind over and over.

I would cross oceans of time to find you.

Mina stirred and woke to see the sun setting. She dressed and sat on the edge of the bed, not ready to face Dracke. A knock at the door pulled her from her thoughts.

"Who is it?"

"Celine, Madam Mina."

"Come in."

"I was checking to see if you are coming down for dinner."

"I… give me a minute, please?"

"Whatever you need, madam."

Mina watched her leave, then retreated to her window nook, looking out at the snow-covered orchard. Her breath sucked in at the sight of so many stars in the sky. She wrapped herself in her arms, knowing she was not ready to see him. She was too ashamed, too conflicted, too angry.

Dracke was waiting for her, she knew that. She left her room and went outside, walking amongst the rose bushes and thinking about her feelings for him. Mina was unaware Dracke was at the window watching her every step.

"How is she?" he asked, continuing to study Mina's movements, as Celine walked in. He remained concerned she seemed so distant, though she was less than fifteen feet away from him.

Celine stiffened but said nothing for a moment. "She seems okay."

"But?"

"She was not eager to come down for dinner. What will you do?"

"I will give her space, as that appears to be what she needs." He finished his drink and retired to his chamber. Celine pulled a cloak off the hanger and took it to Mina.

"Madam, please, it is too cold to be out here."

"I cannot go inside yet. I just… I cannot."

"He has retired for the night, saying he wishes to give you space."

"Why would he do that? He is usually quite forceful about what he wants."

"Yes, he is. However, something about you is changing him… in a good way," Celine added hastily.

Mina gave her a small smile, then wrapped the cloak tightly around herself. "Thank you for this. I'll be in momentarily."

"Yes, madam."

Mina watched her go inside, then continued to stroll around the garden. Duke approached her, lowering his head when he reached her. She scratched his ears and smiled. A chill shivered down her spine, and she decided to return.

Nervous, she walked into the dining room, only to find it was indeed empty. She ate her meal, then went to the library. She grabbed a handful of books and sat to write, but all she could think of were the words he had said.

Your eyes condemn me. I would cross oceans of time to find you. Shaking her head to clear it, she began to catalog books, grateful for the temporary distraction.

Working for another hour, she decided to turn in. She went to place the books on the shelves where they belonged when an envelope with her name on it caught her eye. She picked it up and held it close as she carried it with her. A cramp shot through her side.

Her eyes closed as she placed her arm over her abdomen. *Oh, no. Not here, not now. Please, anything but this.*

Dracke finished the last of his dinner, his tongue doing a quick sweep of his lips. Celine ran in.

"Master, come quickly!"

He followed her up the stairs and into Mina's chamber. She was lying on the bed, uncovered, and curled up in a ball. Her quiet sobs as she trembled in pain struck him like lightning. He rushed to her side, gently raising her head to look at him. Seeing the hurt on her face, he went to bite his wrist.

"No, Dracke," she said quietly. He froze, his wrist to his mouth. "It won't help."

"Mina, you're sick—"

"No, not sick."

He brought his arm down and sniffed. "Blood." His eyes went wide as he studied her in concern. "Where are you hurt?"

"Please, just go. I'm all right."

"You're bleeding!"

"Dracke, please, I can't talk about it."

He cocked his head when understanding sank in. "It's your cycle, isn't it?"

She buried her face in her pillow. "Please go."

"Mina, whatever is the matter with you? I just want to be sure you are all right. Clearly, you aren't."

"We don't… we don't talk about this. It's… private and unseemly. Please, leave me alone."

"Why do you refuse my comfort?"

"I… do you not crave my blood?"

He chuckled. "This is different. I assure you, you are safe around me. I'll be right back."

"Dracke!" She sat up, but he was gone. She curled herself tighter as the cramps wore her down. He appeared a moment later, holding a pouch of some sort. She watched as he carried it to the fireplace, setting it on a rack for a minute, then bringing it to her.

"Mina, uncurl for me."

"Dracke—"

"Please," he said in a soft tone.

She straightened her legs slightly, and he placed the pouch against her stomach. The heat immediately began to help ease her pain. She looked at him with gratitude in her eyes.

"Thank you," she murmured as she curled back up.

"Mina, what you are going through is nothing to be embarrassed about. Why do you feel this way?"

"Our father and mother told us not to mention it, not to show we were in pain, not to ever discuss it."

Dracke sighed as he sat on the edge of the bed, placing his hand gently on her arm. "They are wrong. It is natural, and there is nothing you and I cannot talk about. Do you hear me?"

"Because you care for me?" she asked softly and hugging the pouch tighter.

"Yes," he admitted. "Also, there was a time in my youth when I will confess I thought it was… gross. Having spent so much time in the library, learning and researching, I see now how immature that mindset was." He glanced down when she squeezed his hand. "Is your pain terrible?"

"It's easing some, thanks to you."

He brought her hand to his lips and kissed it gently before laying it back on the bed. "Whatever you need, Mina, I will always give you. I see now how selfish I have been."

"Thank you."

"Are you able to eat?" he asked when he noticed Celine in the doorway with a tray.

"Hmm, I don't want to, but I will try."

Celine was surprised when Dracke appeared before her, took the tray, and quietly dismissed her. He rested on the edge of the bed while Mina sat up. He held the tray while she ate, no words spoken as he lifted the linen and wiped her chin. She smiled at him in thanks and finished her meal.

"Now, rest."

"The library—" she said weakly.

"A night or two won't hurt anything. Please, rest."

"Thank you, Dracke."

His hand caressed her back and shoulders as she drifted off to sleep. He watched her for a few minutes, debating how to tell her… What to tell her… He stood up and vaolmersed into his parlor, angry he knew the truth while she did not. Still, no matter how he chose to tell her, she would always be angry at him.

He sat in his chair, reading the last book he could find in his library on fae history, wondering how much Mina may already know.

A few nights later, Celine knocked softly, then approached when Mina bade her to enter. She smiled at Mina in her pale pink gown and ruby necklace. "You have a guest downstairs, madam."

"I… what?" Mina asked.

"The young man from before."

"I'll be down in a moment." She watched Celine leave then clasped her hands tightly. *Does she mean Gustave? What could he possibly want with me? To risk coming here…*

She gathered her courage and walked downstairs. Before she was on the final step, Gustave rushed to her and took her hand.

"Thank the gods you're all right."

"What are you doing here?" she demanded, pulling her hand away. "Do you know what will happen if Dracke finds you here?"

"I had to be sure you were all right after your accident in the woods."

"It wasn't an accident! You attacked me."

"Mina, you hit your head. You don't remember what happened. It's all right."

"No, Gustave, it most certainly is not. You need to leave, now."

"I am not leaving without you."

"Why would I come with you?"

"I have learned more about your situation here after speaking with Marius. I am here to rescue you. Come quickly."

Mina laughed in his face. "I am not a prisoner here. What are you—" she cried out when he lifted her over his shoulder, carrying her towards the door. "Dracke!" she yelled.

He appeared before Gustave. "Unhand her, now." Mina was worried because his voice was so calm.

"Move, beast," Gustave snarled. "She is mine, and I am taking her with me."

"I am not yours," she called out.

Mina heard the clang of metal as Dracke unsheathed his sword. "I absolutely forbid it."

Gustave put Mina on her feet, roughly pushing her behind him as he drew his own blade. "I will do what I must to free her."

"Please, Gustave, stop," Mina begged. "I've already told you—"

"Silence, Mina," he demanded, watching Dracke as he approached.

Their swords clashed in contact, and Mina could only stand back and watch. Gustave lunged. Dracke pivoted on his heel then stepped to the side. As he brought his sword up, Gustave ran him through his ribcage. The sword fell from Dracke's hand as he placed his palm over the wound and collapsed to the floor.

Mina ran to him, picking up the sword and turning to Gustave.

"Leave now," she commanded, trembling at the thought of facing off against him. "You are not welcome here."

"Whore," Gustave said as he sheathed his sword. "Not even worth a notch on my bedpost."

As soon as he was gone, Mina knelt beside Dracke. Not sure it would work, she lifted her wrist to his mouth, and his fangs sank into her flesh. He gripped her arm as his instinct forced him to feed. Mina's color faded as she grew cold. He immediately pulled away and sat up, catching her when she fell unconscious.

"Mina!"

Mina stepped out of the washroom, happy to be clean and in fresh clothing. She smiled at the pouch resting beside a book on her nightstand, and she was grateful Dracke cared for her, even knowing her own feelings for him were conflicted. He had not mentioned the horrible incident with Gustave since that night, and she was eternally grateful for it.

When she picked up the book, an envelope fluttered to the floor. She set the book down and scooped up the letter, going to her window nook and sitting on the soft cushioned seat. Carefully, she opened the envelope and removed the letter.

My dearest Mina,

I fear you will not return to me. I know your fury is great at the things I have done. I sit at the dining table, looking up and expecting to see your smile, only to grow empty at the loss of your presence.

I have missed you this week, and I do not admit this lightly, but living without you has made me realize how much I care for you. You have grown on me, wrapping me in your beauty as the roses around the pillars do, covering me in your charm and splendor. I am not worthy of you, not of your soul nor of your heart. However I yearn desperately for both.

I doubt you will ever see this letter, because I know in my heart you have chosen to leave me behind. Can I let you go? I know it is the right thing to do, but my heart aches so at the thought, and I cannot ignore this pain.

I am all in a sea of wonders. I doubt; I fear; I think strange things which I dare not confess, even to my own soul. My heart, my body, my very soul longs for you.

What must I do to see you again? I will give you whatever you desire, whatever your heart wishes for the most if only to look upon you one last time.

With love from an unmoving heart,
Dracke

Her breath hitched as her tears landed on the letter, staining the parchment and smearing the ink. Her heart pounded as her thoughts raced, pitying him and hating him, wanting him to be happy while believing he deserved his misery for what he had done to her. Oh, but to be free of such feelings!

"Dracke," she said softly, patiently waiting and keeping her gaze averted when he appeared beside her.

"Mina, what is the matter?"

She handed him the letter. "Is this true?"

He looked at the piece of paper in his hand with disbelief. "Wherever did you get this?"

"It matters not, only whether what you wrote is true."

"It is. Every word of it." He waited with bated breath, hoping to hear the words he desired more than any other.

"I cannot love you," she said at last.

His heart sank. "Nor am I worthy if you could," he confessed.

"That is not the reason. You know how much I care for you. We care for each other. I just… my heart is still shattered in grief with so much pain and agony I cannot feel joy. To do so would be treason against my very soul." She wiped her tears as she finally lifted her eyes to him. "I need time."

"Time is the one thing I do not have to give."

"Are you not immortal?"

"I am, but to a degree. I can only say time is not on my side."

"Please, I need more of an explanation."

He sighed as he turned away. "All I can express to you is things here are not as they appear. My birthday is in less than a month, and things after will never be the same."

"Less than a month?" she asked with a scoff. "Are you… are you giving me a deadline to fall in love with you?"

He took her hand, kissing her palm delicately. "My dearest Mina, no. Please, listen to me very carefully. In twenty-seven days, I will turn one hundred years old. On that day…" Anger filled him as he shook his head. "I cannot say, but please, trust me about this. There is so much I wish to tell you, that I ache to tell you, but I need you to understand. Now more than ever."

Looking into his eyes, she could finally see the fear and pain he had previously hidden so well. She stood up to face him, giving him a small nod as she caressed her thumb along his jawline.

"I will try to understand."

"Thank you."

"Why do you care for me so?"

This was his chance. He could speak the truth, but to do so, she may leave him forever. His heart ached at the thought, and he immediately pushed it away. "Because you do not treat me as the beast I am, even after I have hurt you. I would that you could see me for my heart, but I fear even it is venomous."

"It is not."

"How can you possibly say that?"

"Because a venomous heart would not go to the lengths you have to protect me and care for me. You hide here, in the dark, afraid of the light. I know you do not wish to hurt anyone."

"Mina, there are darknesses in life, and there are lights. You are not only one of those lights, you are my light."

She cleared her throat, continuing. "I do not know what all has been done to you, nor what you have done, only that you do not deserve this torment, least of all from yourself." She gathered her courage as she worked to forgive him. "I understand why you fed from me. It was an overwhelming and primal urge. I do not know if I can forgive you for throwing me into your dungeon without giving me the chance to defend myself. That was downright cruel!"

"I was angry and—"

"I know, but you did not give me one second to explain to you what had happened. I begged my father to let me leave, practically in tears. I demanded he let me go."

"You were so eager to return to the beast who had hurt you? Or was it because you were afraid of my wrath if you were late?"

"Both," she answered, staring him square in the eyes. "And I see now I was right to feel that way."

"I told you explicitly what would happen if you failed to return by sunrise."

"I promised you I would. I see how little you think of me, think of my word to you. Even though I have always done everything in my power to keep it, to honor it? I was held against my will both times! And this time, you kidnapped my sister."

"She is unharmed."

"No, she is traumatized! When I hugged her goodbye, she went tense and did not reciprocate my hug. I am unsure she will ever be able to look upon me again."

"I did not mean—"

"I don't care," she said with a clenched jaw. "I did not mean to break my promise, yet it happened. And you would not give me an ounce of grace. Why do you then deserve it?"

"What are you talking about?"

She snatched up the letter and held it to his face. "You were so sure I had abandoned you that you gave up on me. Do you have so little faith in me?"

"No, I have so little faith in myself. I was sure you would not return after what I had done to you. I did not see how you could face me again."

"It wasn't easy," she admitted. "And I'm still torn on my feelings for you. I will always be grateful you saved me from Gustave, but you have betrayed my trust. I deserved a chance to defend myself."

"Mina—"

"Go away," she hissed, shoving him back. "Leave me alone!" She went to shove him again, but he vanished. Nearly falling, she managed to catch her balance. She sat on the bed, trembling as she picked up the book on her nightstand.

Dracke went to his parlor, where Celine was setting down a fresh bottle for him. He walked up to her and grabbed her arm, spinning her to him. Her eyes widened in fear.

"Did you do this?" he demanded, holding up the letter.

"No, master. I would not do so unless you told me to."

"Then how did she get it? This was locked up in my safe, along with the rest of my letters and papers!"

"I don't know."

Dracke released her arm and continued pacing, debating how best to proceed. He stopped when Mina appeared in the doorway, her face soaked with tears, her eyes red and puffy, and a book clutched tightly in her hands.

"What's wrong?"

She held up the book containing the history of him and his people. His head tilted when she flipped it open to the page of countless victims being impaled and tortured.

"Did you do this?"

"Mina—"

"Answer me!" she screamed in fury. "Are you him? Are you Vlad?"

"I am, but—"

"Then you are exactly the monster you think you are. And you thought I could ever fall in love with someone like you? Knowing you have done this?"

"Mina, wait—"

"You are a beast, and you deserve eternal damnation." She chucked the book at him and ran from the manor, going to the stable to retrieve her horse. The sun was starting its slow ascent as she rode out into the fresh air.

Chapter 12

The Coward

Arriving in Lyndon, Mina was unsure of where to go. She longed to see her family but feared Elise was still traumatized after being kidnapped by Dracke. Taking the chance, she returned to Renfield Manor. She settled her horse into the stable before she knocked on the front door. Delphine gestured her inside. Marius walked in a moment later.

"Bellamina, what are you doing here?" he asked coldly.

"I wanted to check on Elise." She glanced over when Elise and Marie walked in, holding hands. Elise said nothing, keeping her eyes on the ground. Mina stepped forward. "Elise, I am so sorry."

"You should be," she murmured.

"Please—"

"That beast took me because of you!" she snarled as she folded deeper into Marie's protective arms. "You should not have come back here."

"This is my home," Mina said with hope.

"No," Marius responded, deflating the very thought of her returning for good. "I have already lost you. I will not risk your sisters," he said, looking at Elise before turning back to Mina. "I will lose no more."

"Father, please—"

"No, Bellamina. You have made your choice."

"What choice?"

"To stay with the prince."

"You mean the one I saved you from? I took your place, saving your life, and this is how you repay me?"

"I was only taken prisoner because I took a rose for you."

"Did I ask for one? Did I ask you to steal for me?"

"Well, no, but—"

"How short your memory is. I have only ever given myself for this family, for you. I traded myself for Elise, as well. Why do you not see this? Why are you pushing me away now?" Mina asked with a tremble in her voice.

"As I said, it is too dangerous for your sisters. It is better if you go."

"I only wanted to help."

"You have done enough." Marius swallowed hard, ignoring the ache in his chest. "You are banished from this estate. Leave now and never return."

When Mina looked to Marie for help, all she could muster was a sympathetic smile. Mina realized she truly was on her own. The thought ripped through her heart, sawing her veins, and splitting her hope to shreds. Unable to say another word, Mina fled from the manor and mounted her horse.

Tears streamed down her face as she tried to think of somewhere she could go. She realized she was in fine jewels, and she could sell some to pay for lodging. She rode to Rhoem, the next town over. She found a shop willing to buy her earrings, then used the money to secure a room.

The Demeter was a quiet, unassuming tavern attached to the inn. She sat in the corner, eating her beef stew while watching the sailors drink and laugh, enjoying their time home before setting sail again the next day.

"Can I get you anything else?"

Mina offered the barmaid a polite smile. "No, but thank you."

The barmaid could see the fine gown she was trying to hide beneath her cloak. "I've not seen you around here. Where did you say you were from?"

"I didn't," Mina said as she stood up, tossing a handful of coins onto the table. "Thank you." She retreated to her room.

It was small and drafty, but at least it had a fireplace. It took her a few tries, but she lit a fire, sitting and waiting for the room to get warm. Holding her head in her hands, her mind raced as she tried to come up with a plan.

Where do I go next? Alain could always use a governess, and he is a sweet boy, but can I do it again? Thinking of Colin is still so painful, and I do not believe I am ready. However, I only have a few jewels, and some are so valuable the local shopkeepers are unable to purchase them. What do I do?

Desolation crept in, a sense of loss and separation unlike anything she had felt before. She longed to be anywhere she would be loved. She knew Dracke did not love her, only her presence after so much time alone. Her father no longer loved her, not if he could banish her. She was truly, utterly, on her own.

"Hmm, what's a girl like you doing in a place like this?" Dracke chuckled softly as he took in her tiny, sparse lodgings.

Mina sat upright, nearly falling from the bed in surprise. "What are you doing here?"

"What does it look like? We need to talk."

"I have nothing else to say to you."

"Mina, I did not kill those people. My brother, Vlad Sarpe, was the one who inflicted such horrors."

"You are both named Vlad?"

He sighed. "It is a family custom to name the sons after the father. We go by our middle names."

"So, at times when the book mentioned Vlad… it was not always referring to you?"

"That's right. I am Vlad Dracke Dracul. Do not misunderstand. I am not innocent. I did impale soldiers and those who tried to hurt me and my people. Never though, did I do that to an innocent, I assure you." He sat beside her on the bed. "Do you believe me?"

"I want to. So why were you cursed and not him?"

"He is… *was* my identical twin. We were celebrating our birthday, and he was passed out drunk in the ballroom. I could've said something to her, told her the truth, but…" He looked at Mina. "Wait, you said cursed. What do you know about it?"

"I saw a little more in your journal than I originally said because I was scared to tell you the truth when you caught me up there. I only know there was mention of a curse and nothing else, I swear."

"I cannot discuss it, but if you are truly done with me, I at least wanted to clear the air with you. Tell me to go, and I will leave you in peace."

She scoffed. "You and everyone else apparently."

"What?"

"I… nothing. So, what happened to your brother?"

"Mina, please. I don't want to talk about it."

"You said if I tell you to go, you will. So this may be your last chance to tell me everything."

"Fine. After the curse, he realized what I had become, and he attacked me."

"Your own brother?"

"He no longer saw me that way. Instead, he saw a monster to be slayed. Never mind the fact I chose to stay silent when she placed the curse upon me, to take it for him."

"Dracke—"

"It's all right. I defended myself and killed him. Celine saw to disposing of his body. I have never hated myself more than I did that night."

"You didn't have a choice."

"I am damned, cursed as this immortal being. He could've lived a life. Even if he was cursed to stay there, he wouldn't have been a monster like I am."

"Yes, a life full of pain and torture for anyone who crossed him. He got what he deserved."

Dracke immediately stood up. "Who are you to decide who lives and who dies?"

She jumped to her feet, placing her palm flat upon his chest. "Please, I didn't mean it like that."

"Then what did you mean?"

"If I were the person making the choice, I would choose you. Because as you told me, you did not slaughter thousands of innocents."

Dracke went to grip her wrist, but as he clasped her small, petite hand in his own, a spark struck him. His breath shuddered, and he realized she had the same reaction.

"What was that?" she asked.

He pulled away. "Static in the air. That's all."

"You are hiding something from me. What?"

"I have told you exactly how I feel. Laid myself bare only for you to tell me I deserve eternal damnation."

"I was scared of my own feelings." She traced her fingers along the lines on her hand. "I was angry you would feel such things for me."

"Why?"

"Because I do not deserve love and devotion."

"My dearest Mina, that is something I should be saying to you. I am the villain in this story, not you. You deserve the world at your feet, and a love to complete you, all of you. You are kind, giving, and beautiful. Why would you ever believe this?"

"Because…" Her words were lost before she could get them out. "Because I let him die." Her voice cracked.

"What are you talking about?"

"I can't. Please, it's too painful."

"I thought we were being open."

"Dracke, it's too much. I'm not ready."

"Very well. I have to ask. Are you through with me or do you wish to return home?"

"Do I even have a home?" she asked quietly. "My father told me I am banished."

"Hmm, I meant my chateau, but now you have piqued my curiosity. Why did he say that?"

"He said I chose you over my family."

"Did he?" The pain in her eyes sent an ache ripping through him. "How can I help? What do you want?"

"Can I return to the chateau with you? If not, I'll understand. Especially after what I said when I left."

"You will always have a home there. I promise you."

Marius read a few pages, paced a bit, then read some more. Marie entered with a mug of tea and a fresh lemon scone. "Father, please eat and drink something. You've hardly said a word since she left."

He glanced at her, only to turn his nose up to the offer. "I'm not hungry. I'm fine."

"No, you are not. Why is Mina banished? She was correct, she did nothing wrong. Dracke—"

"You are taking his side as well?"

Marie set the plate and mug on his desk before approaching him. "What is going on?"

"Mina is not your sister, and that is all you need to know."

Her jaw dropped at his casual confession. "What do you mean? You cannot say something like that without giving me answers."

Marius looked at her for a moment. "Your mother was pregnant with our third child. You were five years old, so I doubt you remember. She became violently ill, and the baby…" Marius clenched his hand as the lump formed in his throat. "Your mother was heartbroken from the loss of your sister, and she went into the woods to grieve alone."

"I remember her being sad, but you wouldn't tell me why."

"I didn't get the chance. While she was in the woods, she met a fae who made a bargain with her. There was a baby fae whose own mother had perished in childbirth, a bastard. No one knew her paternal lineage. The fae offered her up but warned she was cursed. To take her in was to change the course of the future. Your mother was wary, but once the fae pulled back the blanket and showed her the infant, your mother did not care. She fell in love with her in that moment, and she named her Bellamina."

"Beautiful love."

"Yes."

"Why did we never know this?"

"Your mother swore me to secrecy. I only tell you now so you understand why I must push Bells away. If she were to return here, disaster may strike. I must protect you and your sister."

"She is still my sister! I care not whether she is human or fae, nor about her lineage. I have been immature and selfish with her, but she has always shown me such love and grace. I wish to extend the same to her now."

"We cannot. It is out of our hands. She has chosen her path."

Delphine entered the room. "Monsieur, you have a visitor," she said.

Dracke waited in the foyer. Marius stormed in, his burning anger apparent in his demeanor. "You have to stop this. It upsets my daughters, and you have no right to be here."

"I thought we would speak, the two of us. Inside or out, it's your preference. Just so you know, it's a blizzard out there." Dracke grinned at him.

"Fine." Marius stared at him with distrust. "My study it is."

Dracke followed him, then glanced over the books on the shelf while Marius watched him. Finally, Dracke faced him. "You cannot turn your back on Mina. Not after everything she has been through."

"You have no right to tell me what to do."

"When it comes to her, I think I do. As I reminded you, she took your place. I can renege on her *bargain* any time." He smiled when Marius took the bait, flinching at the word. "Yes, I know what she truly is. Did you think I would not figure it out?"

"How?"

Dracke turned away to hide his shame, refusing to tell Marius he fed from Mina, that her blood told him who she was. "It matters not, only that I know. Shall I take you instead? Let her live her days here with her sisters while you wither away in the dungeon?"

"You wouldn't."

"Try me," he said, staring him down.

"I know you wouldn't because Mina would never allow it. Do you forget? I heard what you said to her. You are wrapped around her finger. She gave herself once for me. She would do it again."

Dracke scoffed. "I am not the only one under a curse."

Marius was taken aback by the unexpected statement. "How do you know all of this?"

"I have spent every night for nearly eighty years researching in my library, trying to regain my humanity. I know a great many things. Her course and mine are intertwined, though I do not see to what end. Will you turn your back on her now, knowing her life as she knows it may be coming to an end?" The guilt on his face told Dracke everything he needed to know. "Ah, that is why you have done so. To protect your own heart. You are nothing but a coward."

"It is not cowardly to do what I must to protect my family. I never would have let my wife accept her, had I known. By the time she returned home, it was too late, and there was nothing I could do."

Marie walked in without knocking. "Dracke, will you take me with you? I wish to see my sister."

Marius stepped between them. "You are not leaving."

"Father, I love you, but you do not own me. Now, I wish to see Mina."

Dracke studied her, suspicious of her intentions. "Is something the matter?"

"No. I only wish for her to know I still care for her. I do not agree with our father, nor do I wish to see her banished. I want her to know I am here for her."

"Dracke can relay your message."

Marie walked around Marius, placing her hand on Dracke's arm. "No, I will tell her myself." She looked at Dracke and nodded. He gave Marius a subtle tilt of the head before they disappeared.

Once in the chateau, Marie stepped back, unsteady on her feet. "Are you all right?" Dracke asked.

"Fine. I'm not used to traveling that way, is all."

Dracke chuckled softly. "It makes your sister a little sick to her stomach." He knocked. "Mina, someone is here to see you."

Mina opened the door, her eyes wide at the sight. "What did you do?" she asked Dracke, her voice rife with anger. "Taking Elise wasn't enough?"

"Mina, stop. I asked to come," Marie assured her.

"Really?"

"Yes." They went into Mina's bedchamber to speak in private.

"You're welcome," Dracke muttered as he sulked down the stairs.

"What's going on, Marie?" Mina asked as she walked to the bed, gesturing for Marie to sit with her.

"We have much to talk about. First, did you know Elise and Gustave have been courting?"

"What? No." Her chest tightened at the news.

"Apparently, he made her swear not to say a word. Father told me you rejected him, and I pieced it together. I guess Gustave figured if he couldn't have you, he would have her, instead. I know you are reluctant to speak of it, but I worry about her. Will you tell me what he did to you?"

Mina shifted for a moment. "It was the first party after Colin had passed. We were still in mourning, and Gustave drank too much." Mina looked down, straightening her already straight gown. "He cornered me in the foyer, asking if he could kiss me before he left."

"What did you say?"

"I told him no, I do not have those feelings for him. He said he was hurting, and my kiss would soothe him. I refused again. He grabbed my arm, pulled me to him, and kissed me. He slobbered all over me, the drunken fool. Then he…" Her jaw clenched. "He brought his hand up between my legs. He started to… he ripped away…" Mina shook her head. "But before he could do anything else, a couple walked in. They were making out and oblivious to what was happening."

"Did he stop?"

"Only because I shoved him away and ran."

"Mina, I am so sorry," Marie said, gently squeezing her hand.

"Thank you, but there's more. He attacked me in those woods. I didn't trip. He shoved me, knocking me to the ground. Then he came here and tried to take me away, saying I should marry him. Elise isn't safe with him." Her worry for her older sister consumed her. "He will hurt her. Or worse."

"I know, but I fear we may be too late. I believe they will become engaged soon."

"She won't listen to me," Mina said.

"I doubt she would even believe me, as she is over the moon for him. He bought her silk gowns and jewels, and that was all it took. She was smitten immediately."

"She doesn't care he is merely a constable?"

"Of nobility from a wealthy family. His occupation means nothing to her, so long as he can lavish her with gifts and a title."

"That's what she meant, when she said my jewels were baubles compared to what she would receive."

"Yes."

"I'm surprised you came here," Mina admitted.

"I know we haven't always seen eye to eye. Even though I am the oldest, you have always had a good head on your shoulders. I will do what I can to show Father you need not be banished. You know how stubborn he can be."

"I do. A trait I inherited from him."

Marie stood up and paced in front of the fireplace. "No one has told you? You really don't know?"

"Know what?" Mina asked.

"It's not my place."

There was a knock at the door. "Madam Mina?"

"Please, Celine, come in."

Celine walked inside. "Apologies for interrupting, but dinner is ready."

"Thank you." Mina looked at Marie. "We should eat."

"Of course."

They walked downstairs and into the dining room where a feast had been laid out. Wine, tea, coffee, meats, breads, cheese, stew, and desserts covered the table.

Marie shook her head. "This smells great."

Mina laughed as they were about to sit down. Dracke walked in. Marie approached him and gave an awkward bow. "Your Highness, thank you for dinner."

He waved his hand dismissively at her. "You're welcome, but call me Dracke. I insist."

Marie looked at Mina, easing when she gave her a small nod. "Yes, Dracke."

They sat to eat while Dracke had his usual goblet. Marie kept her attention on Mina, who was thinking about their previous discussion. "Marie, what did you mean earlier? You said something about me, something I do not know?"

Marie shot a glance at Dracke before turning back to Mina. "As I've said, it's not my place. Once our father has calmed down, the two of you will have a heart-to-heart, I'm sure."

"All right. How long are you staying?"

"I will return tomorrow. I wanted to come today to reassure you I have not turned my back on you. I know what you did to protect Father and Elise both. I am sorry they do not see it as well."

"She is lucky to have a sister like you," Dracke said, drinking the last swig from his cup. "If I could have had a sibling like you…" He shook his head. "Well, it matters not. When you're finished eating I can show you to your chamber for the night."

"Could I stay with Mina?"

Mina nodded and took her hand. "Of course, dear sister. Just so you know, we usually stay awake all night and sleep during the day."

"That's fine. You know me, the night owl anyway." She laughed softly. "Will you show me the library you're working in?"

"I'd be happy to."

They ate the last few bites of their meal and rose from the table. As they walked down the hall, Marie took in the size and beauty of the chateau. She was awed when they entered the library.

"What a beautiful collection. No wonder he needed your help with it."

"You never cared much for reading," Mina commented as Marie examined the books.

"I did read a little, but not like you."

They sat at the table where Mina showed Marie the work they had done. "Thank you," Mina said softly.

"Whatever for?"

"Coming here. For showing me and the family you aren't afraid of him, or me for that matter. The other night, I thought I was alone, and… I hadn't felt like that since Colin passed away."

Marie looked down. "I wasn't there for you like I should have been. I want to be here for you now."

"I cannot tell you how much this means to me."

They talked through the evening, reminiscing about their mother, celebrating holidays at their chalet in the mountains, and the time Elise was nearly swept away by the tides when they visited the shore. Mina looked at Marie when she sighed again.

"Sorry," she offered with a nervous laugh.

"Marie, please. Talk to me."

"I can't, Mina. Don't ask."

"Are you returning home?"

"Assuming I'm allowed to."

"If not, you are welcome here anytime."

"Thank you."

They looked up when Dracke entered. "Apologies, but the sun will be rising soon. Am I returning you to the Renfield Estate?"

"Please," Marie said, hugging Mina tight. "I promise to visit again soon."

Chapter 13

The Wine

racke and Marie appeared in the foyer of the manor. She gave him a sincere smile. "Thank you. I appreciate it very much." He nodded before disappearing. She removed her cloak and went to her father's study, where she found him deep in thought as he sat in front of the fire.

"You've returned," he said without so much as glancing in her direction.

"I have."

He sighed, then looked at her. "Do you think me cruel? A coward? What?"

"Tell me what is going on, and I will give you an answer."

"What do you already know?"

"Only what little you have told me."

"Which was Mina's curse. If she fulfills it, she will bring about the end of King Willam's reign."

"Then why have you lavished so much affection on her, only to pull it away now?"

"I thought perhaps the fae was mistaken, that Mina was not cursed. We have gone nineteen years without incident. Seeing how things are unfolding, I know now what will happen. We must keep our distance."

"But—"

"I have done everything in my power to keep her away from the prince. She has chosen to defy me every step of the way. She chose this path, and I will not help her on it."

"Wait, if she is a fae, why does she not look like one?"

"Part of the bargain was to make her at least appear human, knowing fae do not reside within our lands. However, if she discovers what she is, the spell will break, and her true form will be revealed."

Marie gasped. "What? I almost told her!"

"I am grateful you did not. Now you see, every choice we make can significantly alter the future, could even bring about the end of the current monarchy. We must tread carefully."

"How do you know banishing her will not escalate it?"

"I do not. I can only hope and pray I am making the right decision."

"But you aren't, Father! Regardless of her bloodline, she is your daughter. You cannot turn your back on her now."

"My mind is made up. I have no choice, as my loyalty is to my king."

"That is the wrong choice."

Dracke returned to find Mina pacing in his parlor. "What's wrong?" he asked as the cloak slid from his fingers and onto the hook. His heart sank when she looked at him with tears streaming down her face. He appeared before her and gently wiped them away.

"What is going on with my father? Why has he abandoned me?"

"I don't know, but I intend to make things right. Between him and Elise, both. I am sorry for the rift I caused. I never meant for this to happen."

"Regardless of your intentions, it did," Mina said, pulling away and storming from the room.

Dracke shook his head as his despair only deepened. He wished desperately to change how things had transpired.

Mina slammed the door and wiped the last of her tears, wishing on every star she saw out her window for her father to forgive her, to love her, to accept her.

The loneliness was more than she could bear, and she went to the kitchen. She found a bottle of wine sitting on the counter and used the wax opener and corkscrew beside it to open it. She did not waste time retrieving a glass.

Dracke walked in a half hour later to find her on the floor, slumped against the wall next to a nearly empty bottle. For a moment, his thoughts drifted back to the night of the curse.

"Mina, what have you done?" he asked as he sat beside her, lifting her up and placing her on his lap.

"I let him die," she confessed, her eyes watering and her speech slurred. "It's my fault."

"Who?" Dracke asked, guilt creeping into his heart as he realized he was taking advantage of the situation.

"Colin, the boy who was my ward."

"I thought he died from the blood plague?"

Mina's eyes closed as she hung her head, her tears flowing as freely as her words. "His doctor asked me to give blood for a transfusion." She shook her head. "But when the time came, I was too afraid of the needle and refused. I couldn't do it, and he died because of me."

Dracke stroked her hair. "Mina, regardless of the blood in your veins, a transfusion would not have saved him."

She went still at his words, then she faced him. "Really?"

"I assure you."

"But I didn't know that at the time. I'm a coward."

"It's all right to be afraid. You have nothing to be ashamed of."

She caressed his face, smiling at him with pity in her eyes. "You would know better than most after what you've been through."

He returned her smile but quickly grimaced when she vomited all over both of them. Dracke sighed. "Celine!" She ran into the kitchen, not saying a word at the sight. "Clean her up, please."

"Of course, master."

Dracke slowly removed Mina from his lap and stood. He bent down and gently pushed the hair from her face before vaolmersing into his washroom and cleaning up. Stepping into the main chamber, wrapped only in a towel, he thought of Mina's luscious lips and eyes which could penetrate his soul with merely a look.

His tongue flicked along her neck, then he sank his teeth in. The thought of her warm, sweet blood flowing into his mouth caused him to shudder. He pulled back, staring at her lips and thinking of nothing more than how badly he needed to plant his mouth on hers, to claim her body and soul for himself. He held her tight as his tongue explored her mouth and his hand caressed her side. She writhed under him.

"Dracke!"

He lifted his head and opened his eyes to see Mina standing in the doorway, cleaned up and in a silk nightgown that left little to the imagination. "Mina—" he started to apologize.

"Again?" she demanded as she stalked towards him.

He was sure she was coming to slap him, and he couldn't blame her, not after the impure thoughts he had. Before he could utter his apology, she grabbed him to her and kissed him hard, the way he had envisioned it. He pulled her in tighter, gripping her neck as her fingers caressed his muscular chest.

"Mina."

"What?" she asked, looking at him with want in her eyes.

"Are you still drunk?"

She giggled softly. "Maybe a little."

He shook his head as he pulled away, went into the closet, and promptly dressed. As he approached her again, he couldn't help but admire her lovely form. "You need to sleep this off, then we will talk tomorrow night."

"What did I do wrong?" she asked.

"Nothing. We need to rest for now."

"If you're sure?"

He pulled her to him and vaolmersed with her into her chamber. He tucked her in, then kissed her forehead. "Get some rest."

"Will you kiss me again?"

He shook his head. "Not now."

"All right."

He turned off the light on his way out, the taste of her wine lingering on his lips. Once back in his chambers, he took a long, cold shower.

Mina woke up with her head throbbing as bits and pieces from the night before made their way into her memory. She groaned as she stood and rushed to the washroom, emptying the last of her stomach contents. She rinsed her mouth and took her time showering. The cool water eased her aching head and cleared some of the fogginess from her mind. When she was dry and dressed, she sat in her window nook with her legs tucked under her, watching the snow.

"How are you tonight?"

Without looking at the source of those words, she answered softly, "I'm all right."

"Are you sure?"

She sighed when he appeared beside her. "Fine, I'm a little embarrassed about last night."

"You have no reason to be. What you have been through, you needed to let go."

She wrapped her arms tighter around herself and hung her head. "But I know what's it like to… to be… I'm sorry I kissed you."

"Even though I wanted it?"

She shook her head. "But I was drunk. I had no right to do that."

"Mina, you did nothing wrong. I feel as though I should be the one to apologize because you did not know what you were doing."

"So that excuses it?" she asked as she stood up to face him. "A few drinks, it's no big deal, and everything is excused?" she yelled.

Dracke cocked his head slightly. "Mina, what is wrong?"

She swallowed hard, realizing his words were meant to calm her, not to excuse what had happened to her. "I'm sorry," she murmured.

"For what?" he asked as he pulled her back against his chest, his arm wrapping around her.

"I… Gustave is Colin's uncle. One night after Colin passed, we were hosting a party for my father at the manor." She proceeded to tell Dracke everything. She trembled as she relived the horror Gustave had pushed on her. "I did the same thing to you last night."

"No, you did not. Gustave asked, and as soon as you said no, he should've left. You kissed me, yes, but I wanted to. Only when I realized you were still drunk did I stop."

"Even so."

He spun her around, caressing her neck. "Well, you're sober now. Do you want to kiss me?" When she pulled away, he looked at her in confusion.

She bit her lip as she thought about his question, and she surprised him when she nodded. "Yes, more than anything."

"What's stopping you?"

"I am still trying to figure out how I feel about you after everything you've done."

"Feeding from you?"

"No, I told you I forgive you for that. I'm still angry about the dungeon."

"I didn't know you were claustrophobic."

"I don't mean because you threw me in there, but because you did not give me a chance! You assumed the worst in me."

"Mina, please," he begged as he took her hand and brought her to his side. He kissed her palm, then worked his way up her arm, coming to rest at her neck. "I need you."

Her breath shuddered as she grew warm, her heart pounding furiously at his touch. Unbeknownst to her, it was nearly driving him mad. She ached when his tongue flicked gently along the crook of her neck. His fangs nuzzled her skin as his tongue continued to explore.

"Yes," she responded. His mouth closed as he kissed her neck. At first, she thought she misunderstood until his fangs plunged into her skin. His fingers trailed mindlessly along her side and stomach as he fed from her. Her back arched as she was overcome with pleasure, growing dizzy as he continued to feed.

He pulled his mouth away but held her tight. "I have you. It's all right." He sat her in the chair before vaolmersing downstairs. When he returned, he had a tray with food and tea. "You need to eat after that."

As she ate, her color slowly returned, and he was awash with relief at the sight. "Thank you," she said once she finished, handing him the tray.

"I'll be right back."

As soon as he was gone, she stood and walked about the room, grateful she was no longer dizzy. She thought of his fangs on her neck, his lips on hers. The cold truth slithered in, that she was unable to give him the love he deserved. She wanted nothing more than to love him, to return his affection, but her heart was still too broken.

"Are you all right?" When she didn't respond, he crossed the room and took her in his arms. "What's wrong?"

She looked at him, unshed tears glistening. "I can't, Dracke."

"Can't what?"

"Be what you need, be who you need. I…" She pulled away. "I'm sorry."

"You don't love me?" he asked in disbelief.

"No, and I'm not sure I ever could."

He swallowed hard at her confession. "I understand. I know I am unworthy of you."

"Dracke, no—" Before she could reach for him, he was gone. She bit back her tears as she gathered up clothing, packing what she could into her small bag.

Without looking back, she fled the manor on foot, not knowing or caring where she was going. She only knew one thing for certain, she no longer had a home. Not in Lyndon or Parysse. Her heart ached as she passed through the gate, longing to take one last glimpse at the chateau. Instead, she ran as fast as she could.

Chapter 14

The Sisters

racke glanced at the calendar on his desk, not needing any reminder his birthday continued to loom before him. He was no closer to breaking the curse. His hands clenched as anger flowed through him, anger with Mina for rejecting him, but more than that, anger at himself for giving her every reason to. He froze in place. Something was wrong. Something was… missing.

"Mina," he said softly, closing his eyes and reaching out for her. His skin grew ice cold when he could not find her. Something was holding him back from accessing their connection, perhaps his guilt or anger. He rushed from the chateau, following her scent until the falling snow blew it away. "Mina!" he called out, growing more concerned with each moment that passed.

Finally, he heard a faint voice calling to him through the trees. "Dracke?"

He charged towards the sound of her voice, finding her in the woods. A hungry pack of black and grey wolves had her surrounded.

"Mina!"

"Dracke, don't," she begged as he drew closer. "Save yourself!"

The wolves snarled, chomping at the bit as they circled tighter around her. Mina was against a tree trunk, trapped. A wolf lunged for her throat, and she hastily lifted her bag. His fangs tore the fabric before he hit the ground, watching her and preparing to attack again. Dracke appeared between Mina and the wolves, growling at them. They shrank back.

"Leave!" he commanded. Mina watched in awe as they ran away, the alpha letting out a final howl before disappearing into the woods. "Listen to them," he said softly. "Children of the night. What sad music they make."

"How did you do that?" Mina asked.

"Because I am a vampyr. Now, what are you doing out here?"

Her heart ached as she met his gaze. "I saw no reason to stay. Not after I had hurt you so."

"You have nowhere else to go."

Her teeth began to chatter, and he pulled her to him, vaolmersing them back into his parlor. He sat her in front of the fire, then he knelt beside her, his hand on her arm.

A tear rolled down her cheek. "I do not wish to cause you any more pain than you already suffer."

"My dearest Mina, regardless of your feelings for me, this will always be your home. There is so much I wish I could tell you…" He stood and walked to the window, watching the snow drifting in the wind.

She gathered herself, then she walked to him and placed her hand on his shoulder. "What's wrong?"

He caressed her neck, her pulse racing at his touch. "I know you have feelings for me."

"I…" She backed away. "I don't know how I feel."

"Then let me tell you," he said. "When I touch you, your heart races, your breath comes in short pants, and your body tenses in response."

"That could also be fear," she shot back.

"Are you afraid of me?"

"Of course not."

"Then the only logical choice is love. You love me, as I love you."

"I… what? Dracke, please."

"Why are you fighting this?" he asked, growing angry at her refusal to see what was standing right in front of her. He could be closer to breaking the curse if she would only admit her feelings. "Mina, tell me the truth."

She shook her head. "I'm not ready."

"What is holding you back?"

"Dracke—"

"What?" he demanded, his voice gruff.

"Please," she begged. "Don't push me about this."

She ran from the room, going to her own and collapsing against the door as she wept into her hands.

Dracke stayed in his parlor and read, knowing Mina needed her space after the way he pushed her. "I deserve this punishment and eternal damnation, but please, spare my staff, spare Mina from my pain. What will it take?" he begged, praying the faery would hear his pleas.

"Master?" He turned to Celine when she walked in. "Is there anything I can do to help?"

"It's not fair to you, but can you talk to Mina? I cannot explain what is happening, but she needs to understand we are running low on time."

"My hands are tied as much as yours, but I will do what I can."

"Thank you."

Celine bowed and walked upstairs, knocking softly on Mina's door. "Madam Mina?"

"Come in," she answered.

Celine stepped inside. Mina was in her nook. She gestured Celine closer.

"I come on behalf of my master, who implores your forgiveness and understanding while acknowledging he deserves neither."

"What can you tell me about the curse?"

Celine shook her head. "I cannot. But please, do not turn your back on him. Not now."

Mina nodded. "Yes, I will speak with him." Before she could move, Dracke appeared. "Were you listening in?" she huffed.

"Yes."

"I want to help with the curse. What can I do?"

His hands clenched when he was unable to answer. Helpless, he looked at Celine, who was in no better state than he was. "Mina, if you would but give me the one thing I have asked for."

"Is that what it would take to break it?"

"No, there is more," he admitted.

"What?"

His throat tightened. "I cannot say."

"Then what can I do?" she asked in exasperation.

"We still have time. Please, give me a chance."

"Fine," she said softly.

He lifted her hand and kissed it. "I know I have been a beast, and for that, I am truly sorry."

"Thank you. For now, could we work in the library?" she asked, hoping for a distraction from the pain consuming her heart.

"Of course."

They said nothing as they walked together. Mina went straight to work and kept to herself at first, but she began to soften as the night wore on. She asked Dracke about some of the books she was cataloguing and found herself enjoying his company more than ever before. When Celine brought in a tray with fruits and tea, Mina smiled and thanked her.

Dracke watched her eat, wondering what each piece tasted like on her delicate tongue. She smiled at him. "How is it?" he asked, his voice laden with envy.

She placed a cherry in her mouth, then leaned up and kissed him, pushing her tongue inside. His taste buds erupted at the flavor. She pulled back, smiling at him.

"Well?" she asked playfully.

"But I thought—"

Her smile grew. "Give me a little time." She kissed him again, stroking her fingers through his hair. He stood up, wrapping her arms around his neck as he took her to the wall. His body pinned her own as his kiss intensified.

"Mina, please. I need you.'"

"Again?"

"No, Mina. Not to feed from you. To pleasure you." He immediately backed away when she tensed up.

"I can't."

"I'm sorry," he said.

"No, I started this. I want you, but I keep thinking of that night Gustave hurt me."

He wiped her tears as they fell, holding her against his chest. "I am sorry he did that to you. He had no right to violate your space, nor to take from you without your consent."

"Dracke, I do care for you, but it feels wrong to not be able to say what you need me to say. I see how much it hurts you. I am sorry."

"Mina, it's all right. For now, let's focus on the books and continue to build up our friendship. It means a lot to me, you know, having you as my friend."

"Really?"

"However I can have you in my life, I am honored to do so."

The week passed by, and each night after dinner, Dracke presented Mina with a gift. The first night was a ruby necklace. The second, a bracelet with diamonds and sapphires. The third night, he pulled out a ring box.

She swallowed hard when she realized what he had. He opened it to reveal a ruby cut to the shape of a rose with an emerald leaf on a platinum band.

"Dracke—"

"Mina, marry me."

Her breath shook as she stared at the ring. "I… I thought we were trying this as friends? I don't understand."

"Mina, I love you. I love how your eyes sparkle brighter than the stars in the night sky, how your heart races when I am in the room with you, how you look at the world in awe and splendor. More than anything, I wish for you to look at me the same way. I want you on my arm, as my partner, my wife, my true love."

"Dracke, it's…" She stood up and walked to the window, not seeing the snow but thinking about his words. *Is this because of the curse or does he love me? I am so confused!* Building her courage, she faced him. "I am sorry, but I cannot marry you."

Her head hung when he vanished without a word. She wiped her tears, angry with herself because she could not open up to him, angry she could not be what he needed her to be.

"I'm trying," she said softly to herself.

Mina walked into the dining room, disappointed to find it empty. She went to the library but found no sign of Dracke. Hopeful he would appear, she gathered up books and sat down to work. The next few nights were the same. She worked in the library, thinking he would come in so she could speak to him. One night, she did not leave her chamber.

Celine knocked softly and entered when Mina did not respond. "Are you ill?" she asked when she saw Mina in bed.

"I'm fine," she replied quietly.

"Will you come and eat?"

"I'm not hungry."

"You need to, Madam Mina. You have hardly eaten all week."

"I said I'm not hungry," she snapped as she pulled the blanket over her head.

Celine sighed and went downstairs, seeing the worry on Dracke's face. "You heard her?"

"I did."

"Yet, here you sit."

"What do you mean?"

"I think you need to speak with her."

He scoffed at the notion. "I am the last person she wants to see right now."

"Foolish."

"I beg your pardon?" he asked, his eyebrow arched.

"She quit eating once you stopped joining her."

He vaolmersed into Mina's chamber. At the sight of her in bed, his expression softened. His fingers combed gently through her hair.

"Why will you not eat?"

"I don't see the point."

"Why not?" he asked.

"Why do you not join me?"

"I thought you needed space after everything I said to you."

"That just shows me you were only interested in… in being with me, and you aren't really my friend."

"Mina, I want to marry you because you are my friend. It grew from friendship into love. Why do you not believe me?"

She sat up and looked him in the eyes. "From that night… the night in the shower. I have seen your true intentions with me. I thought it was because of the curse, but thinking back on how you have needed me, fed from me, kissed me, I am unsure of what you want from me."

"I fell in love with you the moment your eyes met mine."

"What?"

"I immediately forced it down, telling myself it was because I have been alone here after being forgotten. Instead, it lay in my heart and grew into true love." He bent down and kissed her forehead. "I am deeply, madly in love with you. Seeing you like this hurts me so. What can I do to ease your pain?"

She pulled him to her, gripping him tightly as she tried desperately to open her heart, to let herself be emotionally vulnerable for him. Her thoughts drifted to Colin in bed, cold to the touch, and the color of death upon his visage. His eyes stared at the ceiling, seeing nothing as his soul was no longer present.

"I can't," she said. "I don't deserve happiness. I don't deserve your love."

"Mina, please get dressed and dine with me. I beg of you."

Seeing the pain on his face, she reluctantly nodded. "I will be down shortly."

He vaolmersed into the dining room, calling excitedly for Celine. She approached and was overjoyed to learn Mina would be eating with him. She hurried to have dinner arranged.

They looked up when Mina walked in, dressed in a tight black gown with red roses along the skirt. Dracke's expression showed Mina exactly how much he liked the way she looked.

She took her seat, unable to hide her surprise when he sat beside her instead of taking his usual spot at the head of the table. From time to time, she would glance at him and smile while she ate her meal. He took her hand and kissed it.

"My dearest Mina, you are radiant in this gown."

"Thank you."

He stood up and pulled her with him. Celine took it as her cue and turned on the gramophone before stepping out to give them privacy.

Mina smiled as she and Dracke slow-danced with his arm wrapped tightly around her, reassuring her and comforting her. When the song ended, Mina stepped back but stumbled over her own feet. Dracke gripped her wrist, drawing her to him so their faces were inches apart. She looked into his eyes, and without hesitation, kissed him firmly.

Her heart ached when he pulled back. "I'm sorry," she said. "I should know better after I rejected—"

His lips crashed on hers, and she gripped the back of his neck. Her body leaned in, and she ached in her very soul to be with him. She was ready to let go of the past, ready to move forward and give him everything he wanted.

"Dracke, I—"

"Master, come quickly!" Celine yelled as she ran in, frantic.

"Not now!" he scowled.

"It's life or death. Please, hurry," Celine begged.

"What? Where?"

"The foyer," she answered as she ran up to him. He vaolmersed the three of them, then stepped back at the sight of Marius as he stood before them. Cradled in his arms, Elise was bloodied, bruised, and barely breathing.

"What happened?" Mina cried out.

"A… a runaway carriage," Marius managed through his tears. "Please, save her. I'll give you anything. I'll do anything. Please, don't let her die."

Dracke looked at Mina, then back to Marius. "Forgive Mina and revoke her banishment."

Before Marius could respond, Mina gripped Dracke's hand. "There's no time to argue! No bargains or deals. Help my sister, please. I beg of you!"

Dracke rushed to Marius, lifting Elise from his arms, and kneeling. He bit his wrist, then held it to her mouth, coaxing her to drink. They watched in wonder as her wounds healed. Marie ran inside, removing her cloak.

"What are you doing here?" Marius asked.

"I followed you. I couldn't sit back at the manor, wondering if she made it or not. How is she?"

Dracke stood up, holding Elise close to his chest. "She is healed. Follow me." He looked at Marius. "I will return in a moment, and we will talk." Marius gave a slight nod. Marie and Mina followed Dracke upstairs into an unused guest chamber. "Clean her up and dress her in whatever you need from the closet there. Your father and I will be in the parlor."

Mina leaned up and kissed his cheek. "Thank you," she said as she and Marie took Elise from him.

Dracke vaolmersed into the foyer, then gestured for Marius to follow him. They sat in the parlor, not speaking for a moment.

"Thank you," Marius said, breaking the silence.

"I didn't do it for you."

"Regardless."

"Is Mina still banished?" Dracke asked.

"She has to be. You know what will happen."

"Actually, I don't. I only know there is a curse. What is it?"

Marius shook his head. "What matters is keeping my daughters safe."

"And banishing Mina does that how, exactly?"

"Fine, I do not know for sure. What I do know, is my daughters—"

Dracke cocked his head, as though listening for something. "Speaking of which," he said after a few moments.

"What?" Marius asked, his eyes squinted in confusion.

"Elise is awake and telling her sisters what really happened." Dracke watched as the color fell from Marius's face. "You didn't think they would find out?"

"I… I had hoped."

"Shall I kill him for you?"

Marius jumped to his feet. "That is inappropriate."

"If anyone hurt my family, what is or is not appropriate would be the last thing on my mind."

Marius sighed as he slumped into the chair. "I have no evidence. It is her word against his, and he is a highly respected constable from a noble family."

"And she is the daughter of the king's personal barrister. Come on, man. For once in your life, stand up for your daughters, and do what is right."

"You have no place to dictate—"

They turned towards the door when Mina walked in and quickly stood as they waited to hear what she had to say. "The damage was only… external. He wanted to celebrate their betrothal, but she refused him, and he tried to take it for himself. She fought him off, and he punished her for it."

"Will she pursue it in the courts?" Marius inquired.

Mina gave a slow shake of her head. "No. She has asked to stay here for a few days while she recovers."

"Whatever she needs," Dracke offered, ignoring the cold, hard look from Marius. "Please let her know she is welcome. She and Marie both."

"Thank you." Mina left to inform her sisters.

Marius cleared his throat. "I will return home then."

"You will not stay for your daughters? There is plenty of room here."

He scoffed. "I will not stay where I am not wanted."

"You are the one who turned your back on Mina. She misses you and wants to speak with you."

"I have nothing more to say to her. I've made my decision. Thank you for saving Elise, but I must return to Lyndon."

"Without even saying goodbye?" They looked to see Elise standing in the doorway, supported by Mina and Marie. "Do you hate Mina so much?"

"I do not hate her at all," he said as he looked down. "But she chose him over her own family."

"He saved my life!" Elise cried out. "After Mina saved yours. When did you become so cruel?"

"I am only trying to protect you and Marie."

Marie scoffed at the notion. "No, you aren't. I know exactly who you are trying to protect. That you would pledge your loyalty to him instead of your own family. Do we mean so little to you? Leave now. We are all three done with you."

"Marie—"

"No, Marius. Just go."

He glimpsed from daughter to daughter, not seeing an ounce of love in their eyes. His hands clenched as he walked towards them. He looked at Marie and Elise. "You two are welcome to come home any time."

"Unless Mina is welcome there, it is no longer our home," Elise said to everyone's surprise. Marius shook his head and swore under his breath as he stormed from the chateau.

Dracke smiled at the three sisters as they clung to each other. "You are all welcome here. Do you need anything?"

Marie smiled at him. "For Elise to rest now."

"Of course."

She and Elise returned upstairs. Mina approached him and took his hand. "Thank you for saving her."

He gave her a sad smile, worried whatever chance he had disappeared the moment Celine interrupted them. "It was the least I could do for you." He kissed softly along the lines of her palm. Her scent tantalized him, and she saw the desire burning in his eyes.

She nodded. "Please, whatever you need."

His fangs sank into her wrist, and his tongue flicked greedily at the blood flowing out. Mina's body tightened. Her core heated and ached as her heart swelled.

"Dracke," she croaked out, unable to utter anything else.

He licked her wounds to heal them. "Yes, my dearest Mina?"

She grabbed his face and kissed him hard, not caring about the blood smeared between them. Her fingers tangled in his hair as his hand caressed her side. He looked at her.

"What do you want?"

"Please, I want you. I ache for you. I want you to do everything you did that night in the shower. Only this time, don't stop."

His hand slid under the fabric of her gown, and his fingers teased along her breast. He smiled as she moaned softly, ready for whatever he would do for her.

"Mina, are you sure?"

"Yes," she said, a shudder of pleasure ripping through her body.

He lifted her up and carried her to the other side of the parlor. After placing her on her feet, he removed her gown and helped her lay on his sofa. He knelt above her, his hands exploring her chest as his tongue did the same in her mouth. His fangs brushed along her teeth, gently scraping the skin of her lips.

Her fingers fumbled with his shirt buttons until she was trembling in response to his touches. Unable to grasp them, she ripped the shirt off him. She traced her fingertips on the scars along his torso and abdomen.

"Mina, stop."

"What's wrong?" she asked in concern.

He stood up. "We can't do this."

"I don't understand?"

His eyes lowered to his bare stomach. "I am a beast. I will not—"

"No, you are not."

"There's another reason I will not continue. I do not know your feelings for me, and until I do, I cannot continue this in good conscience."

The hurt was apparent on her face, the pain in her eyes at his words, but he had to speak the truth. She stood up and approached him, gently caressing his chest.

"Dracke, please. You know how much I care for you."

"I do, and that is why I will stop before either of us do something we regret. Because you do not seem to understand, it is not just you I want. Yes, I love your blood, and I wish to bury myself inside you while you cry out my name. More than that, I want your heart, your soul, your very being. However, I am unworthy, I know."

"Dracke—"

He disappeared. Humiliated and hurt, she quickly dressed and went to her chamber. Her body ran cold while her heart ached at his sudden rejection.

Chapter 15

The Nightmares

ina startled awake to the sound of screaming. She ran into the guest chamber next to her own to find Marie comforting a weeping Elise. She mumbled into Marie's chest and trembled as she tried to calm herself down.

"I'll make tea," Mina offered. Marie smiled at her in gratitude before Mina made her way to the kitchen.

Ignoring Dracke when he walked in, she placed the kettle on the rack in the fireplace and proceeded to get down three tea cups. She set them on the tray, waiting for the water to steam. Dracke stepped up beside her.

"Is everything all right?"

"Elise had a nightmare," she answered, refusing to look at him as she spoke. "We're fine. You can go back to whatever you were doing."

"Mina—"

"Go away," she hissed.

"Why are you being like this? What did I do?"

The kettle steamed, and she turned her attention to it, removing it from the fire and placing it on the trivet on the tray. She added three linens before turning to him. "It's what you didn't do. Because of that, I have no desire to see you for the rest of the night."

She brushed past him and carefully walked upstairs, trying to balance the tray as she did. Almost to the guest chamber, Dracke appeared before her, holding up the pouch containing tea. She said nothing as she took it, shooting him an angry look before going inside.

Once everything was set up, the three sisters sat at the table in the corner, steeping their tea while Marie and Elise chatted. Mina watched Elise from time to time, pity in her eyes after what Elise had just survived. Mina's thoughts drifted to Dracke, but humiliation washed over her.

"Are you all right?" Marie asked. "You look flush, Mina."

She gave her a reassuring smile. "I'm fine."

When they finished, Mina collected the dishes and took them downstairs. She placed them in the sink. As she leaned against the counter, thoughts of Dracke on the sofa invaded her mind. Her fingers trailed the scars on his chest, his breath shuddering at her touch. When her hands went to his pants, she stopped, realizing he could see and feel what she was thinking through their connection. She ran up to Elise's chamber to check on her.

Marie was snuggled with her on the bed, the lights dimmed, as Elise slept in her arms. Mina smiled at the moment of comfort. As she watched them, longing for Dracke's lips overcame her.

She rushed into her chamber, throwing herself on her bed, knowing it was in her head, but if it was the only way to have him, she no longer cared. Her dress practically ripped in her hands as she rushed to lift it. He leaned over her his as his fangs pierced her flesh, then his tongue traced along the vein in her neck as he greedily fed from her.

His hand lowered from her shoulder, slowly, painfully slowly, going down her arm, her stomach, and resting between her legs. She opened herself up, her back arching as his fingers explored. The pleasure of his fangs and his fingers sent her into a dizzying spin, and when she exploded in ecstasy, she could only pant for air.

She calmed her breathing and quickly cleaned up. Her heart fluttered at the thought of Dracke's lips kissing her own. She shook her head, growing cold from the memory of him pulling away from her.

When she stepped into the main chamber, her breath caught in her throat at the sight of Dracke, arms stretched above him as he leaned into her doorway.

"Having fun?" he teased. When she didn't respond, he stepped inside. "Will you talk to me now?"

"We have nothing to talk about."

"Why are you so angry with me?"

"I'm tired. I need more sleep after the night I've had."

"You do know how to wear a man out."

She blushed at his words. "I had really hoped you weren't seeing that."

He appeared immediately before her, leaning down and trailing kisses along her neck. "My dearest Mina, we are tied together. Though I do not know why you fight it so."

"Me?" She scoffed. "Twice you told me you needed me, needed to feed, and I let you." Bitter tears formed in the corners of her eyes. "The one time I told you I needed you, you pulled away from me. I—" She shook her head, unable to continue.

"Mina, I'm sorry."

"Please, I am humiliated enough as it is."

He gently gripped her shoulder. "I never meant for you to feel this way."

She yanked backwards. "Well, you did!"

"What can I do?"

"Leave me alone. That is what I want."

"Very well."

He vanished from the room. She collapsed onto her bed, burying her face into her pillow as she wondered why he rejected her after all his talk of love and desire.

Celine crossed her arms and looked at Dracke. He sighed. "I know. I'm an idiot."

"It's not my business, but—"

"You're right. It's not."

"Master, what if it had led to her saying it to you?"

"I will not trick her, nor will I force this from her. Most importantly, I will not risk her soul for mine. She is… too good for me. I will not take her until she is ready."

"It should be for her to decide."

"I know, but I cannot tell if she truly wants me or if she is simply feeding off our connection. That is the real reason I backed off. I want it to be her decision."

"Yet, you did not tell her the truth?"

"How could I? For now, let us focus on the upcoming ball."

"What?"

"I am throwing a ball in honor of my one hundredth birthday."

"Master, why?"

"The curse started this way. Let it end the same."

"But nothing is ending for you!"

"Do you seriously believe I would live this way? To be a monster for all eternity? No. If the curse is not broken, my life will end."

Celine gasped at his words. "You cannot. Madam Mina has already lost her home since she was rejected by her father. Whether she sees you as a friend or lover, she cannot bear to lose you, as well. You must think of her."

Dracke lifted up a thick envelope. "I already have. Everything is taken care of, I assure you."

"What will become of you?"

He smiled for a moment as he glanced towards the window. "Do you know how long it has been since I have watched the sunrise? To see its hues of pink and red as gold fills the sky? It has been far too long."

"If that is your wish, master. Though I heavily disagree."

"I am sorry beyond words, Celine. While I deserve this punishment, none of you do. I would give anything to stop it."

"It's all right." She gave him a sad smile. "It's not your fault." Her eyes trailed to the window. "At midnight on that night, I will wrap my arms around him and be with him once more."

Dracke swallowed the lump in his throat. "You have always shown me such kindness and patience, even though I have never deserved it." He stood up and surprised her when he hugged her tightly. "Thank you for all you have done."

"And will continue to do until I am no longer able."

His hand quickly swiped at his eyes. He worked in silence, filling out the papers he had prepared for Mina in case the curse could not be broken. Occasionally, he paused and listened for any signs of distress from upstairs.

An hour before sunrise, the silence was broken by Mina's screams echoing through the chateau. He vaolmersed to her room, pulling her from the bed, and waking her. She could only weep in his arms as she trembled in fear, unable to speak.

"My dearest Mina, what happened?" He grew concerned when she clutched him tighter in response. "It's all right. You're safe now. I've got you."

Marie and Elise ran in. "What's wrong?" Elise demanded, eyeing Drack with suspicion.

"Nightmare," he replied.

Elise started towards them, but Marie grabbed her hand. "We'll let you comfort her." Ignoring the cold look from Elise, she dragged her from the room.

"What do you need?" Dracke asked softly, his hand caressing Mina's back.

She wiped her tears, her breath hitching until she finally calmed down. "I'm all right," she managed at last.

"Will you tell me about it?"

"It's one I've had before." Her heart ached as she pulled away from him. "Thank you for comforting me, but you can go now."

"Mina—"

"No, Dracke. Nightmare or not, I am still humiliated. I laid myself bare for you this time, only to have you reject me in return. You say you love me, but you will not show me."

"I wish you would understand I did that to protect you."

"Protect me from what?"

"From me."

"So you made the choice for me? You said you didn't want to continue without knowing how I feel about you. Yet you said you could hear my heart racing. You knew how I felt because you could feel it as well. I told you what I wanted, gave you consent, and still you denied me. You can ignore all of this and pretend it was to be chivalrous, but in doing so you have destroyed whatever feelings I had for you."

"Don't you think that's a bit dramatic?"

When she looked at him, he could see the fury and pain in her eyes. "After what I have been through, I told you exactly what I wanted, what I needed. I was ready to open myself up for you, but you ended it by rejecting me. So no, I don't think it's dramatic at all. I think it is simply the truth."

"Mina—"

"Once Elise is recovered, the three of us will return to Lyndon."

He took her hand. "Please, don't leave me."

The connection between them continued to grow stronger, until Mina pulled away. "I see no reason to stay here now."

"One week from today, I am hosting a ball for my one hundredth birthday. I implore you, please stay. Then you can decide what you want to do after."

"One week?"

"That's all I am asking for. I will give you space, respect your boundaries, do whatever you ask of me. Please, will you stay with me for one more week?"

"Fine, as it will give Elise the time she needs."

"Thank you." He kissed her cheek and walked for the door.

"What is this… this connection between us? You said it was because we have fed from each other. Is that true?"

"In a manner of speaking," he replied, his hand resting on the doorknob.

"Tell me about it."

He tensed and sighed, unable to face her. "You will not have to deal with it much longer. I am sorry for any trouble it has caused you."

"What?" she asked as she scrambled to her feet. "What aren't you telling me?"

He faced her. "You want the truth?" She nodded. "Yes, a bond does form when we feed from each other. However, this one is deeper. I was unsure of your feelings for me, thinking it was the connection making you feel that way. I did not wish to take from you what you may not have been ready to give."

"Wait, what do you mean?"

"Did you really want me or was it simply because of the connection growing between us?"

She stepped back in surprise. "Dracke, I have been attracted to you from the beginning. Even," she blushed as she looked down, "even calling you art to my sisters." Her gaze met his. "Why did you think pulling away was doing the right thing?"

"I have seen how much you still hurt from what Gustave did to you. I would never forgive myself if I hurt you the same way."

She scoffed. "Yet, that is what you did."

"What do you mean?"

"Are you so blind? What you did was not as vile as Gustave, but you still took my choice and made it yourself."

The realization sank in, and his head hung in shame. "You're right. I should've told you the truth right then and there."

She stepped up, her hand trembling as she placed it on his chest. "I cared for you more than I wanted to admit, and it scared me. But I was ready to face those feelings, to confront my past so we could try and have a future."

He gripped her hand, kissing it softly over and over. "Mina, my dearest Mina, please. Let me prove to you I am not the beast you see before you, but I can be the prince you deserve. Will you give me another chance?"

"I thought you said you were giving me space?"

"You asked for the truth, so I am giving it. The decision is yours. Tell me to leave you alone, and though it would break my heart, I will. Because while a thousand armies could not keep me from you, your word is all it would take."

Her breath shook as she stepped closer to him. She caressed his lips and cheek as she looked into his eyes, searching for any trace of humanity within him. When she saw him for who he was, not a beast, but a man who yearned for her love, she smiled at him. He placed his hand over her own, stroking his fingers along her wrist. His hand wrapped around hers, and he pulled her to him, their faces mere inches apart.

"Tell me what you want," he said with a husky voice. "Whatever it is, I will give it. I will give in to every demand you make, give you the satisfaction you so desperately desire. Say the word, my dearest Mina, and I am forever yours."

Her eyes closed as she imagined being on the sofa, his kiss hungry as his hands mapped out her body. Her core ached as her breath caught in her throat. Then he pulled away, telling her no. She ran cold.

"No," she murmured as she pulled away this time, hurting him the way he had hurt her.

"Mina?"

"I owe you nothing. You are nothing to me. Please, go."

Without looking back, she knew the moment he was gone.

Dracke sulked to his coffin, his hands clenched and his jaw equally as tight. *Why does she still deny this? Even without our connection, I could feel how much she wants me. Though it is her heart and not her body I need most. Is all hope lost or do I still have a chance with her?*

Chapter 16

The Connection

ina finally drifted off to sleep, dreaming of the trees by her home in Lyndon. The sun shone on this beautiful spring day. The rays warmed her skin as people strolled along the path. A shadow loomed above her, then engulfed her before she could react.

Blackness encased her, and she could not move, not even breathe. The only sound she could discern was her heart pounding in her ears. She grasped furiously at the velvet prison which held her tight.

"Dracke!" she finally managed. "Dracke, please help!"

Her eyes opened when he pulled her onto his lap, the blackness dissolving as the light of the room took over. She clung to him, her breathing erratic.

"What happened? Another nightmare?"

"Yes. Only this time, I think I was in your coffin."

"Our connection. I didn't realize. I am so sorry. It's okay. You're safe now." He held her tight as his hand stroked through her hair.

"Please," she begged. "Don't put me in there."

"I would never do that to you, Mina. It was a bad dream. You're all right now."

Her scent invaded him, and as she clung to him, his mind drifted back to the night on the sofa when he lay above her and was ready to claim her for himself. She pulled back, wiped her tears, and kissed him softly.

"Don't go," she whispered as her lips lingered by his own.

"Never."

She kissed him again, her fingers in his hair as she folded herself into him. Her legs wrapped around his waist as their kiss deepened.

"Mina, are you—" Marie stopped when she walked in, clearly uncomfortable, and left without another word.

Mina pulled back. "I need to let her know I'm okay."

He caressed her neck as he stared into her eyes. "Are you though?"

"I'm fine," she said quietly, starting to stand.

"Stay," he begged in return. "Stay with me."

Her body eased against his, and she allowed herself the comfort. His lips pressed against her neck, and she gripped him tighter, every part of her wanting to be as close to him as possible.

Dracke wrapped his teeth around her throat, his tongue teasing as he waited for her. He would give her whatever she wanted, and he would not stop until she told him to. She was in charge now, and her every wish was his command.

She pressed him against the bed, and as he laid back, she straddled him slowly. Her thin nightgown provided very little protection, and she smiled as she felt how ready for her he was. His hips thrust when she sped up as the pleasure seeped through her. He pulled her onto him and kissed her hard as she continued to sway her hips.

He lowered her onto her back, teasing along her leg and raising her gown slowly. At the sight of her inner thigh, his blood pounded furiously in his ears until he knew of nothing else he wanted nor needed. He looked at her, and when she nodded, he dove in head first.

His fangs tore into her flesh, and he suckled her sweet blood as she panted for air. He teased her with his tongue, lapping at the blood and healing where his teeth had been. She reached down, pulling on her underwear until he removed it, moaning softly as he did. He then proceeded further up between her legs and began to taste her.

He teased and flicked her desire with his mouth. Her hands gripped his hair, each movement of his tongue sending her further into a whirlpool of rapture. Her head collapsed back onto her pillow as a cry of pleasure escaped her. His lips suckled gently, sending another wave crashing through her. His hands held her hips in place, his tongue swiping again as she squirmed and whimpered in response.

Dracke lowered her gown before he crawled up beside her, taking her in his arms while her body trembled in the aftermath. "How do you feel?"

"What did you do?" she asked.

"I gave you what you wanted without taking what you didn't."

She shook her head. "That was unlike anything I have ever felt before."

His lips pressed to hers. Mina could taste herself on his tongue, and her desire burned again. She stroked her fingers along his chest, reaching for his pants. He gripped her wrist, kissing her palm gently before standing up.

"What's wrong?" she asked as she got to her feet, their faces inches apart. Her breath was warm on his cheek when he pulled back. The breath of life, of comfort, and it reminded him of the humanity he no longer carried inside.

"Nothing, my dearest Mina." He looked away for a moment, ashamed of his beastly appearance and wishing she could see him how he used to be.

"I need to clean up," she admitted with a soft laugh.

"So do I."

She went into her washroom and took a quick shower. When she walked back out, she was surprised he was not waiting for her. Her stomach grumbled, and she decided to get a snack. She dressed before she stopped by Elise's chamber first, watching she and Marie sleep for a moment before making her way downstairs.

In the kitchen, Mina fixed up a plate with bread, cheese, and fruit. She sat at the small table and ate in quiet contentment. Her smile grew when Dracke appeared beside her.

"Hungry, my love?" he asked.

"Famished," she replied, eating another piece.

"How are your sisters?"

"Resting." She took a breath before looking at him. "Thank you."

"They are welcome here."

"No, I mean… of course, thank you for helping them. But thank you for what you did for me upstairs. It was incredible beyond words." Her face blushed at her admission, and she gasped in surprise when he kissed her.

"Mina, I love you," he said. The hope in his eyes reflected the hope in his heart.

She swallowed hard, working up her courage to tell him how she felt. Her hand caressed his jawline, and shame washed over her when she lost her nerve. "Are you excited about the ball?" she asked, popping a blueberry into her mouth.

"Yes. In fact, I have a gift for you." He stood up and offered her his hand.

"Walking, right?" she asked.

When he nodded, she laced her fingers with his. He led her upstairs and into another unused guest chamber. A dress model on display bore the most beautiful gown Mina had ever seen.

"This is… beyond gorgeous. It's too much for me."

"You will look radiant in it, I assure you."

"Thank you. Are we… can we continue to catalog books?"

He turned away. "I see no point."

"What do you mean?"

"I started in the library to research the curse. It was hard to keep track of which books I'd already read, so I started to catalog. The answers have evaded me this long, and I have little hope they will suddenly appear now."

"Dracke—"

"It doesn't matter. Come, I believe your sisters are stirring." He escorted her to Elise's room, then left without another word.

Mina went inside, pushing down her worry at the sudden shift in his mood. Elise and Marie sat on the bed, laughing.

"What are we talking about?" Mina asked as she joined them.

"Nothing. We heard about the ball. Dracke said we are welcome to attend," Marie said.

"Yes. He just gave me a gown for it."

Elise rolled her eyes. "I bet it's gorgeous." She laughed when Mina gave her an angry look. "How easily you believed me jealous! I assure you, that is no longer the case. Not after he saved my life."

"Do you think he is a beast?"

"No. Gustave is more of a monster than the prince could ever be."

"Are you sure you won't pursue this?" Marie asked.

"I am. Can we go down for breakfast?"

Mina yawned. "I did not realize the sun was rising. I will turn in now." She started to leave when Elise took her hand.

"Thank you."

Mina retired to her chamber. She slipped on a nightgown and brushed her hair. Her fingers caressed along the cool silk, and she smiled when she thought of being with Dracke. Her heart sped up. She leaned against the wall, her hand trailing her stomach. She climbed into bed, lying on her back as her fingers explored between her legs.

The pleasure built up as she continued to tease and caress herself, wanting nothing more than to feel the way she had when Dracke took care of her. She realized he was in his coffin, sharing in the experience of what she was doing to herself. Instead of stopping, she moaned his name as she worked faster. Her breath came in pants while her fingers explored inside. The inevitable explosion rocked through her, and she rolled onto her side, gasping for air.

She went to the washroom to finish getting ready for bed. As she snuggled under the blankets, she thought of what she had just done, only this time she imagined it was Dracke's fingers.

Dracke bolted upright, nearly banging his head on the lid of his coffin when her pleasure tore through him. He ran to the washroom but was too late. He quickly showered, then looked at his coffin. The thought of sleeping alone was suddenly unbearable. He called for Celine, instructing her to close Mina's curtains if they were not already.

Once he had her confirmation, he vaolmersed into Mina's chamber. He smiled at the sight of her passed out on her bed before climbing in and pulling her against his chest. His smile grew when she snuggled in tighter with him. He placed a chaste kiss on her forehead before falling asleep.

"What are you doing in here?" Mina demanded as she pulled away from Dracke.

He sat up, giving her a quizzical look. "I wanted to hold you after what we did."

Her arms crossed her chest as she turned away. "That doesn't mean my bed is yours to do as you see fit!"

"Mina," he crawled to her, wrapping his arm around her, "why are you so upset?" He grew concerned when she trembled against him. "Because of Gustave?"

"You should've asked for permission first."

"I didn't realize. I'm sorry."

She let out a heavy sigh. "No, I am. You did nothing wrong. This is me, overreacting."

"Let's get you something to eat. I believe that will help."

"I'll get dressed and meet you downstairs shortly."

As soon as he vaolmersed from the room, she went into the closet to change into a lavender gown. As she looked at herself in the mirror, shame washed through her when she thought of being in bed with him.

It was so improper. We are not even betrothed. What was I thinking? Is he right? Is it this connection between us? He fed from me and… No, I am making excuses so I can blame him. The truth is, I wanted it as much as he did.

She walked to her window nook and sat down, watching the snow swirling in the dark. Her heart sank at the thought of seeing him, while she was still trying to sort out her feelings, unaware of time as it passed by.

"My dearest Mina, are you all right?"

She jumped at his voice and let out a nervous laugh. "Sorry. I'm fine."

"Why are you still up here?" He stepped closer when she didn't answer, worried even more when she wouldn't look at him. "Mina?"

"I'll be down in a moment," she said softly.

"Look at me," he commanded.

Her courage swelled within her, forcing her to meet his gaze. "What?"

He shook his head. "Why are you so ashamed?"

"Would you stop doing that?" she asked as she stood up. "Stop using this connection."

"Mina—"

"I don't want it anymore! What will it take to sever it?"

"You know not what you ask."

She thought for a moment before she responded. "All right, what aren't you telling me?" He disappeared when she stepped towards him. "Really?" she huffed, grabbing her cloak, then running downstairs.

"Mina, where are you going?"

She ignored Marie and ran out the front door as fast as she could. The cold air nearly knocked her off her feet. She tightened her cloak as she walked briskly down the path. She was tired of his cryptic speech, his secrets, the way he took control, and the way he ran his palace. She stopped walking.

He is the prince, and it is his palace, after all. He has every right. Still, what is he keeping from me?

"Why are you out here? Do you wish to catch your death from the cold?"

The voice was dark and low, and it practically rested on her ear. She turned slowly, her face mere inches from his. "I needed air."

"Okay, now let's get you inside. You need to warm up." When she took a step back, he cocked his head.

"No. I will return when I am ready, not because you say so."

"So, you'd rather freeze out here than speak to me?"

"You are the one who disappeared!" she cried out. "What is this connection?"

"I don't know—"

"You said there was more to it. What?"

"Come and eat. While you do, I swear I will tell you everything. I cannot stand to see you shivering."

"Fine."

They vaolmersed into the dining room, and he gestured for her to sit down. Then he retrieved a meal for her, consisting of bread, meat, cheese, and hot tea. He knelt before her, his hand resting on her knee.

"You've heard the story of Cupid and Psyche?" he asked.

"Yes. He was the god of love, and he was sent to make her fall in love with someone. Instead, he fell in love with her himself."

"And?"

"That's all I know."

"There's more. She disobeyed his one request, and he became angry, leaving her behind. She went through a series of trials to win back his love."

"She succeeded?" Mina asked as she took a bite of her bread.

"No, she failed the last trial. But the gods took mercy on her and made her immortal, so she and Cupid could be together forever."

She finished her tea as she thought over the story. "I'm glad, but what does this have to do with us?"

"The legend has it, they blessed one couple. A pair who would have a true love, not immortal, but who would find each other in every lifetime and fall in love again and again. They would know because of a connection between them, binding them."

"What are you saying?" she asked.

"We are the blessed ones, Mina."

She froze in place, and Dracke grabbed the cup from her before it fell. Her mouth hung agape as she stared at him. His hand gripped hers as he looked her in the eyes.

"Mina, please. Say something."

"It's not true," she finally replied.

"Why not?"

"Because I don't deserve to be happy and loved, much less to have a love like that."

"For the last time, what happened to Colin was not your fault. You have to stop blaming yourself. There was nothing you could've done for him."

"Why do you think that? You don't know. Death is brutal and unfair. It—"

"There is beauty in death. A final peace one spends their entire lifetime searching for. To die, to be really dead, must be glorious."

"He was a child!" she cried out. "He didn't get to—"

"Mina, he is dead and gone. You have to let him go."

She stood, shaking in anger as her eyes glistened with tears. "How dare you? You don't decide when I let go of my grief." She ran from the room.

Dracke set her dishes on the table, then began to pace. His heart ached to go after her, but he thought it best to leave her be. He was angry he had hurt her so when all he wanted was to bring her comfort. Marie walked in, and he stopped pacing.

"She has a point, you know. She will carry her grief for the rest of her life," she explained quietly.

"I know, but it weighs heavily on her heart, and she does not deserve it."

Marie sighed as she approached the table, picking up a scone and taking a bite. "You will not convince her otherwise."

"That's my fault," Elise said from the doorway.

"How so?" he inquired.

"When she returned to us after Colin passed, I was cruel to her."

"Why?" Dracke asked.

"Because I have always been jealous of her. First our mother lavished unending affection on her, then the Blanc family, who had massive wealth. They gave her beautiful gifts and treated her like she was one of their own."

"And you bullied her for that?"

"I was… there is no excuse for what I did. I have apologized to her, but she feels she is responsible for his death. I don't know what else to do."

Mina leaned against the wall in the hallway, listening to every word. She knew they were right, but every time she tried to push past the grief, she would see Colin in bed and taking his last breath.

She went into the kitchen and found a bottle of wine. Realizing it wasn't what she needed, she put it back. Nothing would fill the void in her heart nor could anything ease her pain.

Except Dracke's touch. When his lips are on mine, his hands holding me tight, he brings me a peace I cannot explain. Maybe he is right. Perhaps we are the blessed ones. My heart is so torn, and I am unsure what I am supposed to feel. I couldn't save Colin, but can I save Dracke? If I can't...

Her stomach churned at the thought. She quickly sat down as her legs threatened to buckle. She wiped the unshed tears and realized it would come down to her. That she would have to make the choice. To choose to love him may be the key to breaking the curse.

Dracke faced Marie. "Mina is in the kitchen. She needs one of us, and I am sure she does not want to see me at the moment."

"Which is why you should go," Marie argued. "She doesn't need to be coddled."

He vaolmersed into the kitchen, appearing beside Mina. She jumped back in surprise. "I hate when you do that."

"What are you thinking about?"

"Nothing," she said coldly.

"Mina?"

"Fine, yes. I still grieve for Colin. What do you want me to say?"

"You don't need to say anything. I'm sorry. I... it was wrong of me to tell you to let it go."

The sincerity of his words surprised her. "Thank you."

"Now, will you come and join us? Your sisters are worried about you."

"I'll be in my room."

He watched her leave, then returned to the dining room. "She wants to be alone," he explained to Marie.

"Mina has been alone enough." Shaking her head as she stood, she left to check on her.

Dracke studied Elise for a moment, seeing how graceful she was, even doing something as simple as drinking her tea. "And you, do you wish to be alone?"

"No."

He sat beside her. "Mina was a governess, and Marie oversees your father's estate. What do you do?"

"I..." She took another sip as she thought for a moment. "I help Marie."

"How so?"

Her brow furrowed in anger, and he noticed the cup in her hand visibly shaking. "Just... I do. What do you care?"

"Because it seems like Mina and Marie have something to do, a purpose. And you, what is your purpose?"

"Do I need one?"

"Of course not, but you seem lost."

"All I want is to marry someone of nobility, to have them lavish me in gowns and jewels. Why you felt Mina is worthy, I will never understand."

"I thought you were making amends with her?"

Elise sighed. "She has always thought she was better than me."

"She told you this?"

"Well, no but—"

"So you bully her for fun?"

Her shoulders sagged. "I don't know why I have treated her the way I did. I guess because, even though our mother spoiled me with gifts, she lavished Mina with affection."

"Do you know why that is?"

She looked at him as she set her cup on the table. "I didn't know there was a reason."

"Hmm, Marie knows, but you don't. Interesting. I guess you assume it is because Mina is far more beautiful than you, and everyone in your village knows it."

Her anger flared when she noticed Mina lingering in the doorway. She shoved down her disgust at Dracke's appearance, grabbed his arm, and kissed him suddenly. Glancing out of the corner of her eye, she saw the look of horror on Mina's face before she turned and ran upstairs.

Dracke pulled away, wiping his mouth. "What the hell is wrong with you?" He froze when he heard Mina crying. He vaolmersed to her chamber, only to find her in her washroom. "Mina?" He knocked softly. "It wasn't what you think. Please, talk to me."

"Go away!"

"Can we discuss this?"

When he heard the shower, he knew she needed time. He would talk to her when she was ready, and he would convince her nothing had happened.

Dracke sat in her nook, and she froze when she stepped out of the closet to find him there.

"What do you want?"

"Mina, it's been two days. I have given you space, but we are running out of time. We need to talk about what happened in the dining room."

"I know what happened. I wouldn't give you what you wanted, so you decided to try with my sister. Just like Gustave."

"That is not what happened. She kissed me."

"You seemed to enjoy it."

"And you would dare to compare me to him? After everything I have done for you and your sisters?" he asked as he stood.

"Very well. I'm sorry. Now go."

"Mina, why are you prolonging this? You know how we feel about each other. Why do you deny it?" He stepped closer to her.

"I do not deny there is an attraction. That does not mean I love you, or that I ever will."

"What has changed?"

"You! You are putting too much pressure on me," she cried out. "None of this is my fault. Why am I expected to fix it?"

"I have never asked you to break the curse."

"Because you literally couldn't. I've seen how you and Celine are when it's mentioned. But you said it yourself, there is more to this than a simple 'I love you' involved."

"Do you still not understand? This was meant to happen, because if I had not become immortal, we would not have met in this lifetime. This was done for you."

"No! This is not my fault!" she screamed as she pummeled her fists into his chest. "Why are you blaming me?"

He gripped her wrists and held them gently with one hand while the other caressed her cheek. "My dearest Mina, that is not what I am doing."

She stilled at words. "Then what do you mean?"

"Every moment of my agony has been worth it because it led me to you. My feelings are so strong. It's why I am certain we are the blessed ones, that we were meant to find each other.

"We fed from each other, that's all. There is no other connection between us."

He lifted her hand, placing her palm flat against his chest. "Do you feel that?"

"Barely. It's not a heartbeat. What is it?"

"It is a heartbeat, which should be impossible for a vampyr. My heart had not beat in almost eighty years, then at the sight of you, it nearly leapt from my chest. I tried to tell myself it was because you are young and beautiful."

"Dracke—"

"Even now, your skin is flush, your heart is racing, and you long to have my lips on yours. We are meant to be together."

"You were cruel in the beginning."

"Because I was in denial, the way you are now. I refused to believe I could be cursed to look like this, only to be blessed with a love like you."

"I started to fall for you," she said, pulling away.

"But not anymore?"

"I don't know. What I do know is I am not enough. I am not the heroine of your story who will ride in on a white stallion and save you. I'm sorry."

He released her wrists. "Mina—" Helpless, he could only watch as she fled from the room.

Chapter 17

The Ball

ou invited my father?" Mina asked in surprise when reading the guest list. She had barely spoken to Dracke the whole evening. She shook her head in disbelief, eager to see her father but afraid at the same time, wondering if he would even appear.

"Yes. I know you and your sisters want to see him, despite what you've said."

Mina scoffed. "I doubt he will come."

"Are you about to get dressed?" His voice strained as he spoke, and her heart ached to hear it.

"Yes, I'll be down shortly," she responded.

She went into her chamber. Marie helped her while Elise stood back and watched with a pout on her lips. She and Mina had not spoken since the kiss. Elise's eyes dripped with jealousy over Mina's gown. Dracke had refused Elise any of the other dresses in the chateau as punishment. Marie had to run to Lyndon to get one made up, though not nearly as extravagant as Mina's.

"Dracke will be floored when he sees you in this," Marie said as she led Mina to the mirror.

The gown was navy blue with a gold accented corset bust, blue off-shoulder sleeves, a split skirt with gold roses and ruffles, and the blue of the underskirt visible. The piece that most took Mina's breath was a pair of attached wings. They were large with matching hues of blue and gold, shaped like butterfly wings with a sheer, gossamer edge.

"I care little about what he thinks," Mina said as Marie finished pinning her hair. "Elise can have him."

"Oh, don't be a brat!" Elise cried out as Marie cinched up Mina's corset. "He didn't even give me a dress. Now, I won't be as decadent in a costume as the rest of the dancers! Does that not tell you how he feels about me?"

"Why did you kiss him?"

"To make you jealous, of course. The way you have done me all of these years. You flaunt your gowns, your jewels, and our mother's love. I've hated you because of it."

Mina stopped and turned to Elise. "What does our mother have to do with any of this?"

"Please. She made me beautiful gowns, but she was always hugging you, kissing you, telling you how much she loved you. Why are you so special?"

"Both of you, stop," Marie interjected. "Let's focus on having a pleasant evening at the ball. You can kill each other tomorrow for all I care." She shot Mina a grin, who giggled in response. "Now, I have to get ready myself."

"At least Dracke gave you something to wear," Elise said.

"Because I didn't kiss him," Marie teased back.

"That's not funny. Mine isn't nearly as nice as either of yours."

"Get over yourself," Mina snapped. "Shut up already. If I don't see you for the rest of the evening, then it will indeed be pleasant."

Elise ran from the room, hobbling as she finished getting into her heels. Marie laughed a moment before looking at Mina and turning serious.

"Both of you need to do better."

"Whatever did I do, besides defend myself?"

"You've been moody all week. Apart the kiss, what else is bothering you?"

"You don't know about the curse?"

Marie paused for a moment. "A little. How did you find out?"

"He told me."

"What? When?"

"When he—"

"Are you ladies ready?" Dracke asked from the other side of the door.

"Give us a moment," Marie said, but Mina rushed to the door in hopes of avoiding the conversation.

She jerked it open, and Dracke's jaw dropped at the sight of her. "You are magnificent." He held out his arm. "Thank you for agreeing to escort me this evening." He was dressed in a black suit with a silver cravat matching the mask he wore. Mina stared for a moment. He gave her a small smile. "Don't want to scare our guests, do we?"

Without a word, she laced her arm with his, and he led her to the ballroom. The lights were dimmed, red roses were in vases everywhere, and the scent nearly gagged Mina, as it was overpowering. She shook her head, trying to focus on the candles and crystal chandeliers.

"Well?" Dracke asked.

"It looks lovely," she managed.

The room began to fill with partygoers, mostly nobility who came out of curiosity. The small orchestra played, and Mina walked with Dracke as they greeted their guests.

"How did you get so many people to come?" Mina inquired.

Dracke chuckled softly. "People love a good story, and there's nothing like a legend to sate their curiosity. An invite to a ball hosted by someone who should not exist? They couldn't resist coming to see it with their own eyes."

"Of course."

Mina watched people in lavish costumes and feathered masks glide about the dance floor. She hesitated when he led her towards them. He gave her hand a gentle squeeze. "Please dance with me, my dearest Mina."

She followed him, and he held her tight. Her heart pounded when he pulled her in closer, his hand stroking through her hair. He kissed her softly. Mina was grateful no one seemed to notice.

"Dracke, thank you for a lovely evening."

"I love you, Mina." He watched her for a moment. "It's all right. You don't have to say anything. I just want you to know."

They danced through a few more songs, then sat to eat dinner. He drank from his goblet, watching as she enjoyed her meal and observed the party guests. They were returning to the dance floor when Celine approached them.

"Master, come quickly!"

They followed her to the foyer to see Gustave trying to take Elise against her will. She struggled in his arms and cried out for him to leave her alone. Marius ran in front of them and blocked the door. Mina did not even know her father had arrived. She gasped when Gustave aimed his pistol at him.

"Move," he commanded.

"Unhand my daughter this instant!"

Gustave shot him in the stomach, then headed for the door. Elise begged Gustave to let her go, crying out for her father. Marius lay on the floor, unmoving as blood pooled around him. Dracke appeared before Gustave and quickly disarmed him. Gustave shoved Elise. She rushed to her father's side, applying pressure to the wound and looking helpless as she attempted to stop the bleeding.

Dracke and Gustave unsheathed their swords at the same time. Mina watched as Gustave parried. Dracke feinted and deflected Gustave's attack, then knocked him to the floor. When Gustave picked up the pistol and aimed it at Dracke, he lowered his sword, ready to be free of his curse.

On instinct, Mina rushed in front of Dracke as Gustave fired. The bullet lodged in her sternum, and Dracke caught her in his arms, lowering her gently to the ground. He lifted his sword and, in a quick spin, removed Gustave's head from his body. He rushed back to Mina, kneeling beside her.

"It's okay," he assured her. "I'm here."

"Dracke," she choked on the blood as it rose in her throat, "I'm sorry. I love you." Her eyes closed as she became listless.

"It's all right. You'll be fine." He brought his wrist to his mouth, but he was too late. His skin began to revert to its natural hue as the curse was broken. "No! Please, no," he said as he realized what was happening. Panic overtook him as he became human, unable to save her. "Mina—"

"I love you," she said softly once more before taking her final breath.

Her hand went limp and cold. The bells chimed midnight as he leaned down and kissed her forehead, clutching her body to his chest and weeping. A white light filled the room, and he looked up to see the faery had returned.

"You broke the curse," she said with a smile as she studied him.

He gently laid Mina down before he approached the faery. Falling to his knees, he clasped her hand. "Please, I will give anything, do anything. Take my kingdom, my title, my wealth. Whatever the cost. Please, save her!" His voice hitched in his throat, and a strangled sob escaped him.

The faery looked down to see Mina lying in a pool of blood on the ground. "Oh, no. What happened?"

"She died protecting me. Please," he begged, hanging his head lower, "save her. I will do anything, give anything."

The faery approached Mina. "You would give your life for hers?"

"Yes, whatever it takes to save her."

"Very well."

She knelt beside Mina, speaking softly as her light wove around her, engulfing her and healing her. Dracke rushed to her side, taking her hand.

"Mina—"

"Now for your bargain," the faery reminded him.

"One moment, please," he begged as he watched Mina's chest rise and fall with each breath.

"Make it fast, as you do not have much time."

Dracke leaned down, speaking softly into Mina's ear. She stirred in response, and she reached her hand up, caressing his face. He kissed her palm as his tears dripped down her arm. Just as she opened her eyes, he disappeared. Her eyelids fluttered, then everything went black.

Chapter 18

The Faery

ina came to, and her room slowly came into view. When she sat up, Marie rushed to her side. As she helped her, she tried not to stare. "How do you feel?" Marie asked, building her courage to tell Mina the truth.

"Everything hurts. What happened?" Mina groaned.

Marie sat on the edge of the bed, recounting some of the previous night's events. "There's more."

"What do you mean?" Mina asked, bringing her hand up to push her hair back. Her fingers trailed her pointed ear. "What?" she asked, rushing to her feet.

Marie grabbed her to steady her. "Sit back down. You need to continue to rest."

"No, take me to the mirror!" Mina begged.

"Not until we talk about what happened."

Mina reluctantly sat, her hands clenched and her back tightened. She looked over her shoulder, losing her color before turning to Marie with fear in her eyes.

"What is that?"

"Maybe it is best to show you." When Marie took her to the mirror, Mina gasped at the reflection gaping back at her. Her skin shimmered white in the sunlight coming in from the window. Her ears were now pointed and elongated, but most shocking was the pair of golden gossamer wings upon her back. She turned to Marie in shock.

"Is this a dream?"

"No." Marie explained about her mother and the bargain she made with the fae. "I'm sorry no one never told you."

"I… I'm not a muritor?"

"No. We thought you were a fae. We had no idea you were actually a faery until we saw your wings."

Mina stepped closer to the mirror, still taking in her new appearance when Elise emerged in the doorway. Marie helped Mina back to bed before approaching Elise.

"Are you all right?"

"Um, I didn't expect to see this." Elise lowered her gaze. "Father is resting. The doctor said he should make a full recovery. I wondered why you hadn't been in to check on him." She looked at Marie. "She's not our sister, is she?"

"She will always be our sister," Marie stated. "I don't care about blood or lineage."

"Does she know about Dracke?"

"What about him?" Mina asked, overhearing their conversation.

Marie and Elise exchanged a look of concern. "Let's get something in your stomach, and we'll talk," Marie said. "You need your rest. I'll see about food." She shot Elise a warning glance as she walked past her.

Elise and Mina sat in awkward silence, with Elise occasionally glancing at Mina and trying not to stare. Marie returned with a tray of food and drink. She helped Mina eat, then tucked her in under the covers.

"Get more rest," Marie said.

"You said you would tell me about Dracke."

"I can see how exhausted you are. Please, sleep some more, and then we will talk."

"Fine."

Marie stroked her hair as she pulled the blanket higher. "I'll be right here if you need me."

Mina wanted to ask about Dracke again, but between the exhaustion from her change and the warm meal in her stomach, she drifted off to sleep.

Mina awoke as Marie and Elise spoke quietly in the corner. She slowly stood and made her way towards the washroom. Marie walked to Mina to help, but she gestured her back. When she went inside, Elise turned to Marie.

"Is she going to be okay?"

Marie was surprised by the concern in Elise's voice. "I think so. I'm sure all of this is still a shock to her, but she's not alone."

"All right. I'm going to check on Father. I'll meet you downstairs for lunch."

Marie waited for Mina but was worried when she heard her crying. She knocked on the door. "Mina, are you all right?" When she didn't answer, Marie opened it and walked in. Mina was leaning against the vanity, crying into her hands. "What's wrong?"

"Am I really a faery?"

"Yes, and a beautiful one," Marie said, taking her hand and leading her back into the main chamber.

"But it means I can't stay here."

"Why not?"

"They live in their kingdom, ever since the great war. I'll never be allowed to stay here."

"You will, Madam Mina," Celine said as she walked in.

"What do you mean?" Her eyes went to the thick envelope in Celine's right hand.

"His Highness was prepared for this day."

"How so?"

Celine looked at Marie. "I thought you told her."

"I was about to."

"Tell me what?" Mina asked, clearly exasperated.

Marie took her hand. "The night of the ball, when Gustave tried to take Elise, Dracke stepped in to stop him."

"Yes, you told me this."

"Here's what I left out. Gustave picked up his pistol and aimed it at Dracke. You jumped in front of him, saving his life."

"I was shot?"

"You were," Celine answered. "Then you told him you love him, and in doing so, you broke the curse. It took two things to break it. First, an act of pure selflessness, which you did when you jumped in front of him. Second, for someone to fall in love with him and tell him so."

"Wait, if I freed him from the curse, where is he?"

"The faery appeared before him when the clock struck midnight. Dracke made a bargain with her. She used his life force to restore you, bringing you back from the dead. Before he passed, he told you the truth about who and what you are, thus breaking your spell in return."

Mina thought over her words for a moment. "Dracke is… he's gone?"

"Yes, I'm afraid so."

She shook her head as her tears fell. "No, he can't be. I broke the curse! Where is he? I need to see him, please?"

"You can't," Marie said matter-of-factly before her tone softened. "I'm sorry. He's gone."

The thought of never seeing him again ripped through Mina's chest, and she clung to the memory of dancing in his arms as he held her tight. He called her his dearest Mina, kissing her softly.

"I apologize, but we need to take care of this as soon as possible."

Mina was pulled from her thoughts and glanced at Celine. "Take care of what?"

Celine handed her the envelope. "He was prepared for all possible outcomes in case he couldn't break the curse in time. He wanted you to have everything."

Mina sat on the bed. She carefully opened it, removing the papers. As she unfolded them, a ring slipped onto her lap. She picked it up, recognizing it as the ring he had proposed to her with. Her hands shook as she read through the documents.

"This is a marriage certificate."

"Yes," Celine confirmed. "After you sign it, I will notarize it, thus making your marriage legal."

"I don't understand."

"If you sign this, you will become Princess Bellamina and inherit the kingdom and all land within. It was what Dracke wanted for you."

"But he is not here?" She looked down. "He signed this?"

"It is common amongst royalty to sign a marriage certificate before the couple has even met. As far as anyone else knows, Dracke is still alive. He has not been declared dead. That is why it is urgent you sign this before it happens."

Celine handed her a quill. Mina took it and signed her name, then slipped the ring onto her left hand. Celine took the paperwork to the table, finalized it, then returned with a small box. She opened it to show Mina a diamond and sapphire crown.

"You are now Her Royal Highness, Princess Bellamina Dracul, ruler of the L'Evrope Kingdom."

"Wait, I thought that was Willam's title? At least, King of the L'Evrope Kingdom?"

"They inadvertently usurped the throne when the faery cursed Dracke."

Marie gasped in realization. "This is what Father meant when he said you would bring about the end of King Willam's reign."

"I don't want that," Mina argued. "I thought I would just be the Princess of Parysse."

"No, you are now the rightful ruler over all muritor lands," Celine explained.

"Willam will never willingly give it back," Marie stated.

"That is between him and Mina. I will see to it everything is filed properly. Do you need anything else, Your Grace?"

"Thank you for staying," Mina said, her lips trembling. "Did… anyone leave now that the curse is broken?"

"No. Everyone stayed, ready and happy to serve you."

"I'm so grateful. Thank you, Celine." Mina looked at Marie once Celine left the room. "From a governess to a princess."

"A faery princess, no less."

Mina shook her head and swallowed hard. "It means nothing without him."

"You do love him, don't you?"

"Yes. This is all my fault. I should've told him sooner."

"Mina, you need to rest. We'll speak tonight if you are up for it."

"And to plan my approach for King Willam."

"Father may be able to help," Marie offered.

"Oh, what is he going to think of me? He isn't my father anymore, is he?"

"Give him time. None of this was your fault, and he will see soon enough."

The bell tolled, and Mina jerked awake. She got out of bed and went to her closet, where she found a black, shimmering, backless dress, and slipped into it. Downstairs, she joined Marie and Elise in the dining room. She was taking a sip of tea when Celine walked in.

"Evening, Your Grace."

"Celine, please. You don't have to be so formal."

"Yes, madam. Since we can leave the estate, we have purchased new furniture and mirrors to replace what was broken the night of the curse."

"Thank you."

Elise stared at Mina, admiring her crown, her dress, and her wings. Marie kicked her in the shin.

"Ow!" Elise cried out, shooting an angry look at her sister.

"It's not polite to stare," Marie said.

"Sorry."

Mina finished her meal and decided to walk about the chateau, curious to see what else needed to be taken care of. She started outside, removing her cloak when she realized it was warm. Marie joined her.

"Where's the snow?" Mina asked.

"Apparently, it was part of the curse for the land to be trapped in an eternal winter."

"It's so weird." She ran her fingers over a rose, thinking of Dracke's lips consuming hers. Her heart ached at the memory, and she wiped the unshed tears before continuing her stroll with Marie.

"Celine and her husband have been working hard to oversee the repairs to the chateau."

"How was it damaged?" Mina asked.

"Apparently, the night he was cursed, Dracke tore through the chateau and did a lot of damage in his anger.

They walked back inside. "I need to rest."

"Are you all right?"

Mina gave her a reassuring smile. "Yes, thank you." She went up to her chamber, stopped at the door, and felt a pull to go to the third floor. She went into Dracke's room instead, half-expecting to see him there. Her heart dropped at how empty it was. She went to the desk and picked up the journal, only to find he had ripped the pages out.

She walked to the fireplace and saw the scorched remnants. Her body felt like the journal, gutted and discarded. She threw it down before she approached his coffin. His blanket caught her eye, and she clutched it to her chest, wishing desperately to be in his arms.

Grief consumed her as she gave in, realizing she had her chance but blew it. In the same way she had been unable to save Colin, she could not save Dracke. She was unworthy of his crown and title.

The blanket still in her hands, she returned to her chamber. She undressed and climbed onto the bed, lifting it to her face. The scent overwhelmed her as memories flooded in. She would never forgive herself for her loss, and she would spend every single day doing what she could to make it up to him.

She would take his kingdom, growing it and making it into one of prosperity. Her heart swelled as she swore it would be so.

Elise watched Mina from across the table. She had said little during the week and had spent most of her time in the library preparing to meet with King Willam. Elise worried about her.

"Are you going to see Father today?" she asked.

Mina shook her head. "I have tried every day, and each time he has refused to see me."

"I'm sorry," Marie said.

Before Mina could respond, Celine rushed in. "Mina, you are never going to believe it!" In her excitement, she forgot all formalities.

Mina rose from the table when a faery walked in, followed by a fae she did not recognize. That is, until she saw his long black hair, his silver eyes, and the way he stared at her. She slowly approached the fae.

"Dracke?" she asked in utter disbelief.

He smiled and took her hand, kissing her palm. "Hello, draga mea."

"I... How?"

The faery stepped forward. "I am Alyssa, the faery who cursed your prince. When Prince Dracke explained everything to me, I was overwhelmed with guilt for my mistake. I cursed the wrong brother. I abused my power, so as reparation, I granted him a boon. I made him a fae and freed him from his bargain so the two of you could be together."

Mina took his other hand, still not believing he was standing before her. "You're mine?" she asked, her voice a lingering whisper.

His smile spread. "As long as you want me."

Her heart filled with joy, and she leaned up to him.

"There you are!"

The voice startled them, and they turned to see a female fae and two male fae guards storming in. Elise and Marie stayed back, unsure of what was happening. Dracke stepped protectively in front of Mina.

"Who are you?" he demanded.

"There, the princess," she said to the guards, ignoring Dracke. "Get her, and let's go."

Alyssa looked at Mina, then back to the female fae, who had long black hair and silver-blue eyes. "Juniper, what happens if she isn't returned?" Alyssa asked.

"We will not fail our king."

Mina stepped up to Juniper, unafraid. "I will go nowhere with you. Who are you?"

Juniper bowed to Mina. "Your Highness, you are to come with us."

"For what reason?" Mina demanded.

"Your parents are waiting for you," she explained.

"What? No, I won't—" Before she could utter another word, Juniper grabbed her arms and pulled her away from Dracke.

"Mina!" he cried out when they all vanished in a ball of light. Dracke reached for her, but she was gone. He turned to Celine. "Where are they?"

"My best guess? The Faeryland Kingdom."

"I don't know how to get there. I have researched for nearly eighty years, and I never found its location. What do I do?"

Mina's stomach lurched when they arrived, and she leaned against the wall while it settled back down. She glanced up, only to be amazed at the sight of the palace she was in.

The walls and pillars were white marble with gold inlays. The enchanted ceiling mimicked the night sky, complete with shooting stars, and the dark blue floor reflected it all, making the gigantic hallway seem even bigger than it already was. She watched the guards marching by in formation. They wore silver and gold armor polished to a blinding shine.

"Come," Juniper said. "This way to the throne room."

Mina had no choice but to follow, looking about as she walked, searching for the exits. They approached a set of doors, sixteen feet in height. They were gold with relief leaves, vines, and roses climbing all the way to the ceiling. A golden serpent wove in between the roses. Mina blinked in amazement as it magically slithered over the doors.

When they opened a moment later, Juniper took her arm, practically dragging her inside when she refused to move. Fae lined both sides of the aisle, dressed in all manner of nobility. The aisle itself was a dark blue velvet carpet leading all the way to the thrones. Mina looked up to see two fae seated upon the golden dais. The king and queen held hands, watching her with unhidden curiosity as she approached.

The queen stood up, dressed in a regal gown of silver and dark purple, her husband dressed in matching colors. They each wore a gold leaf circlet with flowers made of polished gemstones upon their heads. The queen had Mina's gentle features, while the king had her fierce eyes and serious demeanor. To Mina, the queen was stunning, with her hair shimmering under the circlet. Juniper bowed, then gestured for Mina to continue walking forward.

Mina bowed before them, surprised when the queen rushed down the steps and took her into her arms. "Lily, my precious Lily! Is it really you?" the queen cried as she pulled back to study Mina.

"Majesty, my name is Bellamina." She stood tall, determined she would not give even an inch, not after what she had lost.

"That may have been the name given to you by the muritor, but I would know you anywhere. You are my Lily."

Mina shook her head, angry this stranger would try and dictate who she is. "No, Your Majesty. I will always be Bellamina. This is a mistake. I do not belong here and wish to return home at once." Her voice remained steady though her heart drummed in her chest.

Murmurs of shock went through those in attendance. Mina glanced around before turning back to her mother's gaze.

"Lily, please. This is your home."

Mina stepped back. "No, I am a stranger here. My home is in Parysse."

The king stood, and all murmurs hushed as he walked down the stairs towards them. "That may be where you were picked up, but it is not where you belong. You will stay here. Tonight, you will dine with your betrothed while we celebrate your return."

"I am married."

Everything stopped. The king's face reddened, but he composed himself before speaking again. "It's no problem. We will break your marriage bond."

"You most certainly will not," Mina insisted.

"It is our law. You are the faery princess, heiress to our throne, and as such, you must marry a fae prince."

"I'm already married to a fae prince."

The king looked at her, skeptical. "If it were not for the fact we are incapable of telling falsehoods, I would believe you were trying to deceive me, though I cannot figure out to what end. You seem to believe what you are saying. Yet I know every fae prince, and not one of them is your husband. What is this enigma?"

"Your Majesty," Alyssa said softly as she approached. "I can explain."

"Somebody better!" he declared.

Alyssa proceeded to explain the curse, the boon, and everything in between. "My humblest of apologies."

"You had no right to interfere. Why did you?"

"Because Dragobete instructed me to."

"Who is Dragobete?" Mina asked.

Alyssa gave her a small smile. "You know him as Cupid."

The king scoffed. "The gods abandoned us ages ago, no longer offering us words or aid. Why do you believe this?"

"Because it is true. At the time, he only instructed me to curse the prince who had committed such atrocities. You know how these old gods are, using deceit and trickery to achieve their ends. He came to me during my hour of prayer last night and told me everything. Mina and her prince are the blessed ones."

Murmurs again broke out amongst the crowd. Mina looked at the king with defiance in her eyes. "See? To break our connection is to go against the gods themselves."

"We shall see. For now, Juniper will escort you to your room while we decide how best to proceed."

When Juniper gripped Mina's arm, she jerked away from her. "No, you'll return me to Parysse at once," she demanded.

The king approached Mina, and she refused to lower her gaze. "Listen here, daughter. You are the princess, so know your place. You will do as I say."

"Or what?"

The king raised his hand to silence the audience, shocked by her defiance. "Please, Lily. Go with Juniper. We will talk soon," he implored her with a softened expression.

Mina knew she had no choice. "Very well." Without bowing, she followed Alyssa and Juniper from the room. She said nothing as they asked about her life with the muritor, her heart longing to see Dracke again.

They arrived at her chamber, and Alyssa showed Mina around. "You have everything you need in here. Gowns and accessories, food, drink. Simply think of what you want, and it shall appear, as the palace is enchanted."

"Thank you."

Alyssa hesitated a moment at the door. "It will be all right, Your Highness. You'll see, everything will work out."

"As much as I want that to be the truth, for now, I will settle with being happy you believe it."

Alyssa bowed, then left. The chamber was breathtaking. Branches and vines rambled along the ceiling, and flowers grew in the boxes lining the large, round windows. Mina approached and stared out in wonder. The trees were massive, and a river flowed beside the golden meadow. The sky sparkled azure as the diamond clouds drifted by, twinkling in the sunlight.

Her bed was a canopy of branches and roots, the blanket a blue moss as soft as silk, and her mattress was the most comfortable one she had ever sat on. Her thoughts went back to Dracke, to seeing him alive and holding him again.

At least I know he is still alive. They can do whatever they want to me, but I will not be staying here. I'll stop being so defiant, play along, and sneak away at the first chance I get. I will do whatever I must to see him again.

Her stomach rumbled, and she realized she needed food. She longed for strawberries and bread, gasping softly when they appeared on a tray resting on the table by the window. She sat down and ate the fruit, then began to devour the rest of the meal, taking pleasure in each bite. The berries were perfectly ripe, and the bread practically melted in her mouth. She drank the hot beverage before her, delighted to discover it was a honeysuckle tea with rose petals. The sweet beverage rolled smoothly down her throat.

"Your Highness, do you need anything?"

Mina looked up as Juniper walked in. "Only to know how much longer I will be here," she said as she wiped her mouth.

"The king and his council are still debating how best to proceed. They did not anticipate you would already be married."

"Will they let me leave while they are in their discussions?"

"No," she answered more quickly than she intended. "Apologies."

"What right do they have to keep me here?"

"Because it is our law. You are royalty, and so you are subject to the protections and wards of the palace."

"Wards?"

"Even if you tried to leave, they would not allow you to. Only the king himself can order them lowered."

Mina's heart sank at her words. How could she possibly escape now? "Thank you for telling me this."

Juniper bowed, then left the room. Mina finished her meal, the loneliness gnawing at her heart. She envisioned being in Dracke's arms, holding him tight and kissing him, what she wanted to do before they had been interrupted. She wished for nothing more than to be back at her chateau with her beloved.

Alyssa visited to have tea and educate her on fae history. "There are four courts. The flacari, or fire court. The apa, or water court. The pamant, or earth court. And finally, the court you are in, the vant court, which is the wind court."

"What is the hierarchy within each court?"

"Well, as you've seen, there is a king and queen who rule the Faeryland Kingdom. Then the other three courts are governed by a prince, a princess, or both. Each court is distinct, both in dress and appearance."

"I noticed a variety of fae in the audience, but I couldn't look long as I was giving my attention to the king and queen."

"The flacari are the ones with red hair, pale skin, and clothing of black and blazing orange. The apa have light blue skin with white hair, wearing flowing blue gowns and dress clothes. The pamant wear garments with living flowers and leaves growing on them. Finally, here in the vant court, our clothing is typically white with a combination of the other elements woven in."

"Do all fae have magic, or just you?"

"All fae. Faeries, such as you and me, have the most power."

"What?" Mina asked, nearly dropping her teacup.

"Faeries are exceedingly rare, and they are only born in our court. Legend has it, a faery created the vant court, and that is why. Though who is to say?"

"If they let me leave, which I highly doubt, what will happen here?"

"What do you mean?"

"I assume the king and queen wanted me to marry and take their throne when the time was right. Which I have zero interest in since I'm already married and have my own kingdom."

"They have been training a prince who may take your place. Since fae children are rare, they have a system in place. In case something like this were to happen, where the king and queen were unable to have children or had one who passed away. We are immortal, but we can be killed."

Chapter 19

The Trial

ina paced in her room as the debates raged on. It angered her that they did not seek her input, would not grant her an audience, and completely left her out of a conversation that was solely about her. In the meantime, Alyssa continued to educate her on the fae courts and laws.

"Can I visit the courts?"

"I beg your pardon?" Alyssa asked.

"While they are deciding what to do with me. I can't just sit here."

Alyssa thought it over. "Let me make some inquiries."

Mina continued to pace while waiting for Alyssa to return. A mug appeared on the table, and she enjoyed the melted chocolate drink as she waited. Alyssa appeared shortly after.

"I can take you on a short tour of Faeryland. The king will allow it."

"I'm allowed to leave?"

Alyssa shook her head. "The Faery Kingdom is one large island. North, where we are, is the wind court. To the south is the water court, with the fire court to the east and the earth court to the west. I can transport us to each court so you may see them. Then we will return. He has given us three days to do this."

"Anything is better than pacing in here."

"We'll start with the water court. Are you ready?"

"Yes." Mina braced herself. Alyssa took her hand.

They arrived a moment later. Ponds, lakes, and waterfalls surrounded the sandstone palace. Mina was in awe of the paradise. A fae walked out from the pond, his robes flowing and drying in the sun.

"Your Highness," he offered with a bow. "I am Prince Trystan. Welcome to our court."

"Thank you for having me," Mina said in return.

They followed him into the palace. The floor was made of a glass mosaic with sand as a border around each piece. With the sun's rays streaming in the massive windows, the floor shimmered as they walked on it. Trystan led them to the throne room, which was empty at the moment. The thrones were dark blue and gold with backs made of massive shells.

Mina shook her head. "Are those real?"

"Yes. Those shells came from the ocean off our coast."

"It is beautiful here."

They spent the day walking along the shore, meeting many of the fae and a few faeries who lived there, then returned to the Wind Palace for supper.

Mina sat back in her chair, and Alyssa couldn't help but notice her demeanor.

"Your Highness, is something the matter?"

"I miss my beloved," Mina admitted. "I thought he was gone, then for him to suddenly appear again…" She wiped the tears as they fell. "I would give anything to be taking this tour with him, holding each other, and smiling at the beautiful sights. It's making me miss him even more than I did."

"I'm sure you'll see him soon."

"But what will come of it? Will they force me to marry a fae prince?" She shook her head. "I won't. Not after everything he and I have endured. I would take my own life before I would allow them to break what we have."

"It will not come to that. Everything will be all right."

Mina wanted nothing more than to believe her. She saw Dracke, his long black hair, silver eyes, and his smile at the sight of her. More than anything, she longed to be in his arms. It hurt she could not even feel him, the way she could when they were in the chateau together.

"The magic here is powerful, isn't it?"

"How so?" Alyssa asked.

"That I cannot feel my husband."

"Yes, it is the wards preventing it. I am sorry."

The fire court fascinated Mina. She had expected heat, flames, or maybe even lava. Instead, it was lush forests with a beautiful palace made of granite and marble.

"Your Highness, I am Princess Luminita. Welcome to our court."

"Thank you." Mina cleared her throat. "I've noticed there are no homes at these courts."

"Homes?" Luminita asked. "No, everyone lives in the palace at each court. We are all a piece of the court, from the ruler down to the servants. While our quarters are not equal, we try to ensure everyone has some level of comfort and luxury."

"I like that," Mina said. Alyssa was happy to see her smile for once. "What does everyone do all day?"

"We work towards the betterment of the courts. Some of us use our powers to grow and heal. As you've seen, we are not relegated to our own court. We work together to grow food, keep the peace between our people, and anything else which needs to be done."

"It's amazing."

"It hasn't been easy," Luminita said. "First, we had our own wars, for the throne and to rule our lands and the muritor. When the great war ended two hundred years ago, we agreed to stay in our lands if they stayed in theirs."

Alyssa cleared her throat. "Yes, I'm still not sure how this will work, with fae now the rightful rulers over the muritor lands."

"It will take a lot of convincing to keep the peace," Luminita said.

"Wait, you mean the union between Dracke and myself could lead to war?"

"Not the union," Alyssa replied, "but the fact you are both fae. We are unsure how the muritor will react to this news."

Mina sighed. "You speak as though I will be allowed to leave."

"Why would you think you couldn't?" Alyssa asked.

"Because of this tour. Why else would the king allow me to see the courts? He wants me to see what I will be ruling over when he rips me away from my husband, my family, and the only life I've ever known. It's not fair!"

Alyssa took her arm. "Your Highness, have faith. That is not why I brought you here. This is your home, where you are from, and His Majesty wanted you to see it."

"I know you believe it, but I do not."

Luminita continued the tour, hoping to lift Mina's spirits while avoiding any further unpleasantness. Mina pushed the thoughts away as she focused on meeting more fae.

They arrived at the earth court, and Mina couldn't stop the tears. Roses grew everywhere, along with lilies, hibiscus, and other beautiful flowers. She ran her fingers along a red rose, her heart aching more than anything to see Dracke. She turned to Alyssa.

"Take me back to the palace."

"The tour—"

"I don't care. I cannot be here. Please, take me back."

Alyssa said nothing as she gripped her hand. They arrived at Mina's chamber, and she immediately pulled away from Alyssa.

"Your Highness—"

"I need to be alone." Mina watched her leave, then went into the washroom. She stood in the shower, wrapping her arms around herself, the scent of fresh roses taking over her senses. She wished to walk among her own roses, her hand clasped within her husband's, his soothing voice teaching her the history of his land.

At the thought of being in Dracke's arms, Mina collapsed backward, falling against the shower wall and sobbing into her hands. *How is this a blessing? They call us the blessed ones, but this is worse than any pain I have felt before. Knowing Dracke is alive, is waiting for me, is more than I can bear! I am unsure of how much longer I will last here.*

When the king's decision was finally made, Alyssa came to collect Mina. She dressed in a gown of white and silver, as celestial as any star in the sky.

They walked into the throne room, and Mina stopped at the sight of Dracke. Worry flooded her as she wondered why he was there. She stepped up to him, relieved when he gripped her hand and kissed it softly.

"My dearest Mina."

"My beloved," she replied, holding him tightly for a moment before they approached the throne together.

"We have brought your husband here to determine more about this claim. Since you say you are the blessed ones, you will need to prove it."

"How?" Mina asked.

"One simple trial."

"Which is?" she asked, exasperated at the joy he was taking in dragging this out.

"We will break the connection."

"What?" she cried in shock.

"If you are truly the blessed ones, we will be unsuccessful. If not, the connection will be broken, and with it, your marriage contract."

Mina glanced at Dracke with fear in her eyes. "Please, don't let him do this."

"And if the connection holds?" Dracke asked the king, not looking at Mina. "What then?"

"We will release her into your care as the princess of your kingdom."

"You can't!" her mother cried out. "Please, Alder, do not take her away from me again. I just got her back. You have not even let me see her while you were—"

"Quiet," the king scolded. "Hold your tongue."

The queen slid back into the throne, and her shoulders sagged as she humbled herself at his command. "Yes, my king."

Alder approached Mina, studying her and Dracke as he did so. "You may have tonight together, then tomorrow we will put your connection to the test."

"No, I refuse," Mina said. "You will let us leave right now."

"Absolutely not."

"Why?"

"Because you are bound by contract to your betrothed. I do not have the power to break this agreement. It is not your fault, as you did not know any of this. However, we must prove you are the blessed ones to release you from this obligation."

Dracke squeezed Mina's hand. "Everything will be all right."

Her eyes closed, and she thought it over for a moment. When she opened them, there was fire in her gaze as she stared down the king. "Very well."

"Now get some rest. We will call for you tomorrow."

Alyssa led them back to Mina's chamber. She clutched Dracke's hand firmly in her own, swearing nothing would ever separate them again. Alyssa gestured them inside, then bowed as they walked past. As soon as the door shut behind him, Dracke pulled Mina into his arms and held her tight.

"Are you really here?" she murmured into his chest.

"I am."

"I've missed you," she admitted. "I was happy to know you were alive, but I didn't know if I would see you again. My heart ached from your absence."

"I'm here, my dearest Mina. We will prove our love, then we will return home. Everything will work out."

"How can you be so sure?"

"You may not like my answer."

She stepped back and looked at him. "What do you mean?"

"There is a way to cement the connection between us."

"How?"

"We have to give each other everything, completely. Nothing held back."

"You mean…"

"Yes."

She turned away, hugging herself. "I know we are married, but I don't know if I'm ready for this. Not after everything we have been through. Everything I have been through," she added softly.

"We don't have to."

She paced for a moment, thinking of her grief, and how desperately she had missed him. She would not lose him again. "No, if it will help, I will do it. It's just… I don't know what to do. I've never done this before."

Dracke took her hand and led her to the window. He leaned down and kissed her forehead. "I'll take the lead. If at any point you are uncomfortable, say the word, and I will stop. I promise you. Could we dim the lights?"

Mina focused for a moment, and Dracke chuckled when the lights suddenly lowered. He took her hand, pulling her to him, and kissing her softly.

"Some candles would be nice," he said.

Mina bit her lower lip. "Watch." She closed her eyes, picturing the room filled with candles. Her eyes opened as their wicks flickered about them. Dracke smiled at her.

"How did you do that?"

"The palace is enchanted."

"Hmm, what else can we have?" he asked. She gasped when her gown disappeared, leaving her in a shimmering white corset with matching accessories. His fingers trailed along the bust. "Mina, what do you want?"

"I trust you, Dracke, and I will give you everything you ask for. I will do whatever I must to keep you beside me." Her eyes narrowed in confusion when he backed away. "What's wrong?"

"Are you only doing this for the trial?"

"No," she said, stepping up and caressing his bare chest. He looked down in surprise, then shook his head. "You have proven yourself to me. I want you."

"Then you shall have everything you want. For when I was a man dying of thirst, you were my oasis when I'd lost all hope."

He leaned down, his tongue flicking along the lace of her bust as his hand reached behind to unsnap her corset. When he removed it, her face flushed at being so exposed.

His hand gently cupped her breast as his mouth met hers. His other hand trailed her side, teasing along her stomach then down to her thigh. Her lips parted as his tongue pressed against them. When his fingertips brushed over her ear, she nearly collapsed against him. He smiled as he did it again, then lifted her up and carried her to bed, laying her down before joining her. Slowly, he removed her underwear.

His mouth lowered down, and his tongue trailed her thigh then at the apex of her legs. A shudder went through him as she teased his ear the same way he had done her own while his tongue flicked at her softest spot. She writhed and moaned when his mouth penetrated her. He laughed softly as he envisioned himself nude, only to discover the remainder of his clothes had disappeared.

She grabbed him and pulled him up, kissing him fiercely as he slowly began to enter her, finding her ready for him. It took every ounce of restraint to keep himself from diving in and claiming her completely. He would not hurt her. Never again would he hurt her. She was his, his love, his life, his to protect at all costs.

While his fingers stroked her cheek, his eyes met hers. "Tell me you love me," he commanded.

"I love you, Dracke."

"Tell me you want me."

"Dracke, please. I want you. I want all of you. Whatever you want, that is what I want, too. The fire in your gaze unravels me, consuming my soul, and burning me to my very core."

He smiled at her words, then moved slowly at first, inching his way inside as she braced herself to take him. Her hips swayed as he picked up speed. Their bodies merged, their souls entwining, as the connection between them grew stronger.

She panted, moaning when he went deeper and faster. The pleasure rose in waves, threatening to drown her, and she climaxed as he came inside her. She cried out as he continued to buck his hips until she fell back against the pillow, utterly spent.

He kissed her brow, speaking softly as she ran her fingers along his ear, now matching her own. "I love you, my dearest Mina. They are right. We are the blessed ones, because only a blessing could give me someone like you."

"Dracke, I feel the same way. I'm sorry I didn't say it sooner. I love you so much."

"Come, let's clean up and eat."

He took her into the washroom. They enjoyed the hot shower as he washed her hair and body. His fingers trailed her gossamer wings.

"They're beautiful."

She didn't respond, instead leaving the shower and drying off, picturing herself in a pale pink silk nightgown and smiling when it appeared on her. They left the washroom to find a small feast waiting for them. He enjoyed watching her eat every bite on her plate.

"Were you hungry?"

Her cheeks blushed, and she gave him a shy smile. "Famished because of you."

"How are you adjusting?"

"What do you mean?"

"Finding out you're a faery."

"Oh, that." She let out a nervous laugh. "It was shocking, of course. I'm ready for bed." Yawning and stretching her arms, she stood and went into the washroom.

Dracke sat back, wondering how she really felt about everything. He jumped to his feet when he heard her crying. Without knocking, he walked in to find her sitting on the edge of the tub, and her face buried in her hands.

He sat beside her, wrapping his arm around her. "Mina, what's wrong?"

"Why did my father keep this from me?"

"He had to. He knew the spell would break as soon as you learned the truth."

"So why did you tell me?" she asked as she pulled away from him.

"Because you needed to know, and I didn't know if anyone would ever tell you." He wiped her tears. "We need to get some rest before tomorrow."

He helped her to bed and leaned above her. She smiled at him when he kissed her forehead. "You were right, beloved. We were meant to find each other. You suffered for eighty years under the curse. I can deal with whatever happens." Her fingers trailed his ear. "We both changed, and we'll get through it together."

His hand gently glided along the edge of her wing as he climbed in behind her. "And these? How do they feel?"

"I'm ready to get some sleep." She gripped the back of his neck and kissed him. "You have worn me out," she said with a giggle.

"And you're okay to have me here with you? In bed, I mean."

"Yes. We're married, and we'll do everything together now."

"That is what I want as well." He rolled onto his side. "Hmm."

"What?"

"I want to hold you, but I'm worried I'll hurt your wings."

"You won't," she assured him.

He wrapped his arm over her chest and gently pulled her back against him. "You're all right?"

"Yes, beloved. As long as I am in your arms, where I belong, everything will always be all right." She looked up and kissed him softly. "Good night."

"Good night to you, my dearest Mina. We have a big day tomorrow."

Mina sat at the table, and her stomach turned at the plate in front of her as she worried about the trial ahead of them. Dracke joined her.

"What's wrong?" He noticed she hadn't touched her food.

"What does the trial consist of?" she asked, forcing herself to eat a strawberry.

"I'm not sure. Alyssa only said it isn't dangerous for you, being the daughter of the king."

"Wait, what about you?"

"If the connection isn't real, I won't survive."

Mina rose to her feet. "We have to put a stop to it."

"You know we will be okay. Why are you so worried?"

"Because I will not lose you again. The very thought of it tears through my heart."

Dracke took her hand and gently guided her back down. "Mina, I have no question about this. I know we will be okay."

Unable to eat, she went to the window and looked out at a world she did not recognize. Dracke stepped up behind her, his arm wrapping around her waist as he kissed the top of her head. She wanted nothing more than to stay in the moment with him. There was a knock at the door, and her heart sank.

"It's time," Alyssa announced.

"Kiss me, please," Mina begged Dracke.

His lips met hers as he held her. He took her hand, and they followed Alyssa through the palace. They walked through the corridor, then down a spiral staircase. Mina grasped Dracke's hand tightly, and he gave her a reassuring squeeze as they entered a large training room.

Weapons, armor, and practice dummies were on display. In the center were two circles, several feet apart. The king walked in behind them.

"Good morning," he offered.

Mina said nothing as Dracke bowed to him. She had decided she was done with bowing, that she would not grant him one ounce of deference, not after what he was trying to do to them.

"Morning," Dracke said in return.

They followed Alder to the center of the room. He gestured to Mina. "You stand there." She looked at Dracke, taking her place in the circle after he gave her a small nod. Dracke then went to the other one. "Now, I will engulf you both in magic, and as long as you can endure until it is over, it will prove your connection is real."

"What are the rules?" Mina asked.

"You must stay in the circle, it is forbidden for you to be together during the trial, you cannot stop the trial, you cannot pause the spell. Any of these is an automatic fail." He turned to Dracke. "And you know what will happen."

"We do."

"All right. One last thing, and this is especially important. You cannot—"

"Stop this!" The queen yelled as she ran in. "Please, my king, surely seeing they are willing to endure the trial is proof enough? You can release her from the betrothal."

"I cannot. Believe what you want, Marigold, but only with this trial can she be free of it. My only other option is to revoke their marriage and force her to marry Prince Edvard. Is that what you want?"

"No," she admitted as her shoulders sagged. "Please, don't hurt her."

"You know as well as I do, the magic is in control of this trial, not me." He read from the spell book, his hand swirling about as white magic began to glow and intertwine between Dracke and Mina.

She cried out in pain, clutching her chest as the magic wove through her. Dracke watched in horror, unable to help her or stop the spell. He wanted to demand the king to end the trial, but he knew to do so would be to forfeit his life. Finally, he could no longer take her screaming.

"Stop it!" he yelled. "I know the price, and I pay it to end her suffering. Stop this trial!"

"No," Mina cried out in return. Tears streamed down her cheeks as she clenched her hands until her palms bled. "I can endure this. Do not stop."

The magic began to dissipate, and as soon as the spell ended, Mina collapsed in a heap on the floor. Dracke charged to her, lifting her onto his lap and examining her.

"What did you do to her?" Dracke demanded as Alder approached.

"I swear, it was the spell Juniper gave me. Testing the connection should not have caused her such pain."

Marigold ran from the room. Dracke caressed Mina's face while reassuring her it was over. She opened her eyes and looked at him.

"Are you okay?" she asked.

A nervous chuckle slipped out. "I should be asking you."

"It was horrible, but I'm okay now. Just really weak."

Marigold walked in, dragging Juniper with her. "Tell him!" she yelled as she threw Juniper to her knees. "Tell your king exactly what you did."

"What is going on?" he demanded.

"She intentionally gave you the wrong spell."

"What? Juniper, why?"

She stood with her arms crossed. "Because I have been like a daughter to you through all of these years. I want to marry Prince Edvard. We are in love. She does not deserve him!"

"She is our daughter, taken as an infant by my sister. None of this is her fault," Marigold explained. "How dare you?"

Alder shook his head. "Foolish woman. When they passed the trial and returned to their home, what did you think was going to happen?"

Juniper's jaw dropped. "What? No, I thought this was a farce. I never thought you would actually let her leave."

"That is where you are wrong. I was going to let you marry Edvard. Instead, you are to be tried for attacking the princess. The price for your treason may be death." He made a spinning gesture and bound Juniper with his magic so she was unable to move.

Marigold knelt beside Dracke and Mina. "My poor child. Are you all right?"

"I am. I guess we have to do the real trial now, don't we?"

"No, you need to rest," Dracke answered, helping Mina to her feet.

"It's tied together," Juniper admitted.

"What do you mean?" Alder asked.

"The magic did start to check them before attacking her. If you don't finish the trial within an hour," she looked at Mina, "you will die."

Marigold summoned a guard and instructed him to take Juniper away before she turned to Alder. "What can we do? She is in no shape."

Mina pulled away from Dracke and stood in her circle. "We have to finish this."

"No, your mother is right," Alder said.

Dracke took Mina's hand. "Rest a moment, then we'll resume."

"You can't be serious?" Alder asked.

Dracke turned to him. "Did you not hear what she said? Mina will die if we do not finish this. We have to take the chance. It's the only way to save her."

"Are you all right to stay with her during the trial?"

"What do you mean?" Dracke asked.

"If you are truly the blessed ones, you can draw off each other for strength. Stay with her during the trial."

"You said it was forbidden," Mina pointed out.

"Normally, it would be. However, I will make an exception."

"How?" Mina asked.

"While the rules state the magic is in control, it does not state you must be separate. I did that to protect you in case it failed. I did not want him draining you as he lost his life. I am sorry."

"Thank you," Dracke said to Alder with sincere gratitude.

"No, Dracke. You need your strength, too. Especially since this could hurt you worse than me."

"What did you say last night? We're married now, and we'll face everything together."

"Yes, beloved."

He stood beside her, holding her hands tightly. Alder opened the book, reading until he found the spell he was looking for. He read aloud, crafting the magic needed. Red and pink smoke shimmered around them before passing through to assess them.

Dracke's jaw clenched as the connection waned and grew, but he maintained his concentration, focusing on Mina. As the magic ebbed and flowed, Dracke could feel Mina's exhaustion, knowing she could not take much more. He held her tightly, giving her what strength he could. Once the trial was through, they collapsed against each other.

"The test has confirmed it. You are indeed the blessed ones. You owe nothing to Edvard."

"Thank you," Mina said weakly.

"Please, go and rest now. Will you join your mother and me for dinner this evening?"

"We will," Dracke answered as he lifted Mina up and carried her back to their chamber. He gently laid her down, sitting beside her. "Rest, my dearest Mina. You've earned it."

"What happens now?" she asked, her voice thick with sleep.

"Now? We rest, eat dinner with your parents, then plan our return trip."

"Hmm, I am ready to go home."

"To Lyndon?"

"No, Parysse," she answered with a yawn. Dracke smiled at her answer as she drifted off to sleep.

Dracke kissed Mina on top of her head. "Are you ready for dinner with your parents?"

"Do we have to?" she asked as she snuggled into him.

He laughed softly as he helped her out of bed. "Yes, we do, unfortunately. It's rude to ignore royalty, don't you know?"

She looked at her nightgown and envisioned a pale pink gown with silver embroidery in its place, smiling when it appeared on her.

"I don't know if I'll get used to that," he said, heading for the closet.

"Well, hopefully we won't be here too much longer. So you won't have to."

"I'll stick to the old-fashioned way." He walked inside and quickly dressed.

They stepped into the corridor where Alyssa waited for them. She led the way to the dining room, where Mina's parents joined them. The table was a fallen tree, carved to shape with roots for chairs. Leaves and vines were etched into the furniture. A hand-carved wooden candelabra was the centerpiece, holding six silver candles. The wax melted red as the wick burned lower. A feast with salad, cheese, and breads had been laid out. Mina noticed there was no meat but said nothing.

"Mina, Dracke, how are you?" her mother asked as she stood up and hugged Mina.

"We are well," Mina responded. "Thank you."

"For what?"

"My name."

"I don't agree, but it is the name you have known your entire life. I would not take it from you now."

They sat at the table, eating in uncomfortable silence for a few minutes before Mina looked at her mother. "How was I taken from you?"

"Oh, of course you wouldn't know. My labor was long and difficult, and as I was falling unconscious, my sister stole you away. I thought she was taking you to clean you up, then she would bring you back to me. Once I awoke, she was gone, and so were you. We searched everywhere in the kingdom, not knowing she had crossed into the muritor lands. She found the woman you knew as your mother and made the bargain with her."

"Wait, what bargain? I thought she just gave me to her."

"Iris made a bargain. At least, that's what she called it. The woman you knew as your mother would take you and raise you as her own, and in return, my sister would claim the throne from us. It doesn't work that way, but my sister was clearly not in her right mind. She was always jealous of me. She wanted my husband, my title, and my child. Since she couldn't have any of these things, she knew the next best thing was to hurt me by taking you away."

"And making me appear human?"

"She knew you would never be accepted in the muritor lands, plus it would make it difficult for us to find you. Which it was."

"I'm sorry. I can't imagine how hard that was for you," Mina said.

Marigold wiped away a tear. "Thank you. When she returned, she told us you died shortly after your birth and refused to say anything else."

"But I thought fae couldn't lie?" Mina asked.

"She didn't come right out and say it. The way she worded it, that you were 'gone' and 'couldn't be saved' and such. I should've pressed harder, but I was recovering from labor and grieving for you."

"How did you find out she was still alive?" Dracke asked.

"I could feel it. When the spell broke, and she returned to her true form, the very wind was knocked from my chest. I knew my daughter was alive. Alder lowered the wards for me, and immediately I could sense her."

"Do all fae have the ability? To feel each other?"

"No, but my grandmother is a faery, so my magic is a little stronger. Then to find out you are a faery, it was a shock."

"How do you think I felt?" Mina mumbled.

"Thank you for having us," Dracke added quickly, trying to break the tension.

"You are always welcome. We are grateful to have you here."

"I'm sorry I can't stay," Mina said. "We don't mean to be rude, but we miss our home."

"About that," Alder said, pulling apart his bread and spreading butter on it. "What are your intentions, as the rightful rulers of L'Evrope?"

"I plan to build it up for the people, to make it a kingdom of equality and prosperity. After seeing your courts, I want to model our lands in a comparable manner."

Alder chortled. "Too bad it won't last. Those of the muritor lands are stupid and greedy."

"I grew up there, and while I did see that, I also saw kindness and compassion. I have faith we will work together."

"Then you're a fool."

"Alder! This is our daughter you are speaking to."

"I am only speaking the truth."

Dracke stood up, pulling Mina with him. "We have been held here long enough. Your daughter is the bravest, kindest, most loyal woman I have ever met. If anyone here is a fool, it is you. You should be ashamed," he added as they hastily left the room. Once in the hallway, Dracke leaned Mina against the wall, pinning himself above her. "Are you all right?"

"Yes. He is a stranger to me, so I care not what he thinks of us or our people. We can work together, I know it."

"Then we'll make it happen."

Dracke awoke to find himself alone in bed. Mina stood in front of the window. He walked up behind her.

"Whatever is the matter?"

"I am ready to return home."

"We will in the morning. For now, you need to continue taking it easy, after what you suffered through at the trial."

"I'll rest easier once we are home. Something is wrong, I know it. We need to get back."

"The ward is up. We cannot leave."

Mina laughed. "Do you really think that will stop me?" She quickly changed from her nightgown into a dress, changing Dracke's clothes as well.

He shuddered for a moment at the sudden shift but said nothing. Mina went to the door, opened it, and saw the guards posted outside. "Take us to see the king," she commanded.

"But he is sleeping, Your Highness."

"Yes, and you will wake him."

"But—"

"As your princess, I command you."

"Yes, Your Highness. Follow me."

Dracke took Mina's hand as the guard led them to the king's chamber. He knocked softly.

"See? He is asleep."

Without hesitation, Mina approached and pounded loudly on the door. Horrified, the guard reached for her hand. Dracke gripped his wrist, twisting it behind his back.

"Do not touch her!" he snarled, releasing the guard's arm.

"Yes, mi'lord. Apologies," he said as he rubbed his wrist.

The door slammed open, and Alder stood before them in blue and gold silk robes flowing around him in the still air.

"What is the meaning of this?"

"We're returning home," Mina responded.

Alder scoffed. "You certainly are not. We have not decided—"

"I have decided. Now."

Marigold appeared, gently taking Alder's hand. "Please, Mina. Will you not stay with us for one more day?"

"I need to return home."

Marigold stepped forward and hugged her tightly. "We will let you leave." She gave Alder a warning look. "But may I come and see you?"

Gratitude filled Mina when Dracke nodded. "You are welcome anytime," he answered.

"Thank you."

Alder sent for Alyssa. "I will let you leave, though I am unhappy to do so."

"Why? You care not for me."

"Do not presume to tell me my feelings."

"I presume nothing. You made it abundantly clear at dinner."

"We may not be as affectionate as the muritor, but you are my daughter. I am glad you have been found, and I care deeply for you."

"I would doubt it, except I know you can't lie."

"No, but you can."

Mina turned to Alyssa. "What do you mean?"

"Since you have both been muritor, you have some of their abilities, including lying. You are the only two fae who can."

Alder smiled. "That may prove advantageous for bringing peace."

"Is it really peace if it is built on a lie?" Mina asked.

"Does it matter?" he snapped back.

Mina looked at Alyssa. "Please, take us home."

"Mina is correct. Return them to Parysse," Marigold instructed.

"Yes, Your Majesty."

Marigold hugged Mina once more. "I will come and see you soon."

Alyssa gripped Dracke and Mina's arms, and they disappeared into a bright light.

Chapter 20

The Father

ina's stomach lurched when they landed in the foyer, and she fell to the floor, sprawled out. Dracke quickly picked her up. Her head went fuzzy for a moment before she was able to collect herself and calm her pounding heart.

"Are you all right?"

"Yes, but I do not believe I will ever get used to this."

"Come, let's get you to bed. You need to rest. Tomorrow, we'll—"

"You've returned! Please, come quickly," Marie called from the top of the stairs.

Dracke carried Mina and followed Marie into her father's chamber.

"He was getting better but suddenly took a turn. Nothing is helping him." She wrung her hands in despair.

Dracke put Mina on her feet. She looked at Marius, who was curled up on the bed, reminding her of her first day at the chateau. His hair was matted with sweat and his face contorted in a grimace of pain. He glanced at her as she approached him.

"Go away," he said hoarsely. "I have no interest to see you."

Mina ignored his hurtful words and put her hand on his. She closed her eyes, thinking of the magic now flowing through her veins. White magic sparked from her hand and into her father, healing his wounds and the deadly infection. She collapsed backwards, caught in Dracke's strong arms.

Marie ran to the washroom to wet a cloth and wipe her father's forehead. "You're better?" she asked him in disbelief.

"Yes," Dracke answered. "Now, Mina must rest." He vaolmersed her into her chamber.

"You can still do that?" she asked.

He laughed softly. "I did it out of habit, but apparently I can." He laid her on the bed.

"Are you joining me?" she asked with a yawn.

"Yes. I'll be right back." He vaolmersed to the kitchen and returned a moment later with fruit and bread. "But first, you need to eat."

"Thank you."

Mina startled awake but quickly calmed herself once she remembered they were home. She looked over her shoulder, smiling at the sight of her husband sleeping peacefully beside her. With a sigh, she left the bed and went into the washroom, stripping down, then stepping into the shower.

The hot water helped ease her sore muscles. She knew she should tell Dracke she still hurt after the trial but decided he worried enough over her. The pain would pass in time, she assured herself.

"Mina?"

"I'll be out in a minute."

"You don't want me in there?"

"I'm almost done," she replied.

"Are you all right?"

"Yes, beloved."

She shut off the water and stepped out, surprised to find him waiting for her. Her cheeks blushed when he lifted the towel and dried her off, carefully finishing with her wings. She clung to him, trembling in his arms, and he held her tighter.

"You aren't all right! What's wrong?"

"I love you," was all she responded, her voice strained.

"Mina, what aren't you telling me?"

"Nothing," she said as she pulled away. "I need to get dressed." She went to the closet, sighing as she looked through her gowns. Deciding on a pale blue one with silver shoes, she smiled when Dracke placed a diamond tiara upon her head.

"My beautiful princess," he said, taking her hand and kissing it. They walked downstairs together. Mina stopped in the doorway of the dining room to rest for a moment. "You are not as recovered as you acted," he pointed out as he helped her to the table. "You will eat, then rest some more."

"I'm fine," she responded.

Celine walked in, setting down the kettle and pouch of tea. "Welcome back. We've missed you."

Mina smiled at her. "We are happy to be back."

Elise and Marie walked in. They ran to Mina, each taking their turn to hug her. "Where have you been?" Marie asked.

Mina explained what happened while they ate, and neither sister could believe what they had been through. Marie shook her head. "Father is recovered and will be returning home today. He asked to see you."

The surprise was apparent on Mina's face. "Really?"

"Yes."

She started to stand when Dracke gently guided her back into her seat. "Finish eating, and rest a moment."

"Yes, beloved." Mina finished her bread and tea, then stood up. Dracke was instantly beside her. "I'm all right on my own. I'll be back shortly," she assured him.

Dracke said nothing as she left the room. Mina gripped the stair rail as she slowly made her way. Exhaustion washed over her, but she was determined to see her father. At his door, she knocked softly.

"Come in."

Apprehension filled her as she stepped inside, and she lowered her head. "You asked to see me?"

Marius approached her, overwhelmed by her new appearance. He collected himself, then rested his hands gently on her shoulders. "Is it true you healed me?"

"Yes."

"Why?"

Her head jerked up, and she met his gaze. "Because, regardless of your feelings for me, you are my father, and I love you."

Shock washed over him as he stepped back. "How? After all I've done, you couldn't possibly." He glanced at her pointed ears and the golden wings on her back. "So you really are a faery?"

"Yes, Dracke told me the truth."

"You're beautiful."

She shook her head. "What do you want?"

"I wanted to thank you before I returned to Lyndon."

"Yet you haven't. Let me guess, Elise mentioned what happened, and you had to see me for yourself? That was the real reason you asked me here."

"Fine, yes. I wanted to see—"

"Goodbye, Marius," she said as she turned away. Tears fell down her cheeks, but she ignored them as she made for the door. She was nearly there when she collapsed.

"Bells!" her father cried out, rushing to her side. He looked up when Dracke appeared.

"What happened?" he demanded.

"She was leaving—"

Dracke lifted her up. "She is still weak from the trial and healing you. I told her she needed more rest, but she insisted on seeing you. Though, for the life of me, I can't imagine why."

"She told me she loved me."

"And you rejected her?"

"Well… not exactly."

Dracke shook his head as he carried Mina to their chamber, laying her on the bed and removing her tiara. Marie walked in.

"Is she all right?"

"Too much excitement in a short amount of time. She will be all right once she sleeps."

"I'll let her rest. Let me know if you need anything."

"Thank you, Marie."

She smiled at him, then left the room. Dracke sat on the edge of the bed, taking Mina's hand between his. He kissed her palm, wishing desperately she would open up to him.

Mina left the closet to find Dracke waiting for her with concern written on his face. "What's wrong?"

"I should be asking you."

"I'm much better, I assure you."

"Are you really though?"

Mina sighed as she sat down to slip on her shoes. "Why do you doubt me?"

"Because you haven't been honest with me."

"I'm hungry," she said, making her way to the door.

"Mina, I'm not upset with you. I worry, especially after these past few days." He took her wrist, pulling her to him and vaolmersing them into the dining room.

She sat at the table, pouring water for her tea. He took the kettle and joined her, his hand resting on hers.

"What's wrong?" she asked again.

"You are so pale. Are you sure you're better?"

"You mean paler than normal since I changed?" She took a deep breath. "I'm fine. Anyway, has my… has Marius left?"

"Yes, about an hour ago. Marie begged him to stay, but he said he had matters to attend to."

"That's all right."

Celine walked in, handed Dracke a message, then promptly left. He read it and looked at Mina. "Willam will grant us an audience tomorrow."

"I'm glad."

"What do you plan to say?"

"I want to show him we are going to unite the kingdoms, fae and muritor. We can live and work together in peace, no longer separated."

"The fae king will never allow it."

"If we are the rulers here, rulers of the muritor realm, he'll have no choice. He'll surely make a treaty with his own daughter."

"Willam will need assurance of this before agreeing to relinquish the throne."

"Regardless of what he thinks he needs, the power is not his. Once your curse was broken, the right automatically reverted back to you."

"To us, my dear princess."

She smiled at him. "Yes, to us. He doesn't have a choice."

"You've been working on this, haven't you?"

She took a sip of tea. "I needed a distraction."

"From what?"

The cup nearly fell. "From everything," she admitted as she set it down. "From my grief over your loss, my guilt because I didn't save you, dealing with… with what I now am."

"You had no reason to feel guilt."

"I didn't save you. I thought I had failed you the way I failed Colin."

He took her hand, gently tracing the lines of her palm with his fingertips. "My dearest Mina, you have never failed me. Look at all that has happened! If you said you loved me sooner and broke the curse, we would be muritor. At least, I would be. They said being the blessed ones is a blessing, but to me, it sounded like a curse. Searching for each other lifetime after lifetime? Now, that's not the case anymore."

"Right," she agreed as she began to gather dishes.

Dracke watched her for a moment. "Celine will get those."

"I don't mind," she said, lifting them and leaving the room.

He sat back, knowing she had not come to terms with everything that had transpired. He was unsure of what to say and wished he could comfort her.

In the kitchen, he found her looking out the window. "Admiring the view?"

"To think, this all started because of a single rose," she said softly.

"Mina?"

"I'm going for a walk."

"Would you like some company?"

"No, thank you."

She stepped outside, taking in the last few golden rays of sunshine. As she walked through the garden, the smell of spring lingered in the air. She could tell it would rain soon, though she wasn't sure how she knew it, since there wasn't a cloud in the sky.

Gooseflesh crept over her when she realized Dracke watched her every move. She cut through the path and into a private part of the garden, sitting on the bench, and grateful for the moment to herself.

Even having him with me, I feel empty. I grieved for him, believing he was gone, and now to have him returned to me. If… if I lose him again, it will be more than I could bear. How do I handle this? Do I keep my distance to protect my heart, which could push him away? Or do I open up, and tell him what I am feeling? I am so lost.

She laughed when Duke approached, covered in black fur with brown eyebrows, his dark eyes studying her. Her hand trailed over his square head and powerful back.

"Hi, boy," she whispered, laughing again when he licked her face. She watched him run after a bird then disappear from her sight.

When it grew dark, she knew Dracke would come for her if she did not return. Reluctantly, she stood and made her way back to the chateau, going inside and up to her chamber to freshen up. She went into the closet, trying to decide on a gown for meeting Willam the next day. *I wonder what he will think when he sees me.*

"Need any help?"

She swallowed hard before she continued her search. "No, thank you." A shimmering pink gown caught her eye, and she took it out from the closet to hold it up before the mirror. It was ankle length, covered with embroidered silver roses and vines, and low cut in front and back.

"You will look magnificent."

"Thank you." She hung it up, retrieved a nightgown, and went into the washroom.

The water was heating up when Dracke walked in. He sauntered to her and took her into his arms, kissing her fiercely as his hand explored her bare chest. For a moment, she wanted to step back, to tell him no. Her thoughts and worries soon melted away as she focused on being with him.

He cleaned her in the shower, smiling when she stepped out. "Dress or don't dress, that is up to you," he teased.

She dried and went into their chamber, dimming the lights, and lying on her back on the bed. Dracke walked out, wearing only a towel. It fell from his hand at the sight of her. He planned to make her forget about everything she had been dealing with.

He climbed onto the bed, kissing her softly as his hand went to her thigh. She parted her legs, and his fingers explored as his tongue trailed down the crook of her neck. He leaned above her, his mouth kissing along her flat stomach when she pulled him up to kiss her.

Her hand wrapped around him, teasing as his fingers continued to build her up. He kissed her again as he entered her slowly, her breath catching with every inch. His thumb circled her while his hips swayed back and forth. The combination of sensations sent her over the edge, and when he finished, she cried out as well. His lips teased along her neck, and he playfully nipped, causing her back to arch in response.

She held him tightly as she panted for air. Her heart thumped against his chest, and he stroked his fingers through her hair.

"Good girl," he murmured into her ear. "Sleep now."

Chapter 21

The Kingdom

ina moaned softly as the sun invaded their bed. She smiled at Dracke sprawled out beside her and snoring softly. His eyes popped open when she kissed him. Her fingers stroked through his hair as she kissed him again.

"Morning, my dearest Mina."

"Morning to you, beloved."

"Are you ready to see the king?"

"Hmm, am I not looking at one?"

Dracke laughed as they sat up. "Not yet, at least. One thing at a time. What about you? Are you ready to become my queen?"

"I am," she said with confidence.

"And everything else?"

She pulled the blanket tighter around her. "What do you mean?"

"Have you dealt with all of these changes?"

"Yes," she said as she stood and went to the closet, grabbing a gown. "What about you?"

"Me?"

"Yes, you. You went from a muritor to a vampyr to a fae. That's a lot for one person."

"We're not talking about me."

"Why not?"

He appeared beside her, taking her hand. "Because I know you are still hurting, though I don't know why."

"I told you, I will always carry grief for Colin."

"And me?"

"I thought…" She looked down. "It doesn't matter. We need to eat and get ready to depart. Our meeting with Willam is at ten o'clock." She walked around Dracke and went downstairs.

Dracke changed into black slacks and a dark blue shirt, smiling as he glanced at the bed and thought of the night before, of his mouth on her while she writhed and moaned under him. His smile grew when he realized she was seeing it the way he was.

He continued to think of her, lying open and exposed for him, waiting for him to fulfill her.

"Dracke!"

He chuckled softly as he vaolmersed downstairs, finding Mina flushed and leaning against the wall.

"My apologies. I was looking at how disheveled the bed was and couldn't help myself." He went to her and helped her sit, pouring her a glass of water.

"Do I need to leave you here?" she teased.

"No, I'll behave."

Breakfast was served, and she enjoyed her mint tea while he drank his coffee. "Are you used to eating and drinking again?" Mina asked.

"I am. And being in the sun."

"I bet you are glad. I love the warmth of it."

"It certainly makes you glow."

She blushed as she finished her tea. They held hands as they strolled through the garden, taking in the fresh air and sunshine before he vaolmersed them to the faery gate.

"Nervous about going to the Ceil Kingdom?" he asked.

"Only that this isn't a trap," she responded as they stepped into the rings of glowing blue light.

On solid ground, she nearly collapsed into his arms. He steadied her and grasped her hand as they walked to the palace. "Hmm."

"What's wrong?"

"I can't vaolmerse us there. It must be another ward to protect the palace and its inhabitants."

"I don't understand."

"A ward is—"

Mina laughed. "No, not that. The palace itself. Why weren't you cursed here if this is your palace? I thought I read it somewhere."

"The Ciel Palace is the main palace. The chateau is our summer home. We were there having the ball when I was cursed. I had heard rumors the Ciel Palace was destroyed. I think it was to keep me from trying to return here."

Once they arrived, the guards parted and gestured them inside. Alain ran up to Mina, excited to see her.

"Mina, wait, is it really you? What happened?" he asked as he walked around her, shocked by her appearance.

She gently gripped his arms and leaned down to meet his gaze. "Alain, yes, it's me. This is who I am. A spell was placed upon me when I was just a baby. It made me appear muritor, but the spell has broken."

"Awesome!"

She couldn't help but smile as he pulled her towards his father's office. "Thank you," she said once he left them outside the door. After knocking softly, Willam called out for them to enter.

He approached them, studying each before speaking. "So, the rumors are true," he said. "You are both fae?"

"We are," Mina replied.

"And you are here to take back your kingdom?" Willam asked, looking at Dracke.

"We wish to discuss it with you, yes."

"Discuss what? You will claim it is natural birthright. I have no grounds to dispute it, though my army is quite powerful if we chose to fight."

"It would be a fool's errand," Dracke assured him. "Between the size of the fae army and the magic at their disposal, your people wouldn't stand a chance. Mina wanted to come here so we could discuss a peaceful transition of power. She believes the fae and muritor could live together once more."

"How would that work?"

"We would use our magic to help," she explained. "Even in winter, we could grow produce, and we could help with illness and injuries."

Willam shook his head. "In theory, it sounds like perfection. Especially after the blood plague that ravaged our youth. If we could have had their help then… But it's in the past. Unfortunately, too many muritor are jealous of the fae, of their beauty, their immortality, and their magic. What would start out innocent enough would quickly turn to jealousy and outrage. One spell gone wrong or a sickness immune to magic, and chaos would erupt. They may accept you as their rulers, but they will never live side by side."

"I was afraid of that." She glanced at Dracke. "Perhaps it is best to simply let Willam continue his reign?"

"That is not up to you."

Mina looked at Willam in surprise. "I beg your pardon?"

"Dracke is the rightful heir. Even if both of you abdicate the throne, it would then go to a distant cousin in Rhoem. The only reason my family inherited the throne was because of the curse. All mentions of Dracke, his family, and his lineage vanished when it set in. My great-grandfather was Steward to the Throne, and he was crowned after the curse took hold."

"You'll hand over power, just like that?" Dracke asked, skeptical it would be so easy.

"Well, we have to ensure peace, regardless. The people need to see you are not the warmongering legend your brother was and that you intend no harm towards us."

"You said all mentions of them had disappeared?" Mina asked.

"Yes, but since the curse has been broken, the history has been restored. In fact, some of it had remained, somehow."

Mina thought of her talk with Alain when he came to see her at Renfield Manor. "Almost like things were meant to happen."

"Yes."

"So, to ensure peace, what do you propose?" Mina asked.

"First, we will have a proper coronation for you both, and I will crown you to show the people you have my full support. Then we will work together. How do you propose to bring about prosperity?" Willam asked Mina.

"By growing food year-round and building additional shelters, we will eliminate hunger and homelessness. Thus, they would be strong enough to work, to earn an income, and the cycle would continue until no one is impoverished."

Willam nodded, trying to hide his surprise. "That's a promising idea. I would be curious to see how it works. Maybe we can work together."

"What do you ask in return?" Dracke inquired.

"Let my son and me continue to live here, to oversee the palace. This is the only home we've ever known."

Mina looked at Dracke with hope in her eyes. "Yes," he agreed. "That will be fine. After we are crowned, you will resume the title of Steward to the Throne."

"Thank you."

"We shall plan the coronation together, ensuring fae, faeries, and muritor are all invited," Dracke said.

"Yes, let the people see they mean us no harm, and we could work together," Willam agreed.

"We may yet unite the kingdoms," Mina said.

"I wouldn't consider that just yet. If it is to happen, it will be a long while in the making."

"You never know," she said with a smile.

"Will you be returning to Parysse?"

"Yes, we have affairs to attend to," Dracke said as he took Mina's hand.

"The gate is now open to you both. You need not wait for an invitation to return."

"Thank you."

"Mina, Alain has expressed he misses you. Will you come and visit him when you can?"

"Yes, Your Majesty. I promise."

"Hmm, I'll have to get used to not being called that," he said with a chuckle.

"We have all had to make adjustments."

Willam observed Dracke's ears. "Right, you were a muritor, too. Then the curse was broken, and you became a fae?"

Dracke shifted on his feet. "It's a little more complicated than that. Begin making arrangements for the coronation. We shall return in two days to go over your plans."

"Yes, of course."

Dracke squeezed Mina's hand as they left Willam's office. "Can you breathe easier now?"

She laughed softly. "I think I can."

"We need to meet with my... with the king and queen. What would you suggest?" Mina asked.

"Invite them to our coronation. Let the people see all the rulers together."

"Good idea," she said as she sat at the vanity, pinning in her tiara.

"Now, are you ready to talk to me?"

"About what?"

"You."

Her smile faded as she focused on her tiara. "What about me?"

"Mina, it wasn't too long ago you thought I was dead, and you turned into a faery."

"And you thought you lost me, then you were turned into a fae." She sighed. "Why do you keep bringing this up?"

"Because I can tell you're still struggling with it."

"What? I've never said a word."

"You didn't have to. Our connection, my dearest Mina. I have felt your fear and worries."

"About the kingdoms," she tried.

He pulled her up from the vanity, their faces only inches apart. "Why will you not tell me?"

She swallowed hard. "There is nothing to tell."

"I'll make you a bargain."

"A fae bargain? For what?"

"For one hour, we must speak the truth to each other. Then the bargain will break. I do not want to continue in this marriage with someone who constantly lies to me."

Hearing the anger in his voice, she stepped back. The fear in her eyes flooded him with guilt. "I have not lied to you," she said.

"You haven't been open, either."

"Fine, you have ten minutes."

"What?"

"I will speak the truth for ten minutes. Once those ten minutes are up, I will leave."

"No—"

"That is the terms of my bargain. Take it or leave it."

"You are being unreasonable! With my bargain, we would both have to be honest."

"I already know everything about you. That is an unfair bargain."

"Do you though? You aren't curious about whether I enjoyed what I did to the enemy soldiers or what thoughts went through my mind the first time I saw you?"

"Why are you doing this? After what we went through to prove our love, you now wish to destroy it. Why?"

"Because I am worried about you!"

She shook her head. "You want the truth? Fine. You don't even need a bargain. I woke up, and Marie took me to the mirror. What I saw in the reflection was a stranger, and it terrified me. I thought you were dead, and I grieved for you. I wanted nothing more than to lay down and give up, believing I had failed you. There, are you happy now?" she cried out, turning away from him.

"Mina—" His hand gripped her arm.

"Don't touch me!" she yelled as she faced him. "I am not ignoring these things. I just wasn't ready to talk about them."

"You need to."

She closed her eyes, focusing with everything she had, and vaolmersed herself into the library. Her breath shuddered when she landed, as she was unsure it would even work. She pulled five books from the shelf and sat at the table, ready to give her attention to anything besides Dracke.

"Of all things."

She ignored him as she continued to transcribe the information. He walked up behind her, reading over her shoulder.

"You need to eat." His anger grew when she continued to ignore him. "Mina, you are better than this. Talk to me."

"I already did," she answered. "I wish to be alone now. Surely, you can grant me that." Her eyes closed when he vaolmersed from the room.

She resumed cataloging books, paying no attention to the plate of food when it appeared. At midnight, she nearly dropped the book in her hand when she stood, exhaustion creeping in. She let it fall to the table before going into her chamber and finding Dracke asleep. She slipped on a nightgown and looked at him, but her anger was too great to be around him. Remembering the guest chamber next door, she slipped out into the hallway.

Mina woke up when Dracke's arm wrapped tighter around her waist. She glanced behind to see him sound asleep. Moving quietly, she slipped from the bed, went to her room to change, then went downstairs.

She was drinking her tea when he appeared before her. "My dearest Mina, why are you so vexed with me?"

"Because you wouldn't give me space."

"I left you alone in the library."

"No, space from what I am dealing with. You forced me to open up about it, and now—" She gave a small shake of her head. "I am thinking over everything that has happened, and it hurts me so."

He seated himself beside her. "Why does it hurt?"

"My grief is amplified, along with my guilt. Knowing I lost you once, and it was my fault…" She buried her face in her hands.

"None of this was your fault. Not the curse, not Colin, not what happened the night of the ball. What's the matter?"

"Because you made me face it, after I told you I wasn't ready!"

"No, you didn't tell me anything. It's why I asked for the bargain. Asked, not demanded. I forced nothing from you, asking simply for you to open up to me."

She wiped her tears. "And now you're angry with me."

"No, I'm angry you feel this way, when all I want is to comfort you."

"It's my pain to carry."

"We are husband and wife," he said, taking her hand. "In times of joy and despair, in times of good tidings or ill, we are one body, enduring all things together."

"Those vows. I… It doesn't feel like we're married. We didn't even have a ceremony."

"Is that what you want? We can have a wedding and coronation together. Share in our joy with all the people, fae and muritor alike."

"Really?"

"Of course. We'll meet with Willam tomorrow to plan everything out, then we'll go together to invite the king and queen of fae."

"Yes, I think it would help."

"Why didn't you tell me? I want us to be comfortable talking about anything, to be a team."

"How come you never talk about your brother?" she asked unexpectedly.

He froze in place, setting the scone back on his plate. "What about him?"

"You told me you were cursed in his place, and he tried to kill you. You never talk about life before that."

"Hardly appropriate breakfast conversation."

"Dracke, you wanted me to open up. Of course, I expect the same of you."

"Can we talk about happier things for the time being? I would appreciate it."

"Like planning a wedding?" Mina offered with a smile.

Chapter 22

The Vow

ell, I think everything looks in order. The invitations will be made up and sent out this afternoon," Willam said, closing the book on wedding customs. "And the king and queen of Faeryland? Have you spoken with them yet?"

"We are going there today to invite them personally," Mina assured him.

"Very good."

"I'd like to visit with Alain before we go."

"Thank you. Dracke, would you stay a moment?" Willam asked.

"Of course."

Mina left the room to find Alain waiting for her in the hallway. "Are you excited about everything?" she asked.

"I am."

"You're not upset you won't be the prince anymore?"

He bobbed up and down. "No, because now I can just be me instead of the future king. Plus, I get to see you crowned as queen!"

She laughed softly. "Thank you."

"Can I show you the latest addition to our library?"

"I would love to see it."

Once back in Parysse, Mina lingered a moment in the foyer. Dracke held her tight. "Still not liking it?" he asked in concern.

"No," she admitted with a small laugh. "I keep thinking I will get used to it, but it makes me so dizzy."

"Even when you do it yourself?"

She nodded. "I've only tried a few times, and I never go very far, but it does."

"We'll rest a bit before traveling again."

"I wonder how they will react."

"To what? They know we are married, and they know we are the rightful rulers of the muritor lands, so what can they say?"

"I think it would be better if I went alone."

"Absolutely not," he said as he led her into the dining room. "That is nothing against you. I know you would do fine by yourself. It's because I don't trust them, especially after what happened during our trial. We will go together when you are ready."

"You're probably right. Yes, we'll go together."

Marie and Elise came in, excited to talk about the upcoming wedding ceremony.

"Oh, have you and Jonathan set a date?"

"We have. With everything that happened, we are waiting for the summer solstice."

"It will be nice."

"By the way," Elise said quietly, "something happened earlier."

"What do you mean?" Dracke inquired.

"I don't know. There was a bright, white light."

"Lightning?"

"No, there wasn't a cloud in the sky," Marie said. "It flashed through the whole chateau, then vanished."

"Are you all right?" Mina asked in concern.

"Yes, we don't feel any different, but it was weird to see."

Dracke took a sip of tea. "We'll find out what it was. Don't worry, I'm sure it was nothing."

"Thank you."

Mina clasped his hand and stood up. "We are going to visit the Faeryland Kingdom. I'm not sure when we will be back."

"We are heading home."

Dracke and Mina exchanged a look of concern before she turned to Elise. "If you are ready."

"I am. It's been long enough. I know Marie misses Jonathan, too. She sleeps with his letters."

Mina smiled at her sisters, leaning down and kissing them each on their foreheads. "We will see you soon. You are always welcome here."

"Thank you, dear sister," Elise said.

Dracke walked Mina from the room, concerned when she wiped away tears. "Mina?"

"I'm okay. I did not expect such a response from Elise, is all."

"Let me speak with Celine for a moment, then we will go."

Mina looked out the window, thinking of the morning of their wedding, and picking a dozen red roses for her bouquet. Her smile grew at the thought of walking down the aisle, holding his hands, and repeating their vows. Dracke appeared beside her.

"Whatever has made you so happy?" he asked.

"Our wedding day."

He took her hand, kissing her palm and working his way up her arm. "You will be a beautiful bride."

"I'm ready whenever you are."

"It's not for another—"

"I mean for travel," she said with a giggle.

He shook his head, held her tight, and vaolmersed her to the fae palace. The guards lowered the ward and led them inside. At the throne room, the king and queen stood when they entered.

"Welcome back," Marigold said as she approached them. She glared at her husband when he sat back down before she hugged Mina. "To what do we have the honor?"

"We wish to invite you to our wedding and coronation on Saturday the twelfth." Mina turned to the crowd. "Everyone is welcome. It will be at our chateau in Parysse."

Alder stood at this news and walked to them. "Wedding, you say? You told us you were already married."

"It's a long story, but we were unable to have a proper ceremony at the time," Mina explained.

"Why should we attend?"

"Because it is our daughter's wedding," Marigold snipped at him.

"And?"

She sighed. "Ignore your father. We will be there."

"Thank you, Your Majesty."

"Mina, please. I am your mother. You need not be so formal with me. Now, will you and your husband join us for lunch?"

Mina turned to Dracke, smiling when he gave her a nod. "Yes, we will."

"Wonderful." Her mother hugged her again. She took Mina's hand, ignoring Alder's cold look, and led her from the throne room. Dracke followed close behind. They went into a small parlor. "I felt this would be more comfortable."

"Yes," Mina agreed. "Thank you."

They sat and said nothing while tea was served. Dracke leaned against the wall, watching them intently while giving them the space to speak together. Finally, Marigold broke the silence.

"What was it like, being raised with the muritor?"

"I had a good childhood. I was raised with love and kindness, along with two sisters whom I love dearly."

"What are your… parents like?"

"My mother passed away a few years ago, and my father hasn't forgiven me."

"Whatever for?" Marigold asked as she dipped her cinnamon scone in her tea.

"For breaking my spell."

The cup nearly slipped from Marigold's hand. "I beg your pardon?"

"Marius, my father, works for King Willam. He sees this," she gestured to herself, "as a betrayal to his king."

Marigold shook her head in disbelief. "That is sad. I'm sorry he feels that way. None of this is your fault."

"Even so, he refuses to see me."

"Did you invite him to the wedding and coronation?"

"An invitation has been sent, though I do not expect to see him there."

"He will attend," Dracke assured her.

They both looked at him. "What?" Mina asked.

"If Willam himself has to command him, he will be there. For this to be successful, the people need to see all of us together, united."

Marigold gestured for Dracke to join them. He paused a moment before sitting beside Mina.

"You are right," Mina said. "Whether he comes for me or not, I do want him there."

Dracke squeezed her hand. "He will be."

"How did you two meet?" Marigold asked.

Her question surprised Mina. "Alyssa didn't tell you?"

"She told us about his curse, but that was all."

Mina started at the beginning, leaving out a few details, and explained their time together. "I gave my life for him, and he did the same," she said, giving Dracke a small smile. "I woke up the next morning and found out I was a faery. I believed he was dead. It was all quite a shock."

"I'm right here, and I'm not going anywhere," he assured her.

Marigold smiled at them both. "No one can deny you are the blessed ones. Even without the trial, you can see the love flowing between you."

Dracke kissed Mina's hand. "We are truly fortunate to have each other."

Marigold took a sip of tea. "We need to talk about your ceremony."

"What about it?" Mina asked, her chest tightened in worry.

"To us fae, marriage is a bargain. You are giving each other your life, your heart, your soul. Hence, it cannot be broken, even in death. If one of you dies, the other can never remarry."

Mina shook her head. "I wouldn't want to. He is the only one for me, and I will never want anyone else the way I want him."

Dracke smiled before kissing her softly. "And I feel exactly the same about you."

"The other thing, the fae ceremony is a private event. I'm not saying you can't have your wedding ceremony with your coronation, but you need to go to our chapel to exchange your vows. Otherwise, our people will not accept it."

"Then we will," Mina agreed, smiling when Dracke nodded. "Just tell us when."

"We will eat lunch, then I will take you to the chapel."

As if on cue, lunch was served, and Mina failed to hide her surprise when Alder joined them. She shifted uncomfortably in her seat when she realized he was staring at her.

"Your Majesty, can I help you with something?" she asked in frustration.

"Apologies, but faeries are rare. We did not know our own daughter was one."

"What?" Mina asked.

"Maybe one in a thousand births results in a faery, always female. It's amazing you are one."

Dracke looked between them, noting Mina appeared uneasy. Alder resumed his meal. "What are the different fae?" Dracke asked, hoping to take the attention off Mina, even if only for a few moments.

"Well, we are the wind court. Hence the faeries being from here. The fire court are the white-skinned, red-haired fae. They can summon fire, bend it, and use it for healing or destruction."

"Healing?" Mina asked.

"Yes, they can draw from the fire to heal. The water court can breathe underwater, manipulate it into ice or steam, and can also use it to heal, by freezing the fae until the wound heals over time. Finally, there is the earth court. They can grow anything, anywhere, with a simple touch."

"They sound amazing," Dracke said.

"We rule all the courts, but each one has its own leaders for the day-to-day affairs."

"Princes and princesses?" Mina asked, thinking of her meeting with the fae in their courts.

"Well, yes and no. The fire court has two princesses."

Mina smiled. "That is good to know."

"It's unusual," Alder said, spreading the rich butter across his bread.

"Because it's two women?" she asked.

"Oh, no. Because one princess is of the fire court while the other is from the water court. Their magic together is truly a remarkable sight."

"I wouldn't want to be there when they have a fight," Dracke added, drawing a chuckle from everyone at the table.

"Very true," Alder said.

"Steamy," Mina said softly, causing Dracke to bark with laughter. She smiled at him, and he kissed her in response.

Dracke caught Alder staring at her wings. Mina squirmed in her seat. "Are you all right?"

Mina stopped and resumed her meal. "Fine," she whispered. She looked at Alder. "Did you need something?"

"Still trying to adjust to seeing my daughter sitting before me."

Mina gathered her courage. "You are coming to our wedding and coronation, aren't you?"

"I will." He took a deep breath. "Am I walking you down the aisle or will your… other father have that honor?"

"I will walk by myself."

"May I ask why?"

"I do not know you," she stated plainly, "and my father is angry with me."

"Very well. I will be honest, this hurts my feelings."

"What? A minute ago you acted like you didn't want to come at all. Besides, last we spoke, you thought me a fool."

He sighed. "I see now how strong and determined you are. The spell Juniper gave me should have killed you. The only way you survived was because of your strength. I am sorry for how I previously spoke of you."

"Thank you."

They finished their meal. Marigold smiled as she led them to the chapel, holding Alder's hand. When they arrived at the ornate golden doors, she looked Mina up and down.

Mina gasped softly. "This is not what I wore here," she said with a small laugh. She and Dracke were decked out in royal dress. Her gown was a shimmering white with red roses embroidered on the lace skirt. Dracke was in black slacks and a crimson silk shirt. He took Mina's hand and followed the king and queen into the chapel.

A priestess approached them, and then bowed. Her robes were silver, and the circlet she wore upon her head was encrusted with sparking crystals.

"To what do we owe this honor?" she asked.

"They are to be married at once," Marigold explained.

The priestess nodded. "And they understand what it entails?"

"We do," Mina answered.

Marigold kissed Mina's forehead, then left with Alder. A bell rang, signaling the start of the ceremony. Dracke and Mina walked up the aisle, hand in hand, then stopped at the altar.

The priestess lifted a silver ribbon. She wrapped it around their hands and wrists with a white magic weaving in and out.

"This bond is unbreakable, and your marriage is tied to your life and your love. Once you say these vows, you are forever tethered to one another in marriage. If you wish to stop it, say so now."

"We wish to continue," Dracke answered.

"Princess, you will go first. Repeat after me, please." The priestess said the vows.

"I, Princess Bellamina, take you, Prince Dracke, to be my forever love. I will be yours from this day forward, as you will be mine. Our souls and our lives are entwined, joined together by this vow, now and for all time."

Dracke repeated the vows, then looked to the priestess. "You will seal this vow with a kiss," she said with a smile.

He leaned forward, grasping Mina by the back of her neck as his lips met hers. Her grip on his arms tightened as the final strands of magic wove in between them.

"You are now one," the priestess announced when they broke apart.

"Thank you," Dracke said, taking Mina's hand. He led her from the chapel, where Marigold and Alder awaited them in the corridor.

"Will you be returning now?" Marigold asked.

"Yes," Mina responded, blushing when Dracke pulled her tightly to his chest.

"Are you all right?" Alder asked.

"I am," she said softly. "This travel always makes me a little sick."

"One moment," Alder said, then abruptly left.

Marigold smiled at them. "You are positively glowing, Mina. Your love for each other must be so strong right now."

"It is," she answered.

Alder returned, handing her a silver and ruby amulet. "This is enchanted and will help with your sickness."

Cautiously, she took it from him and looked it over. "That's all it will do?"

"And offer a small ward of protection."

"Thank you," she said as she slipped it on. "We will see you again soon."

Marigold kissed her forehead. "Be safe, my daughter."

Dracke vaolmersed them to the chateau. Mina waited a moment, then looked at him. "No sickness." Her fingers trailed over the amulet. "I guess it really works."

"Good."

She left without another word and went into the library where she began to gather books. Dracke walked up behind her and laced his arm around her waist.

"Mina, you need to rest now."

"I'm fine," she said, frustrated when his grip tightened as she tried to walk away.

"Talk to me, please."

Her body went limp in his arms. She turned and faced him, caressing his neck as she leaned up to kiss him.

"Is this what you had in mind?" she teased.

He took her hand from his face, kissing her palm. "It was, but I see now it is not what you need."

"What do you mean?"

"You are trying to appear relaxed, but I feel your tension. What are you so worried about?"

"Seeing my father. Marius, I mean, knowing how he feels about me."

"I thought you wanted him at our celebration?"

"I don't really know how to feel. On one hand, he knows I love him. Yet he still refuses to see me." Her eyes reflected her pain. "What did I do that was so wrong?"

"My dearest Mina, you have done nothing wrong. Marius is a fool to turn his back on you. We will talk to him before the ceremony, and only if you are comfortable with his presence will we invite him."

"Really?"

"I swear it."

"Thank you." She smiled at him as she bit her lower lip. "Now, about relaxing?" She kissed him again, and he led her to the table. "Do you feel that?" Her back hit the edge, and he lifted her so she was sitting on it.

"I do. I need you. I need your lips, your heart, and your body. Will you give me everything I desire?"

"Always," she responded, teasing him as she lifted her gown and spread her legs. "I love you so much."

"I love you, too."

His hand caressed up her thigh, reaching her underwear and giving a gentle tug. She lifted her hips, and he swept them down. He smiled as his fingers explored.

"You are ready for me," he said as his other hand unbuttoned his shirt. She removed it, then went for his pants. He took her hand. "One thing at a time, dearest. For now, let me savor this."

He picked her up and turned her around, bending her over the table. Her palms were flat as he knelt beneath her, his tongue teasing and tasting her as she writhed. He stood and removed his pants, circling her for a moment.

"Are you ready?"

"Yes," she panted out.

He guided himself in, holding her hair as his hips thrust. She squealed when he sped up, then cried out when he teased her slowly. "Say my name."

"What?" she asked when he gave a gentle nudge with his hips.

"If you want to finish, say it."

She realized he was toying with her. She was so close but was being denied. "Please," she whimpered. Her body trembled in anticipation.

"Say it."

As stubborn as she was, he thrust again, and she couldn't take much more. Her hands gripped the table top as her resistance faded away. "Please, Dracke," she cried out.

He thrust once more, holding her tightly while his finger circled around her tender bud. Stars exploded in her eyes, the world blurred, and the only thing she knew was immense pleasure. Everything else vanished as she was overcome.

Mina awoke to see Dracke sound asleep beside her. She caressed his face, kissing him softly before slipping away from the bed. As she dressed, she knew he would be angry when he woke up and realized she was gone. Regardless of risking his wrath, she had to see her father by herself.

She rushed downstairs and ate a biscuit with some tea to help settle her stomach. Her eyes closed as she grasped the amulet, focusing with everything she had and vaolmersing outside her father's manor. She knocked softly, stepping back when the door opened.

Marie ran out, hugging her before leading her inside. "We are so excited about the wedding and coronation."

"Thank you." Mina swallowed hard when Marius walked in. "Father," she started.

"What do you want?" he asked casually. Marie shot Mina a look of pity before leaving to give them privacy.

"Dracke and I—"

"Yes, we received the invitation. Willam insists I appear."

"It's for the good of the people."

"Mine or yours?" he quipped.

"Both," she answered honestly. "I grew up here, played with the children who are now nobility and leaders. I governed those with money and have spent my entire life amongst these people. Only you are denying me."

"That's not quite true," he admitted, meeting her gaze.

"What do you mean?"

"There have been talks of rebellion if this coronation goes forward. Some of the muritor refuse to serve fae overlords."

Mina sighed. "Do you even hear yourself? We are not overlords but the rightful rulers. We want peace and prosperity, to build a bridge between our people. Why do you not believe this?"

"I am only repeating what I have heard."

"Do you truly hate me so much you would risk open war?"

"I do not hate you at all. But how would I bring about war?"

"If the people do not see us all together, me, Dracke, you, Willam, Marigold, and Alder, they will not trust us. They need to see us working together, to reassure them. They will see us as a united front."

"Hmm, fae cannot lie, so I must believe you."

Her breath sucked in as she thought carefully about her next words. "That is true, fae cannot lie," she answered, not fully divulging herself. "We only want peace. More than that, I desperately wish to have you at my wedding."

"If I come, I will not walk you down the aisle."

"No, no one will. I am my own person, and I do not need anyone to give me away, especially since we are already officially married, here and in the Faery Kingdom."

"Mina, what have you done?" he asked in concern.

"What do you mean?"

"The fae marriage is unbreakable!"

She gasped softly in surprise. "How could you possibly know about it?"

"After your… after she told me the truth about you, I spent hours researching all I could find on fae. King Willam has quite the collection on the subject."

"What do you care if we have said our vows?"

"Because you are now tied to him forever."

"Yes, and he is tied to me. It's what we wanted."

Marius shook his head. "No, you do not understand. There is more to it."

"Please, enlighten me."

"If one of you dies—"

"The other cannot remarry. Yes, Marigold explained this to us."

"Do you know why you cannot remarry?"

Mina started to answer, only to discover she had no words. She shook her head. "No," was all she could muster.

"Because you will be broken."

"What do you mean?"

"You will wander, lost and heartbroken, wallowing in your grief for all time. You will be a shell of your former self. To lose your love is to lose your life. In other words, you will physically live, but you will not be alive."

"I don't care," she responded, defiance lighting a fire in her eyes. "He is worth everything, and I will endure what I must to be with him."

"He really has his claws in deep."

"I love him. We are the blessed ones. The fae king confirmed it himself. There is no doubt."

"Still, the way he treated you…"

"How he treated me? Yes, he was cruel at first. That changed once he realized how he felt about me, and he has sincerely apologized with all his heart. He is a changed man, inside and out. We are fated to be together, and our love will withstand the test of time. I wish to see you there as we rejoice and share this with the people." She wiped her tears as they fell down her cheeks. "You will always be my father."

"I will not attend your funeral," he retorted.

Her breath quickened as an ache rose deep in her chest. "Father, please—"

"Begone with you."

Mina turned and fled from the manor, running through the woods as the tears poured out. She paused beside a tree, resting her hand against the rough bark while she tried to calm herself enough to vaolmerse back to Parysse. Her father's words continued to pierce her heart, and she hugged herself tightly.

"Mina?"

She turned to see Dracke approaching, anger and worry both apparent in his gaze. "Please," she tried, shaking her head as the tears began to fall again. "Why does my father hate me so?"

The anger he carried melted away at the sight of her, so small and lost. He hugged her and vaolmersed them home. When she started to pull away, he gripped her tighter. She turned to him, burying her face in his chest as she let out the last of her tears.

"Why did you go without me?" Dracke asked softly as he wiped her face. "I was worried when I woke up, and you weren't beside me."

"I had to see Marius alone. I knew you wouldn't understand, but it was something I had to do."

"And how did that work out?"

She pulled away, turning her back to him. "You see for yourself," she snapped as she headed for the stairs.

Dracke appeared before her, taking her hand. "I am sorry for whatever transpired between you two, but it does not give you the right to simply go as you please. I didn't know where you went since you didn't even leave a note."

Her gaze lowered. "You're right. I… I woke up and knew I had to see him. I really thought I could get him to see reason. If he does attend, and that's a big if, it will only be because his king commands him to." She shook her head, biting back tears, as she was done crying for him. "I don't understand what I've done wrong."

"I told you, when it comes to Marius, you have done nothing wrong. This is all him, and I do not know why. Nor do I know how to fix it."

"You can't," she admitted, meeting his gaze. "All we can do is give it time and see if he may change his mind."

"I hate to see you like this and would give anything to ease your pain."

She kissed his cheek while her hand caressed his chest. "Anything?" she murmured, her lips nuzzling his neck.

He lifted her up and vaolmersed her into their chamber. Once on her feet, she began to strip down.

"Wait," he commanded. He dimmed the lights and approached her. "I am here to ease your pain, and I will be taking care of all your needs."

His hands worked gently to remove her gown. He trailed wet kisses from her mouth down her neck, his tongue tracing her bust as his fingers unfastened the corset. It fell to the floor, and his teeth nipped along her peak. She yelped in surprise at the pleasurable pain it sparked.

He took her to the bed, laid her down, then climbed up before her. His lips caressed her thigh as his fingers slowly worked their way inside. He kissed along her tenderness, his tongue flicking as his fingers worked faster.

"Dracke, please, I want you."

"You have me, Mina."

"I want you inside me."

"Then you shall have what you want." He sat up, removing his shirt then undoing his pants. Once he was undressed, he knelt before her again. "You are the only woman who can bring me to my knees. You are my wife, my blessed mate, my goddess. I would burn the world down for you."

"Dracke, please."

"What?"

"No, I want you to help me build it up, not burn it down."

He thrust into her, causing her to whimper in surprise. "I will work with you, give you whatever you want, but you must understand. I will always put you first. Nothing will ever change that."

She went to reply, but his hips worked faster, and all she could do was gasp as the waves began to consume her. He buried his tongue in her mouth as she gripped his hair, holding him tightly and bucking furiously in response.

He pulled back. "Open your eyes, Mina." When she didn't, he smacked her hip. "Open them. I want us to watch each other when we finish."

Her eyes flew open, focusing on his face as they both rode the euphoria erupting between them. He smiled as her eyes rolled back, her mouth open, and her body trembling under him. His lips brushed her forehead.

"That's my girl."

Chapter 23

The Magic

After a quiet lunch, Mina walked about the gardens, admiring the rose bushes and thinking about the events of the past few weeks. *I am now a faery, I am going to be queen of L'Evrope, and I still feel lost. I thought my grief would ease, but it hasn't. I mourn for Colin and for Dracke, even having him with me. So much has happened, and Dracke…he just…he doesn't understand my pain, my grief. How can he? I know he changed, too, but my heart aches every time I think back, hearing Marie tell me he was gone.*

Her thoughts went to her father when her fingers trailed over a red rose. He took one of these, and that one choice led to her entire life changing in the blink of an eye.

Marius started this. I saved his life, gave myself for him, but he's angry with me? He has banished me for things beyond my control, and it's not fair! I wish never to see him again, but I know that's not true. He will always be my father, and I will never turn my back on him, regardless of his own feelings for me.

She looked up and saw Dracke. He watched from the window, wondering what was going through her mind. He wanted to go to her and comfort her, but she had asked for space after lunch. Confusion tore through him as to why she kept opening up to him in the bedroom, only to pull away from him when it mattered most.

Her sorrow flowed through him, and he could no longer stay back. He appeared beside her, pulling her into his arms, and comforting her.

"I'm okay," she murmured into his shirt.

"Mina, whatever is the matter?"

"I… I miss my father."

"Why are you thinking of him so much? Either he will come or he won't, there is nothing else you can do. Let us focus on the upcoming ceremonies and rejoice in the happy times ahead. Please?"

She gave a small nod before kissing him softly. "Yes, beloved. That does sound nice."

Marie smiled when Mina brought her a rose from the bush. "I will have a bouquet of these for the ceremony, and Marigold is taking care of my dress."

"Everything is coming along well," Elise said with a smile.

A flash of light caught their attention, and Alyssa approached them, offering Mina a bow. "Your Highness."

Mina gestured for her to sit with them. "We are finalizing a few things for the ceremony tomorrow."

"Ah, yes. That is why I am here. Her Majesty, the queen, asked me to see if you need assistance with anything?"

"I believe we have everything under control."

"The light…" Marie started.

"What do you mean?" Alyssa asked.

"We saw a light like that last time we were here, only it was much brighter."

Alyssa's mouth opened, and she hastily closed it. "My sincerest of apologies! Then you do not know."

"Know what?" Mina demanded. "What is going on?"

"I meant to return to speak with you and Dracke, but something happened, and I forgot."

"To tell us what?"

Alyssa looked the sisters over before giving her attention to Mina. "I felt bad for Dracke's staff, suffering as they did. I do not have the power to turn anyone else fae, as that was a large boon. It took most of my magic. However, I wanted to make it up to them, as well."

"What did you do?" Mina asked, worry flooding her nearly to the point of panic.

"I made everyone who was in the house that day immortal."

"What?" Elise and Marie cried out at the same time.

"I stole so much of their time with the curse, and I wanted to give it back the only way I could."

"Is Alder aware of this?" Mina finally asked.

"No," she admitted.

Mina glanced at her sisters, seeing Marie's eyes wide in fear while Elise appeared to be in shock. "I think you should leave."

"Your Highness—"

"Now!" Mina cried out.

Dracke appeared beside her as Alyssa vanished. The two older sisters clung to each other as they wept. "What's wrong?"

Mina explained what happened. "How could she do this without asking first?"

"Her intentions—"

"I don't care!" Mina stood up, brushing him back. "These are my sisters, and what she did is unthinkable. How dare she presume that immortality is something everyone wishes for?"

Dracke could not hide his confusion. "Mina, you are immortal. Did you want to lose them over time?"

"Of course not! How can you even ask that?"

"Then I don't understand why you are so upset."

Marie gasped. "Oh, no. Jonathan," she murmured. "What will he think? And I will live forever without him at some point?" She wept harder into Elise's shoulder.

Mina looked at Dracke, helplessness drawn across her face as she shook her head. "What can we do?"

"Marie, Elise, I am sorry this happened to you. Since it has, I will do everything in my power to ensure you are always taken care of."

Elise gave him a sad smile. "Thank you."

Mina knew it wouldn't stop their tears but was grateful it at least brought them a small measure of comfort. She went to her sisters, enveloping them and reassuring them as best she could. Once the tears stopped, Dracke gave them privacy.

"Elise, are you all right?" Mina asked.

She turned to Marie. "We will be. It was just… such a shock to find out." She took Marie's hand. "We don't have to live forever."

Mina's eyes went wide. "Elise, what do you mean?"

"You know exactly what I mean."

Marie shook her head. "No, Elise. We would not do that to our sister. She has given everything for us, protecting us and our father, and the least we can do is stay with her now."

"Do you mean to live here?" Mina asked.

"No, I don't mean to literally stay with you, unless Marius kicks us out once he learns the truth. I simply mean we will support you and be with you."

"I can't bear the thought of losing either of you," Mina said, squeezing Marie's hand.

"We need to head back," Elise said softly, still coming to terms with what she'd learned.

"Do you want me or Dracke to take you?"

"Dracke, please. No offense."

Mina laughed. "I am still learning, I know." She gestured to Dracke, who watched from his parlor. He appeared outside. "Will you see them home, please?"

"Of course, my dear." He kissed her forehead. The sisters hugged and said goodbye, then he vanished with them.

Mina carried the dishes inside. She nearly dropped them when Celine ran to her, taking them.

"Madam Mina, we are here to do this!"

"I don't mind—"

"Mi'lady, you are the princess. Dracke has instructed you are no longer to perform any menial tasks."

Mina sighed. "Has he, now?"

"Yes. I will see to these at once."

"Actually," Mina said with a grin, "would you look in my closet? I wish to wear my favorite blue gown tonight, but there is a tear in the hem of the skirt."

"I will go at once."

As soon as Celine left, Mina went to the sink, knowing Dracke wouldn't be too much longer. She began to wash dishes, not saying a word when he appeared behind her.

"What are you doing?"

"Celine is mending a gown for me, so I decided to take care of these."

Dracke gripped her wrist and pulled her hand from the water. "Mina, we've talked about this."

"It's just a few dishes—"

"No, you will be the queen. Menial jobs like this are beneath you."

Her mouth opened in surprise. "What? I thought it was just because you wanted to take care of me. Is this really how you feel about this sort of work? That it's low and should be treated with disrespect?"

"No, but—"

She stepped back. "I can't believe this. They are dishes."

"And you will be queen!" he snarled. "You will be in a position of regality and beauty. As princess, you already are."

"Where is this coming from? Because the man I love wouldn't care what I am doing, as long as it was something I chose to do, something which made me happy."

"You can't possibly enjoy washing dishes."

"Really? Standing here with a view like this," she nodded towards the garden, "doing something helpful and productive? But I can't possibly enjoy it?" She scoffed. "When was the last time you raised a finger to do something helpful around here?"

"Well, I…" he stammered. "I see to things."

"Other than pointing and barking orders, what was the last actual thing you did for this estate?" she asked, leaning against the sink with her arms crossed over her chest.

"Mina, you know how hard we have worked in the library."

"Yes, and I have planted roses with Celine, cooked you a surprise meal, and am now doing dishes. I understand this is your manor to do as you please, and I don't care what you do or do not do, but do not judge me for being hands-on."

Dracke slinked right beside her and kissed her palm seductively. "I love when you are hands-on."

She jerked her hand away. "I am being serious!"

"Mina, please, you have seen how I treat my staff. You know I am only ever respectful to them. No, I do not look down on them, nor the jobs they do."

"The menial jobs," she reiterated, picking up a plate.

His shoulders slumped as he sighed. "You know what, you want to wash dishes? Wash every single one. You want to mop, to plant flowers, do whatever makes you happy. You are right though. After all you have been through, I am sorry I only wanted to take care of you."

"Dracke—" She slammed the dish into the sink when he vaolmersed from the room. The glass shattered, cutting her hand. Mina grabbed a towel to wrap around it while applying pressure.

Dracke immediately appeared beside her. He gently took her wrist, kissed it softly, and used the same magic she had to heal her father. Mina removed the towel to see there was not even so much as a scar.

"I'm sorry," Dracke said.

"Why did you say those things?" she asked quietly, a tremble in her voice. "You tried to make me feel guilty for doing simple things around here. It was manipulative, and I don't appreciate it!"

"You're right. I… I was raised a spoiled prince, handed everything. After being cursed, I learned to appreciate the people in this chateau. How I could suddenly revert back… I am terribly sorry." He picked up a dish and handed it to her. "Go ahead."

Mina shook her head. "What?"

"Come on." He picked up a clean towel. "You wash. I'll dry."

"Really?"

"Really."

She smiled as she began to hum softly, washing a dish and handing it off to Dracke who dried, then put it away. When they finished, he leaned in, kissing her forehead.

"I am really sorry about before."

"It's all right. I know where you're coming from, but I want to be useful."

"You saved me from the curse, saved the staff."

"What do you mean, saved the staff?"

"You didn't know?"

"What?"

"They were cursed as well. If the curse had not been broken, they were going to turn into statues as a permanent reminder of my failure."

"Living here forever. No wonder she granted them immortality."

"Yes, and I will speak with them. Hopefully, they react better than your sisters." He chuckled when Mina shot him an angry look. "That was not a jab at them. You know what I mean."

"I guess."

"Are you ready for tomorrow?"

"I'm trying to be. Willam has said Marius will be at the wedding, but what sort of mood will he be in? Who knows?"

"Hmm, we need to clean up now."

"What—" Before she could finish, he had them in the washroom, removing her dress. "Dracke?"

"Trust me?"

"Yes, beloved."

They stripped down and went into the shower. Her hand reached down, but he gripped her wrist, holding her hands above her head and pinning her body to the shower wall. He kissed her neck, flicked his tongue along the crook and down to her chest. He knelt before her, his fingers and tongue stroking the desire building within her.

"Dracke—"

"No, dearest. We are saving that for tomorrow night, remember?"

"Then why are you teasing me so?" she cried out, her back arching in response to his tongue penetrating her repeatedly. He lapped at her wetness, indulging in her sweet, floral flavor when she trembled and nearly collapsed on him.

"Gods, you taste delicious." He held her to his chest, his hand running over the point of her ear as her breathing slowed down. "Because you needed to relax after the day you've had. Did it help?"

She gave him a wicked smile. "As only you know how."

"Are you ready for tomorrow?"

"Like I told my sisters, I am. Everything will be perfect."

Chapter 24

The Altar

ina paced the floor while she eagerly awaited her mother's arrival. Marie spoke softly, trying to reassure her. "She'll be here soon." Her words fell on deaf ears as Mina wondered about everything that could possibly go wrong. After all, this wasn't about the wedding but keeping alliances between fae and muritor.

"What if Alder changed his mind? What if none of them are coming?" Mina asked, panic apparent in her voice and demeanor.

Marie gripped her elbow. "Mina, it will be all right."

They both turned to the door when it opened, and Elise rushed in. Their disappointment was obvious.

"Gee, nice to see you, too."

"We thought you were my mother," Mina explained.

"Oh, she's here. She was right behind—"

Marigold appeared in the doorway, holding a silver garment bag. Elise couldn't help but stare for a moment before stepping back to let her in, bowing as she passed.

"Your Grace," Marie offered as Marigold approached her and Mina.

She handed Mina the bag. "I believe this is most appropriate for today."

Elise shook her head as she walked up to them. "I still can't believe you haven't even seen your own wedding dress."

Mina took a breath. "I trust my mother."

She opened the bag and removed the gown. All eyes widened at the sight of it. Marigold sighed, nostalgic.

"I have not seen this gown in… near a thousand years."

"Can I ask about that?"

She looked at Mina. "Whatever do you mean?"

"Why didn't you have another child after me?"

"As fae, we are only blessed with one child, and conceiving is extremely difficult."

"I'm sorry," Mina said as Marie helped her get dressed. They approached the mirror, and Marie stepped back to let Marigold look her over.

"Oh, Mina, you are absolutely lovely," her mother beamed. The gown was white, off-shoulder with silver embroidered vines climbing from the hem of the skirt to the bust. The skirt was split and billowed on both sides.

Marie took her to the vanity, where she rolled her hair and pinned it into place. She added the veil last and helped Mina to her feet. Elise and Marigold shared a smile at the sight.

"Beautiful," Elise said.

Marigold took Mina into her arms and held her tightly. "I am sorry for the time we lost, but thank you for letting me have this with you now."

"You are my mother, and that doesn't mean I loved my other mother any less, but I am blessed to have you with me."

"Do you mean it?" Marigold's voice hitched as she asked.

"I do."

Marie smiled for a moment before her face contorted in confusion. "Wait a moment, why would you ask that? I thought fae can't lie."

"Dracke and I can. Don't ask," Mina said.

"Very well."

"I'll walk you to the start of the aisle," Marigold offered, bringing a smile to Mina's face.

"Thank you."

Marie handed Mina her bouquet of red roses, then she and Elise followed behind to help with her train. Once they arrived at the ballroom, Mina was surprised to see Alder and Marius waiting for her. Alder was dressed in a suit of black and gold, with a gold leaf circlet resting on his head. Marius was in charcoal pants with a matching shirt and a black jacket.

"They both wish to walk you down the aisle. If you will have them," Marigold explained. Mina could only nod as Marigold wiped the tears that fell. "Oh, daughter. This is a happy day. One we will all share in as a family."

Alder and Marius each took Mina's arm, ready to escort her as the music began to play. She smiled at Dracke, waiting at the altar, and dressed all in black with a silk cravat. A white runner with red rose petals was laid out for her to walk on. When she approached him, he took her hand and nodded to her escorts. They stepped back, with Marius taking her bouquet and giving her a smile before going to his seat. Alder joined Marigold.

The priest wore black pants, a grey dress shirt, and a white collar. He cleared his throat as everyone sat down.

"Today is a day of union. Not just one of love between two people, but to bring all muritor and fae together. This union will serve as a reminder. As these two come together, our lands can join together as well. For while they are both fae now, Prince Dracke was once a muritor. Yet here he stands, ready to wed a faery himself. Their love will pave the way to peace.

"Before we get to our vows, I must ask if anyone has any objections to this union." Mina held her breath, praying no one would speak. The crowd remained silent. "Thank you. Princess Bellamina, repeat after me."

She listened carefully. "I, Princess Bellamina, take you Prince Dracke, to be my husband. In times of health and illness, in times of joy and times of sorrow, whatever we face, we will face as one body."

Then Dracke repeated the vows. The priest smiled as he blessed them both. "Prince Dracke, you may kiss your bride."

Their lips locked tight as they gripped one another, joyful to have this final wedding ceremony behind them. The audience cheered. When they parted, King Willam stepped up.

"I will now officially abdicate the throne and restore it to its rightful rulers, to whom I have the honor of presenting the crown." Willam removed the crown from his head, bowed, then held it above Dracke. "I hereby reinstate Dracke's title, as King of L'Evrope, thus giving him all rights to the land and laws within." He placed the crown on Dracke's head before turning to the audience. "Arise and bow before King Dracke."

The audience did as instructed. Mina began to bow when Dracke caught her, keeping her beside him. "My dearest Mina," he said softly, "you are my equal. You neither bow nor kneel to me or anyone else."

Celine approached and bowed, holding a pillow with a sparkling crown. Dracke lifted it carefully and held it above Mina's head.

"From this day forward, Bellamina shall be known as Queen Superiour, equal in status and laws to the king, and shall be treated with equal accord." He placed the crown upon her head, smiling as she trembled in his arms.

The audience stood and bowed again. The priest waited as everyone returned to their seats. "Now, we celebrate this union and coronation with food and drink."

Dracke held Mina's hand as he led her into the parlor. "What are we doing?" she asked.

"We will stay in here while everyone gathers in the garden. We will make an entrance, dine, and dance until the light of morning comes up."

Mina kissed him fiercely. "Hmm, you'd better save something for me tonight."

He smiled back as he devoured her lips. "Always, my dearest Mina."

She removed the crown to examine it. "This is stunning! What kind of stone is this?"

"It is stea."

"I'm sorry?"

He laughed softly, helping her place it back atop her head. "It's from a meteorite that crashed in the barren lands. The stones in this crown came from the heavens themselves."

"It's incredible."

Her hand caressed his neck as she stared into his eyes. "I know we were already married and have celebrated being husband and wife, but I am enjoying this celebration, as well."

"As am I. Were you surprised by your escorts?"

"I was."

They talked for a few minutes until Celine came to retrieve them. They followed her to the gardens, waiting as she stepped in first, announcing the newly anointed king and queen.

The last rays of sunshine slowly faded behind the hill, and balls of magic light floated above, giving enough illumination throughout the evening. The guests were dressed in their finest gowns and suits, with the fae in clothes that shimmered and fancy robes of delicate silk. Mina and Dracke went to the middle of the floor to share their first dance.

When the song ended, she was handed off to Alder, who danced stiffly, uncomfortable in his movements.

"I know we didn't start off on the right foot, but I want you to know, I am proud of you. I think living among the muritor again may someday be achieved."

"Thank you, Your Majesty."

"Mina, I understand if you never call me father, as I know how much Marius means to you. I am grateful for all he has done for you. Please know, you do not have to address me so formally."

"Thank you," she answered. When a new song began, she was surprised to wind up in the arms of Marius. "Father, thank you for coming today."

"I would tell you that Willam commanded me, and it is the truth." He saw the hurt in her eyes, and his hand rested under her chin. "But the truth is also this. I came because I wanted to. I owe you an apology for everything. You did not cause the curse nor the bargain, and you did what you could to fight for love. Not a day goes by when I don't miss your mother, and I am sure I would do anything to have her back. So I cannot blame you for making the choices you did."

"Thank you." Mina glanced across the garden. "What are your feelings about that?" she asked as she nodded towards Elise.

"Who is he?"

"A fae prince."

Marius stopped. "Surely you jest."

"I do not."

"They seem… cozy."

Mina laughed softly. "Who knows? This may be a new beginning."

"Is it true, are she and Marie immortal now?"

She swallowed hard. "Yes. It was a mistake—"

"I am grateful."

Now it was Mina who stopped. "What?"

"I was worried about you, knowing you would lose all of us. Instead, you will have your sisters with you, and this fills me with joy." She reached up to wipe her tears, but he was faster. His hand caressed her cheek. "Mina, you are and always will be my beautiful daughter. I am sorry I ever saw you as anything less."

"It's all right. You're here now."

The evening went without incident, with fae, faeries, and muritor engaging in dance and discussion. When they'd had their fill of celebrating with the crowd, Mina and Dracke shared one last slow dance before retiring. They said their goodbyes and walked towards the chateau. Dracke lifted Mina and carried her inside.

"Dracke?" she asked when he continued toward the stairs.

"I see you aren't wearing your amulet, and I didn't want to make you sick."

She laughed as she wriggled in his arms. "You can put me down now."

"Mina, allow me this, please."

Her lips met his as she stopped moving. "Yes, my beloved."

He carried her upstairs. Confusion crossed her face when they continued to the third floor. Dracke smiled at her.

"Close your eyes," he said as they approached the door to his chamber.

"Yes, Dracke." She did so, her blood pumping with excitement at what he had planned.

He opened the door and carried her in. "You may open them."

Her eyes slowly opened, and she took in the room. The coffin was gone, replaced with a large round bed, covered in a blue and gold duvet with silk sheets. To the side was a matching dresser and armoire.

Mina smiled at him. "It's gorgeous."

"This is our royal chambers." He tilted his head when she frowned. "My dearest Mina, whatever is the matter?"

"I like my room," she admitted softly.

He let out a chuckle. "We will continue to enjoy it, then. However, for tonight, I thought we might enjoy the space and privacy while the festivities below rage on."

"Hmm, good point."

"Now, if you go to the armoire, you will find another surprise," he said as he put her on her feet.

She kissed him before she ran over to look. She opened the doors to find a white corset covered with silver embroidery, similar to her gown. "It's beautiful."

"Your mother sent it. I'll let you change, and I'll return momentarily."

Before she could say anything, he vaolmersed from the room. She laughed softly as she stripped from her gown, hanging it in the armoire, and fastening the corset. The silk undergarments slipped lithely between her fingers. She bit her lip as she imagined lying on her back, Dracke on top of her, as he dominated every inch of her.

Dracke appeared, nearly dropping the tray in his hands. "Mina!"

She giggled as she blushed furiously, having forgotten he would feel what she was imagining. He set the tray on the dresser, then approached her, eyeing her and taking her all in.

"That you are mine, still doesn't seem possible."

"Why not?" she asked, her fingertips caressing along his jawline as he stared at her lips.

"Because, my dearest Mina," he said, leaning down and kissing her neck. "You are a blessing from above."

His tongue flicked along her collarbone as his hand gently teased her hip. He knelt before her. Planting soft kisses along her leg, he gently removed her underwear. His fingers teased at first, and her head rolled back as she was hit with wave after wave.

"Dracke, please," she begged.

"What, my dearest, do you need?"

"You, inside me. Now," she commanded, pulling him up and kissing him fiercely. "I need all of you."

"Then you shall have me. I will worship you, my dearest Mina. I will kneel at your altar, paying homage to your body, worshipping you every chance I am given."

He climbed over her, smiling as she helped him inside. She was warm and ready, her mouth opening when he pulled back and slammed in.

"Yes," she said. He did it again. "Oh, yes!"

His hips moved faster as his mouth was on hers, kissing her passionately with each movement. She turned her head, panting for air, her nails digging into his back as she cried out again. She gripped his shoulders, her head rolling back onto the pillow as she succumbed to the waves of pleasure. When they finished together, he snuggled with her.

"Draga mea," she whispered, placing a chaste kiss on his mouth. "I love you so much." Her smile grew as she realized he was ready again.

"I love you, too. My dearest Mina, you are everything to me."

Epilogue:
(Twenty Years Later)

ina smiled as Elise and her prince played with the newest addition to their family. When Elise announced their engagement, no one was surprised. Marius was the first to hug her and congratulate her. Dracke had hugged the prince, who was taken back by the gesture but quickly recovered.

When Elise announced her pregnancy last year, everyone was a bit apprehensive, as this was the first human/fae hybrid born in a millennia. Everything went well during her pregnancy and birth. Mina loved playing with her niece, named Lacie after Laecilla, their human mother.

"Fae-ry!" Lacie would cry out when Mina approached, laughing.

"That's right!" Mina knelt before Elise, looking at Lacie. "And what are you?"

"Baby!"

Everyone laughed. "Very good," Elise said.

"I can't believe how big she is already," Mina commented.

"Apparently, that's from the fae side. Along with her ears." Elise glanced at Mina. "So, when are you having one of your own?" she teased.

Mina smiled at Dracke, knowing they had previously discussed it. "We aren't having a child," she announced.

Marie nearly dropped her glass. "What?"

"It's not something we want."

"Maybe you'll change your mind," Elise offered.

Mina shook her head. "No, we probably won't. Our life is perfect how it is." She looked at Dracke and saw the love reflected in his eyes, knowing she had his support. "But, if we ever decide to give up the throne, we know we will have a niece to take over."

"Queenie!" Lacie cried out, reaching for her crown. Everyone laughed again.

"See?" Mina confirmed with a smile. "Everything will be fine." She walked to Dracke, who lovingly wrapped his arm around her waist before kissing her forehead.

"My dearest Mina."

"Yes, my beloved?"

He leaned down, so only she could hear. "Are you sure you do not want children? I know I have made it clear I do not, but you know there is not a single thing in this world I would deny you."

"I am certain. As long as I have you by my side, I am fulfilled."

"Same for you."

She smiled at him and kissed him softly.

"Ew!" Lacie cried out as she pointed at them, causing everyone to laugh once more.

"No, Lacie. Not ew," Elise scolded.

Marie squeezed Jonathan's hand, her features frozen in time with her immortality while his hair had turned salt and pepper. Small wrinkles graced his forehead as well. She smiled at him, only seeing the love of her life beside her. They had tried but been unable to carry, and now they lavished their affection on the beautiful baby in Elise's lap.

Dracke took Mina's hand. "We'll be right back." He led her outside to the garden. "You looked like you need a little fresh air."

"Thank you." She kissed his cheek. "And for letting me have time to grieve."

"Marius hasn't been gone four months. You take as long as you need. I will always comfort you as best I can."

"Thank you."

"You never have to thank me for that. I told you, I will always take care of you. My dearest Mina, the love of my life."

"Next month we will celebrate our twentieth wedding anniversary."

"What would you like?"

She laughed softly. "We have peace in the kingdoms, a wonderful, happy family, and a love no one else can understand. I have everything I want."

"Everything?"

She blushed. "Well, a new bookstore did open in Lyndon."

Dracke chuckled softly. "Then we shall go there to celebrate."

He gripped her hair as he kissed her, holding her tightly to him, silently promising he would always be whatever she needed him to be. She accepted his bargain, offering herself in return. No grief, no loss, no weapon could ever break apart the love given to them by the gods above.

Special Acknowledgements:

I wish to thank Bram Stoker, author of *Dracula*, and Madame de Villeneuve, author of *Beauty and the Beast*. I have been reading *Dracula* since I was 8, and I grew up with my Gran telling me the story of Beauty and her cursed Beast.

Since Prince Dracula is Romanian, I incorporated some of their language (taking a little liberty) into this story to add to the imagery of Vlad Dracul.

I hope you have enjoyed reading about Bellamina, her cursed prince, Dracke (pronounced Drake), and a love that will never die. Thank you.

Glossary:

Vaolmerse: to walk in the shadows, meaning to disappear from one location and appear almost immediately in another.

Muritor: A mortal being.

Nemuritor: An immortal being.

Draga mea: My dear

Ciel: Cloud

Legatura: Connection or bond

Flacari: Fire

Apa: Water

Pamant: Earth

Vant: Wind

Acknowledgements:

To my husband, Kevin. We are the blessed ones, and I am so thankful to have you by my side.

To my sister, Lisa. I would not still be here if it weren't for you. Thank you for all of your support.

To Emily, who continues to take my rough work and polish it.

To Yesenia, thank you for being such a great book cheerleader!

To my alpha readers, Brittany, Traci, Bonita, and Ronda. You were willing to read a fairly rough draft to help with plot points and story structure. Thank you for all of your help!

To my beta readers, thank you for all of your feedback and support.

To my ARC reviewers, who accept my book and are happy to let other readers know what you think, I appreciate every one of you.

To the enchantress, Samantha. (Check her out on TikTok @Samazon)

To my closest friends and family, who have supported me along the way. Thank you for everything.

Finally, thank you, God, for a grandmother who loved to tell me fairytales and inspired a love of reading in me.